NINTH SQUARE

Novels by Gorman Bechard
NINTH SQUARE
GOOD NEIGHBORS
BALLS
THE SECOND GREATEST STORY EVER TOLD

Web-novels by Gorman Bechard
THE HAZMAT DIARY
www.hazmatdiary.com
SLOW FADE TO BLACK
www.gormanbechard.com

NINTH SQUARE

Gorman Bechard

A Tom Doherty Associates Book   New York

NINTH SQUARE

Copyright © 2002 by Gorman Bechard

Lyrics from "Lowest Part Is Free!" reprinted by permission of Eric Bachmann, Archers of Loaf.

Lyrics from "New Drink for the Old Drunk" reprinted by permission of Eric Bachmann, Crooked Fingers, www.crookedfingers.com.

This book is printed on acid-free paper.

A Forge Book
Published by Tom Doherty Associates, LLC
175 Fifth Avenue
New York, NY 10010

www.tor.com

Forge® is a registered trademark of Tom Doherty Associates, LLC.

Book design by Jane Adele Regina

ISBN 0-765-30146-6

First Edition: January 2002

Printed in the United States of America

0 9 8 7 6 5 4 3 2 1

To the memory of Ovie and Leonard Laferriere

Acknowledgments to the people who gave input but would prefer to remain anonymous . . . I thank you.

Thanks also to Frances Skelton of the New Haven Colony Historical Society for information on the numbering of the town's original nine squares.

To Fred Russo, whose notes were invaluable. You're still a teacher, Fred . . . at least to me.

To my beautiful wife, Kristine, who gives me amazing dialog without even realizing it. I steal all of your best lines.

To Kathy Milani, Bob Dixon, Steve Manzi, Steven Handwerk (www.designsinflash.com), Irina Gorb, Maya Rossi, Nicholas Watson, Frank Loftus, the Covellos, Bill Roberts, Gary Bechard, Debbie and Stan, Jamie Shugrue, Casey Prestwood, Andy Jackson, Jay Russell, Mike Poorman, Melissa Beverage, Peter Soby Jr., Fran Fried, Lauren Fay, Dean Falcone, and anyone else who's offered support, encouragement, and friendship over the years.

To my agent, Matthew Bialer, of the Trident Media Group and Milissa Brockish of the Monteiro-Rose Agency, and my manager, Matt Luber, the greatest support group in the world.

To Paul Stevens and the people at Tor/Forge for believing in this book.

And lastly, there's the music playing in the background as I write and rewrite. This time around, thanks to Eric Bachmann and both his new band, Crooked Fingers, and his old band, Archers of Loaf, and to Hot Rod Circuit, Elizabeth Elmore and Sarge, Wilco, the Replacements (of course) and Elvis Costello, and most important, the Clash. (This book would never have worked if I hadn't realized that like William Shute, I, too, always wanted to be Joe Strummer.)

Blessed is he who comes
in the name of the Lord!

—Matthew 21:9

It was the title that first intrigued her. Not so much the word itself. But its meaning. This usage. How it applied in this very specific situation. The thickest dictionary in Yale's Sterling Memorial Library defined it as a noun in four different ways: (1) a group of persons, or a single person, accompanying another or others for protection, guidance, or courtesy; (2) an armed guard, as a body of soldiers or ships. And here the word was used in a sentence to illustrate: The President traveled with a large escort of Secret Service agents. Then there was (3) a man or boy who accompanies a woman or girl in public, to a social event. And (4) protection, safeguard, or guidance on a journey. It was the last of these that she felt best fit. Guidance on a journey. Because, in a way, an escort's job was to guide semen along on its journey out of the penis and into, or onto, whatever the customer's pleasure.

The same dictionary defined the adjective *professional* in a few too many ways, only a few of which really pertained. Definitely (1) following an occupation as a means of livelihood or for gain: a professional builder. Perhaps (4) engaged in one of the learned professions: A lawyer is a professional person. Definition (5) seemed to fit: following as a business an occupation ordinarily engaged in as a pastime—a professional golfer. As did (9) done by a professional, an expert, a pro. *Professional hand jobs, professional blow jobs, a professional fuck.*

But in her mind, Midori Strumski saw it as an exercise. It appealed to her sense of drama, like a casting call in *BackStage Magazine:*

Independent Production Company making low-budget feature-length black comedy, seeks beautiful young woman for the role of a lifetime. Some nudity required. Send photo and resumé to . . .

Every client would be a director. What would he want? How could she please him? From what angles would he find her most attractive? She had talked herself into believing she could learn from this adventure. A different role every time, on a different stage. She had talked herself into believing it could be fun. She had talked herself into forgetting how badly she needed the money.

To prepare, she first answered one of the Adult Employment classified ads in the back of the *New Haven Advocate*, a weekly alternative paper that most people picked up mainly for the bar ads. It was from an "established & very busy" escort service and promised, in big, bold letters, "$4,000+ WEEKLY."

A woman named Loretta ran the service. She was a forty-year-old with a voice like a machine shop, who told Midori that someone with her *qualities*—that was the word she used—would be very popular with the mostly older clientele. It was safe. She'd visit them at their homes or hotel rooms, but only after Loretta confirmed that the home phones or hotel room numbers or both were listed in their names. It was lucrative. Massages started at $125; full service escort, at $250. The split was sixty-forty, with the girls keeping the larger share of the pie. "When would you like to start?"

Midori told her she needed to think about it, that she really wasn't sure if she could do this. "Yeah," Loretta had told her, "A lot of girls feel guilty, at first." But with Midori, it wasn't guilt. It was free enterprise. She knew that if she ran the ads herself, she could keep the entire take. And she wouldn't have to deal with the likes of Loretta calling the shots.

Her ad was simple: "Beautiful girl for massage or escort." And there was a beeper number. But instead of competing with the dozens of similar ads the *Advocate* offered, with *Sweet Virginia* or the *Foxxy Blonde*, Midori chose to advertise on the

World Wide Web, on one of the many adult bulletin boards where other professional escorts—women just like her, she assumed—did likewise. It was free. It was anonymous.

Tonight was her third and probably last call for the week. Her first week. Midori liked limiting her exposure. She didn't need four-thousand-dollars-plus a week, just some extra cash. A new pair of jeans. New tires. Books. Food. A little relief from the sting of tuition. She had come to Yale to study.

Her rates were high; a number of men told her so. Massages started at $150; full service was double that. Those same men told her that girls out on their own usually charged $175 to $200 for everything. "If you don't think I'm worth it when I come to your door," she told them. "I'll leave." But neither of her first two clients had sent her away. The first said, "Oh, my." The other's jaw dropped a little, until she said, "Am I okay?" and he grinned from ear to ear.

Both had asked for a description first, on the phone, when she returned their calls. "Tell me a little about yourself," one said. "What do you look like?" asked the other. Loretta had warned Midori about that. Embellish, she'd said. Tell them you're eighteen, instead of nineteen. A B-cup, instead of an A-cup. But Midori chose instead to describe herself as honestly as she knew how. "I have straight dark brown hair which just brushes my shoulders. My eyes are hazel. I have a very round face, with full lips. I'm five-ten, a hundred fifteen pounds. Very, very slender. My measurements are thirty-four, twenty-two, thirty-four. I wear an A-cup, but I'd be lying if I said I was overflowing. I'm very flat-chested. My age? I'm nineteen. Who do I look like?" That was the easy one. "Audrey Hepburn," she'd answer, "In *Sabrina*."

She knocked three times. Lightly. It was a small motel, the Elm City Motor Lodge, located on the New Haven–Wood-

bridge line, just off exit 59 of the Merritt Parkway. It had probably seen better days, back before Interstate 95 took all the
traffic away. Now it offered hourly rates, Jacuzzis, heart-shaped
love tubs, mirrored rooms, and, of course, the ever-popular jungle room. They ran an ad in the *Advocate*, opposite the Adult
Services classifieds. "Good placement," she thought, hoping she
could keep a straight face if room 112 turned out indeed to be
the jungle room. Trying to recall a Jane, any Jane, swinging
through the jungle in the arms of Tarzan.

He opened the door a crack.

"I'm Midori," she said. Not a stage name. It wouldn't feel
right. Though the agency owner had warned, Never give your
real name. Loretta had been especially impressed with Midori.
Thinking it was a concoction. "Like the drink," she had said.
"Tasty. I like that. Shows imagination."

He looked at her for a moment. He was in his late fifties, at
least, with a head of thick salt-and-pepper hair. He was well
dressed, in a dark suit, with wingtips. He still had his tie on. She
hadn't expected him to be particularly good looking. And he
wasn't letting her down.

Midori lowered her eyes and bit down at her bottom lip.
When she looked up again, she touched a hand lightly to her
mouth. Her voice was but a whisper. "Am I okay?" she asked.

The man smiled. His voice was low but powerful. An actor's
voice, Midori thought. Someone with stage experience. A voice
that could boom to the rafters. A voice that could seduce an
audience to tears.

"You're perfect," he said.

"In a fucked-up way," she thought.

O nce inside the room—not the jungle room, no mirrors,
Jacuzzis, or heart-shaped tubs, just a room—Midori asked
the man for some identification. It was another tip from Loretta,

to see that the name he gave her on the phone was real.

He reached into his back pocket for his wallet, and from it pulled a Massachusetts drivers license. According to the laminated ID, his name was Ralph Dillard. He was fifty-seven. And he lived in the town of Quincy.

"Thank you, Mr. Dillard," she said, handing the license back.

He returned it to its place in the wallet behind a clear plastic window and then took out the cash. He held out a wad of twenties, fresh and crisp, probably from the ATM advertised in glowing neon at the gas station down the street.

"You're not a member of any state or local police force, or the Federal Bureau of Investigation?" she asked.

"God, no," he said with a nervous little laugh. "I run a funeral home."

Midori smiled slightly at the irony. In a way they both worked with stiffs. Then taking the money, she folded it and put it inside a large pocketbook, which she then laid on its side atop the closest night table. Its flap open toward the bed, easy access to condoms, lubrication, massage oil—whatever she might need. And even a can of pepper spray, just in case.

Then she sat down on the edge of the bed and waited for his instructions.

Ten minutes later he was inside her. She lay on her back on the double bed, her eyes closed, reviewing what she'd learned in drama class that day. Wishing that she could perhaps apply it here. Wishing she could at least enjoy this more. But he was too small, too inept, and it was all too rushed for her liking.

Dillard tried to kiss her once, but she turned, giving him her cheek. She would not have, if she found him the least bit attractive. It would have made it easier. More like a date. More like cruising for cute guys on a hot summer night, back home in Billings, Montana. Making out, and going all the way—or not. That would always depend on the boy, or her mood, or on how many drinks, or perhaps on nothing much at all.

It would have made it less like a job. Less like an exercise gone wrong. A great scene with an acting partner who could only stumble over every phrase.

"Oh, God, forgive me," he was saying now.

She usually thought the same thing, but not until after. A mental act of contrition saved for the ride home.

She opened her eyes. Something was different now. Something was wrong. Instead of the look she expected, that edge of climax from which most men were so eager to leap, Dillard looked enraged, his eyes wide and frightening as he moved inside her. He was still moving inside her.

"What's wrong?" she asked, her voice breaking just a little. A hard swallow. "Am I not making you happy?"

"I'm sorry it has to be this way," he said.

He raised his left hand then, high over his head. Her eyes darted in its direction. Just in time. Coming fast. Something in his hand. She snapped her head to the right as his fist crashed into the pillow near her head.

She moved fast, as she would have if one of those cute hometown boys needed to learn quickly the meaning of no. Reaching down, she grabbed his balls with her right hand and twisted hard, digging her nails in.

The scream. His scream. "You fucking little whore." His words garbled as he fell out of her, shrinking in the lubricated latex, raising his fist again.

Her right arm up, locked straight. Gripping his left wrist. Her eyes wide. Trying to make sense. A rock. That's what it was. A goddamn rock in his hand. But that made no sense at all. And his mumbling. Not a curse, but a prayer. For her soul. For his. Something like, "This is the gate of the Lord through which the righteous may enter—"

She struggled to get out from under him. But he was holding her, pressing into her shoulder. Screaming into her face. Not noticing her other arm outstretched. Her left hand reaching, fingers stretching into her bag. If she could just reach the pepper spray, she knew it was in there, but—a tampon. Christ! Lipstick. Goddamnit! A compact. There had to be something—the hard rubber end. The point. Her fingers wrapping around it. Gripping it. Pulling it from her purse. Making it count. All of her strength. One jab. Just one stab, sideways. Catching him in the neck and then yanking forward. Yanking hard. Screaming as loud as he. Her rage ripping wide his wound.

Dillard dropped the rock now. Clutching at his throat. No words, no prayers, just a gurgling. Midori pulled herself away. Crawled off the bed, arms and legs flailing. Anything to get away. She'd have chewed off a limb to get away. Falling onto the floor. To the far side of the room. To the wall. Pulling herself in. Tucking her long legs underneath.

He turned his head and looked at her. The blood everywhere now. A small cough, where words might have been. Probably not what he expected. Probably not his plan. And Dillard fell forward finally, landing on the pillow where Midori's head had just lain. Landing on the pencil's sharpened tip, pushing it that much farther in. That much farther home.

When she could breathe again, when she was certain the man on the bed never would again, Midori stood. Her legs were a little shaky. Her eyes stained and burning from the panic. She stepped into the bathroom. The light harsh, like her image in the mirror. Blood had splattered her arms. Not that much, considering. She must have pulled away fast. Pulled away, be-fore—

She ripped off a few sheets of toilet paper and used them to turn on the water. She became suddenly aware of fingerprints.

Fingerprints dancing in her head. Wasn't that how every criminal was caught? Criminal. What she did was criminal. What she did was self-defense. What she did—

She splashed water on her arms, washing away the blood. She splashed water onto her face, washing away the sweat, the fear. She splashed water into her mouth, washing away the taste, the bile that had lodged somewhere in the back of her throat. She wanted badly to brush her teeth, there was a toothbrush in her purse, but—no time. She rubbed fingertips over her teeth and gums. Using her fingernails as floss to dislodge or scratch away what really wasn't there. Then drying herself with one of the threadbare once-white motel hand towels, Midori returned to the bedroom.

Dillard hadn't moved. She wondered if she really expected him to. Like in a play, like in a movie. The curtain falls. The director yells, "Cut!" And the dead actor rises again. From the dead. Ready to perform, to live, love, to die again.

Her panties and bra were on a chair near the bed; her dress, draped over the back of the chair. She put them on quickly, still watching Dillard. She slipped on her shoes doing the same.

Then Midori set about removing her traces. She picked up the black-and-gold foil condom wrapper from the floor near the side of the bed. Then using the toilet paper she wiped off everything she could remember touching. The arms of the chair, the edge of the nighttable near where her purse lay. And the pencil. She needed the pencil. Using the towel as a buffer between herself and the dead man, she pushed his head to one side and then grabbed the little nub of eraser that poked out just to the side of his Adam's apple. She yanked it out in one fluid motion, the small suction sound sending shivers down her spine. Then, dropping the blood-soaked pencil onto the open towel, she wrapped it as completely as she could, finally putting the weapon in her purse.

Next, she lifted Dillard's pants from the floor, wiping the

brass of his belt buckle, which she had undone. Retrieving his wallet from the back pocket, carefully holding the leather in tissue-covered fingers, Midori pulled out his license and wiped that down as well, and the clear plastic window, too. Then she checked his cash. There was over fifteen hundred dollars, all in fifties and hundreds. Why had he paid her in twenties? Was it to make him seem real? Less threatening? As if someone with smaller bills was less likely to murder?

Midori fingered the edges of the bills for a moment and then pulled them free of the leather. What was a little larceny, when compared to murder and prostitution? She threw the bills into her purse, along with the roll of toilet paper. Then taking one last look around, she walked to the door and, with tissue-covered fingers, turned the handle, wiping it down and pulling the door open in the same moment. She switched off the light, stepped into the night, shut and locked the door behind her.

There was no one in the Elm City Motor Lodge parking lot. Just a few cars. Her gray Ford Escort, a gift from her grandparents, given to her long before its model name had taken on another meaning for her. More than ten years old, and rusted in far too many places, it got her from point A to B, usually. It was parked a few doors down, in the shadows. She walked to it swiftly. Not looking back. Not thinking. It was a perfect exit. Stage left. The crowd awed by the power of her performance. Unable to gasp. Unable to understand. Unable to even blink.

And she drove. Back toward downtown New Haven. But not home. Not to her dorm room. Not to the ivy-covered stone walls of Yale. Her roommate would know. Her roommate would sense. She'd notice the way Midori brushed her teeth. Midori always brushed her teeth when she was nervous, or frightened. Before tests, or first dates, or a Christmas flight back home. For ten, twenty minutes at a time. Until her gums bled and she couldn't stand to brush anymore.

She brushed them now, pulling the toothbrush from her

purse at the first red light. No toothpaste, but it didn't matter. What mattered was the repetitive motion, the sound of the bristles moving against her teeth, the tightness of the muscles in her forearm as she moved the brush in a static motion inside her mouth.

She headed now to a bar. One where she knew her ID would never be checked. Her age never questioned. And she would drink. She would find a cute college boy. One who would take her to his room. And make love to her all night long. His youthful enthusiasm burning away the stench. His passion diluting the horror. His appreciation obliterating the memory that she should be dead now. Could be now dead. That a middle-aged man from Quincy, Massachusetts, had tried to bash her head in with a rock while he fucked her for money.

"What's up with that?" Midori said aloud, forcing herself to laugh, saving her tears for later.

MONDAY

Yʏou've all got it wrong. It isn't about gentrification. It's not about beautifying the goddamn city. It doesn't have a thing to do with bringing in tourists. Or making New Haven seem safe for the hicks from out of town. It's politics. Pure and simple. That's why it's so messed up. That's why it's never gonna work. That's why it's all so half-assed and greasy. Look at the mix. You've got a four-star restaurant around the corner from a hard-core all-ages bar, which is around the corner from a Dunkin' Donuts, which is around the corner from a check cashing dump, which itself is down the block from a porno shop and a jewelry store which specializes in melting down gold teeth. Add in more empty storefronts than this town will ever need, throw in a lack of safe parking. And what you've got is ten times worse than it was before. Because at least before, everyone stayed away. It was like a great big sucking black hole in downtown New Haven, and everyone knew better."

"So, what exactly are you trying to say?"

"Fuck the Ninth Square. They should just level it and be done."

"Like the old Malley Building?"

"Yeah, add a couple of blocks to the green. Make it run from Elm all the way to North Frontage Road. This town needs more wide open spaces."

I took a seat at my desk, in a chair that leaned back too far and was beyond adjusting. But new chairs weren't in the budget. Already rubbing at my temples, and it wasn't even ten. Welcome to *one of those days.* The other detectives just sort of looked at me, their never-ending debate about the never-ending revitalization of the city's Ninth Square cut short. They had expected a bad mood. They had expected testy. Just not this testy.

"Let me ask you a question, Shute," Joseph Mazzarella said, "What do you want?" He was sipping at some Willoughby's coffee—one of the three reasons God put New Haven on the map in the first place—and Yale ain't one of the other two. There was already a stain on his tie. And though the tie itself didn't necessarily match, the stain helped it relate to the wrinkles in his suit. His ever-present cellular rested on the nearest corner of his desk. His Palm organizer peeked from the breast pocket of his suit jacket. His beeper hung from his belt. Mazz was connected.

I thought for a minute, shaking my head. Shaking free the anger, brushing it away. *What do I want*? Such a loaded question. Such a loaded word. Perhaps *need* was more appropriate. But what was *need* other than *urgent want*? *Want* with a little *desperation* tossed in for good measure. That certainly fit. What did I need? Unequivocally? Seriously? Desperately? I let the question play in my head until finally the answer became pretty obvious. "A cup of coffee," I said.

"Shute," he said, smiling, reaching back, lifting something from his desk, and placing it on the corner of mine. "Did you know a male gypsy moth can smell a virgin female gypsy moth from one-point-eight miles away?"

At least my brethren were looking out for me. Thinking about me in my hour of, the word again, need. I brought the cup to my face. Took a whiff, then a sip. The jolt. "Thanks," I said, then, "Your point."

"It's over and done with," Mazz said. "You should be happy." He pushed back his horn-rimmed glasses and tapped the side of his Karl Malden nose. "You can go out and use it all you want."

I forced a little clownish laugh. Maybe a big Bozo laugh, from the looks it got. "Yeah," I said, banging my fist a few times against my desktop. I wasn't feeling too sorry for myself. "Happy."

And all that happiness had not a damn thing to do with the Ninth Square, with the original plans for the city of New Haven: nine squares and in the center, a green. No, city planning had nothing to do with it. All that happiness was a direct result of my recent divorce—twenty-three minutes, and counting—from my wife, make that *ex-*, Charlene. She couldn't just end it easy. Leave it uncontested. Nothing was ever uncontested with Charlene. And despite appearances, nothing was ever easy. She couldn't keep what was hers, while I took what was mine. She was a registered nurse, made as much money as I did. More, when you counted the overtime, and she seemed to put in a lot of overtime. She had a degree. There were no kids, just a condo with a hefty mortgage. And she was the one screwing around. She was the one who screwed up. Not that I didn't have temptations. We all have temptations. But the object of the game is to resist. The object of the game is self-control. The object of the game is that it's not a freakin' game.

I caught her. Sending and receiving e-mail. It wasn't that hard to figure out her America Online password—The internet is one of my specialties. It came in handy as a lot of crime seems headed online. It came in handy when my wife started screwing around. She'd used our wedding date—*june6*—Charlene always had a romantic sense of irony. Click on the CHECK MAIL YOU'VE READ heading, and PRINT. Then CHECK MAIL YOU'VE SENT. They were so pornographic and rude, I was turned on, wishing they were written by someone other than my wife. Or at least written by my wife to me.

"How'd it go?" came a raspy Barry White tone that could knock the bottom out of any other sound. Aaron Brown, my partner.

"It went," I said. "Old Judge Branson made the call. He wasn't all that impressed with Charlene, no matter how high she hiked her skirt when she sat in the witness chair."

"Isn't he a fudge-packer?" Mazzarella asked.

"The PC term is *vaginally challenged*," said Gracie O'Toole. She rode with Mazzarella, his partner. A redhead, just turned thirty, whose body made pantsuits look hot.

"You and your PC terms," Mazz said. "You know what she told me the other day? That I'm not balding, I'm just *follically deficient*." He looked to Brown, cracking a smile at my partner's Yul Brenner do. "Wonder what that makes you?"

Brown shook his head. "No wonder they stuck you two together."

"Yeah, Branson's gay," I said. "But Charlene doesn't know it. He didn't give her an inch. Just her due. No alimony. No nuthin'. We never have to see one another again for as long as we both shall live."

"So, why are you so pissed off?" O'Toole asked.

She seemed to be looking at me differently today. Appraisingly. Maybe I looked good. I was wearing my best suit. And unlike Brown and Mazz, I had no gut hanging over the belt.

"I hate paying for my mistakes," I said, returning her look. Maybe it was because I was a free man. Free and clear. Maybe it is all in my head.

"How much the divorce set you back?" she asked.

"Three grand."

"And you were married for?"

"Four years."

"How many times you guys have sex?"

"Y'know," Brown said. "He's my partner and even I wouldn't ask that question. It's his wife. Have some respect."

"He's not *my* partner," O'Toole said. "So, I can ask all I want. And she's his *ex*-wife. Ex-wives have no secrets. Ex-wives are public domain."

"You should know," Mazzarella said, shaking his head, looking away. He wasn't fond of O'Toole's ex.

"I should know," she said, then looking back at me. "Well?"

I grabbed a pencil from a chipped New York Mets coffee

mug on the corner of my desk. I did a little calculation. Took my time. Even erased one of the figures to make it look good.

"Nine hundred," I said. "A thousand times, if you count quickies and encores."

"Five times a week," she said.

"Give or take."

Brown let out a long, low whistle.

Mazzarella said, "And you didn't beg her to stay?"

I ignored them. "What's the point?" I asked O'Toole.

"Well, the going rate with a good-looking pro—"

"A hooker?" Brown asked.

"A professional escort," she corrected. O'Toole's specialty, getting girls off the street, locking away the guys who put them there. "You're talking two, two-fifty an hour. Sometimes three, depending on the girl. That's close to a quarter of a million bucks."

"When you look at it that way, I got a bargain."

"Three bucks a pop."

"Think of the money I saved."

"Best goddamn deal of all time," she said.

Lt. Theodore Klavan interrupted our coffee, yelling as he lumbered toward us, "Got a body in a motel room on upper Whalley," he said. "Victim stabbed in the throat."

"We'll take it," I said, glancing over at Brown, already standing. I had my coffee, now I *needed* to revel in someone else's misery. I *needed* to know that people were still being murdered. That people were still being stabbed in the throat. God bless America.

"I want all four of you out there on this," Klavan said.

"What the hell for?" Mazz said. "Probably just a drug deal gone bad."

"Or a domestic," O'Toole said. "Someone not happy with the jungle room."

"You speaking from experience again?" I asked her.

"None that I'd like to recall."

"I want it handled and closed out," Klavan said. "Clean, quick, and easy." That was how the lieutenant liked everything. One of these days we'd get him an engraved plaque for his desk. "And this is coming from above."

"Would that be from the chief, the mayor, or Jesus Christ himself?" I asked. They seemed to be one and the same in the lieutenant's mind.

Klavan just stared at me a minute, shaking his head. A thought seemed to occur to him. "Weren't you getting divorced?" he asked.

The lieutenant had been married to the same woman since his senior year of high school. Three decades, eight children later, he still beamed when they talked on the phone. Still ended every conversation with an *I love you*. Perhaps *clean, quick, and easy* was his secret to thirty years of bliss.

"All done," I said. "Clean, quick, and easy."

"Painless that way," he said.

"Definitely," I said.

Klavan nodded and then came back full circle. "We've got sixty thousand plus heading into town this weekend," he said. "And I want each and every one of those people to look at New Haven as the promised land."

"Better order sixty thousand pairs of rose colored glasses," I said.

TWO

Y ou really okay?"

We were riding in Brown's unmarked Chevrolet Caprice Classic. It was white. I drove one, as well. It was navy blue. Only grandfathers and cops drove Caprice Classics. Not really *unmarked*, when you thought about it.

We were leading the chase. Whizzing up Whalley, past potential drive-by victims and antique shops. O'Toole and Mazz in his unmarked Crown Victoria, a car that even grandparents wouldn't drive, about five feet back.

"Y'know how it is," I said. "No matter how bad it was, you still think for a while there that you're making a mistake. Like, how can I possibly live without her? I loved her once. I know I did. I probably still love her now. I never liked kissing anyone as much as I liked kissing her. That's when I knew I'd marry her. That first time we kissed. There was something so soft, so gentle about her lips. And the way her mouth tasted. Charlene's mouth tasted like strawberries. All the time. That's how she smelled, too. Like strawberries. It was like biting down into a big, fresh juicy one. There's no better taste than that. I could have kissed her forever. We didn't even have to have sex in the beginning. I didn't even care. I just, I—ah, shit, I even liked her parents, for Christ's sake. Where am I gonna spend Christmas now? And Thanksgiving? And, I don't know, Aaron. I'm watching my goddamn lawyer, and her goddamn lawyer, and poor old gay Branson, and all that's going through my head is, where will I ever find another woman who'll love me like Charlene? To cook for me, clean my house, give me babies, sleep with me, for Christ's sake. I was standing there, before Branson, thinking I'd never get laid again."

I rolled down the window all the way and let the smells of

the city slap at my face—nothing at all like strawberries. The Caprice's air-conditioning didn't seem to be catching. Maybe it needed a recharge. The sun was beating down. One of those spring days with summer pounding on the door. High eighties on May third, when it had snowed just a week and a half back. Four inches of a slushy mess. At least the weather in Connecticut kept us on our toes.

We drove a few blocks without saying anything. I sipped at my coffee. Brown tapped his fingers in some sort of funky rhythm against the steering wheel. He broke the silence.

"She didn't cook for you," my partner said.

I went to speak, but he cut me off.

"Frozen dinners don't count," he said. "You want to see real cooking, you come to my house for dinner sometime. A Sunday afternoon."

A tradition at the Brown residence. Sunday Mass followed by a day of eating and football, or basketball, or baseball, or any combination thereof. "You never invite me."

"Didn't want you to see what you were missing. Bernie—"

That's what he called his wife. Her full name was Bernadine Benedetta Brown. Their kids were named Enid, Tyrus, Hester. The first time he told me, all I could think of was what there were no more John and Jane Does. Now they'd be Octavia Doe, or Eustace Doe, or Hildegarde Doe, or—

"—sets up a feast like she was feeding Henry the Eighth."

"You're getting there," I said, smiling down at his paunch.

"Watch it," he said, then, "I'm talking turkey with all the stuffing, prime rib, those little shrimp wrapped in bacon, scallops wrapped in bacon. We've got everything wrapped in bacon. Potatoes au gratin, sauteed cauliflower, broccoli with cream sauce, deep fried onion rings, apple pie, cherry pie, lemon meringue pie, and Boston cream pie—"

My arteries were clogging up just listening. "Okay, okay."

"That damn Charlene wouldn't even make you a grilled

cheese sandwich after you came off working a twenty-four-hour shift."

"I love grilled cheese sandwiches," I said.

"You're missing my point."

"I get your damn point. All I'm saying is, I love grilled cheese sandwiches."

"Your house was a pigsty." He sure liked putting things in perspective. "She would have made a piss-poor mother. And let's come clean—you've probably been with your share of women since the two of you walked down the aisle."

"Not a one."

"Don't shit me," he said.

"It's the truth."

He glanced over to make sure I wasn't smiling. "You sure have a roving eye."

"Looking don't mean touching," I said.

"How about since you've moved into your place?"

"Nothing."

"How long's that been?"

"A little over three months."

"After five times a week—that was till the end right?"

"We did it twice the day I was packing."

"Your idea?"

"Hers."

"Shit."

"Yeah."

"So," he said, stretching out the word into a grin. "I know what you're really missing."

"I'm missing everything," I said, then a lot softer, "I'm missing nothing."

"But you're surviving?"

"Thanks to loud rock and roll," I explained. "I put the volume on eleven and let it rip."

"Your neighbors must love you."

"I'm all alone in the building after six P.M."

"Lucky you."

"To one side of me is an office building. Insurance. They're out of there by four-thirty. To the other side, a house filled with college students. They're out drinking, dancing, having sex all night long."

"So that's what college students do."

"Besides, I'm playing music so cool they don't even know about it yet."

"Then you get to work on a couple of cold ones," Brown said, knowing me a little too well.

"A six-pack," I said. "The beer's my painkiller."

"The pain's in your head."

"Then I flip on the computer and surf. The other night I logged on to a divorce chat line."

"You'd think you'd stay away from America Online after what you found out about Charlene."

"I never learn," I said.

"Least you've learned that," he said.

"I listened to some poor old SOB go on about how his wife of forty years had told everyone she knew that he was impotent. Then she goes and runs off with their neighbor. Even took his dog. And now his kids and grandkids aren't speaking to him, as if it were all his fault."

"How'd that make you feel?"

"Pathetic," I said.

THREE

The Elm City Motor Lodge was an L-shaped building. Two stories. Twenty-four units in all—twelve up, twelve down. Room 112 was around back, about as far away from the street as the motel afforded, unless you counted room 212 just above it. Either way, privacy at twenty-nine bucks a night, or twenty even for a three-hour stay. Plus tax, of course. Jungle room not included.

The yellow crime scene tape seemed like an out-of-place designer accessory against the dull grays of the exterior walls. The Lodge hadn't always been gray. Once the doors to the rooms had been red. The wood trim, maroon. Once the curtain liners visible through the windows had been snow white; the curtains themselves, a lively flowered print. Once the room numbers nailed to each of the doors had been black; the doorknobs and knockers, a polished brass. But not anymore. The years of sun, rain, snow. The decades of neglect and one-night stands. The tens of thousands of strangers who needed a bed, for whatever reason. Their tears, desires, nightmares. Their secrets. The colors didn't stand a chance.

Two cruisers were parked just outside of 112's door, their front bumpers only inches apart, forming a V. The first cop on the scene had been Brian Luponte. We all knew him well. He was the bad example. The sort of buzz-cut, pumped-up, egohead who gives cops a bad name. His uniform was so sharp, his shoes so shined, his stance so rigid, always at attention.

"Wha'cha got?" I asked.

Luponte was standing by the door to room 112. With him was a rookie. An officer named Juanita Pérez. A small woman with stocky shoulders and wide hips. She was looking a little pale, perspiring heavily.

"Dead white guy. Late fifties," Luponte said.

I turned to Pérez. "You okay?"

"Yeah, I just, ah . . ." She couldn't finish.

"The first time's always the hardest," I said.

"I hope so," she moaned.

Mazz and O'Toole walked up behind us. I noticed the immediate change in Luponte's attitude. With the sharpness and the shine came a slick cool. His eyes moving from me, skipping over Brown, appraising O'Toole from the neck down.

She nodded an acknowledgment and then rolled her eyes the moment Luponte turned around.

I told Pérez to stay outside, to keep any curious civilians away. She thanked me. Luponte then led us into the room. "Looks like he was stabbed in the throat during intercourse," he said, motioning over toward the bed.

Not a pretty sight. A pasty white guy with a gaping hole in his throat. He didn't look as if he'd died a happy man.

"Nice watch." My partner was looking down at the victim. Or, more specifically, at his right wrist.

"What is it?" I asked.

"Gold Rolex Presidential," he said.

"Could be a fake."

"Could be," Brown said, leaning closer, squinting at the watch, tapping it with the tip of a Bic pen. "But it isn't."

Nodding, I looked away. There was a framed Patrick Nagel poster on the wall over the bed—my ex loved Nagel. This particular print was of a black-haired woman, all cheekbones, with one breast exposed. She wore severe ice-blue earrings. I hoped that it wasn't the last thing this poor SOB saw before he died. Then turning, I noticed the other Nagels, one hung on the opposite wall, another hung near the bathroom door, all more or less the same. Someone else must have appreciated his work.

Looking over at Luponte, who stood at attention near the

door. "How do you know it was *during* intercourse?" I asked.

"Nothing in the reservoir tip," he said.

As O'Toole snapped off a few choice Polaroids, something with which to identify the dead man, Mazz talked to the motel manager, a Iranian man in his forties or fifties—I couldn't really tell. He had a thick accent, and a look of horror in his eyes. Not because of the dead man. He just wanted to know, "Who's going to clean up this mess?"

While the clicking of the word *clean* bounced around inside my head, my partner and I looked for anything that might explain why this poor bastard bought it at a fleabag motel on Whalley Avenue before he got a chance to come.

His driver's license identified him as Ralph Dillard of Quincy, Massachusetts. There was no cash, probably cleaned out, or maybe he spent it all. No bank card. No credit cards. Perhaps he hid them, left them at home, whatever, for fear of getting robbed, or worse. There was just a receipt with the name Elm City Motor Lodge printed in script letters along the top. The room had cost him thirty-two dollars and forty-eight cents.

"Nice pants," my partner said. He fingered the material, turning toward the suit jacket hung on the back of a chair. He pushed open the left side of the jacket. The label over the inside breast pocket read ARMANI. "Nice suit."

"If no one collects it, it's yours," I said, dropping the wallet into a clear plastic evidence bag.

"I'd prefer the watch," he said.

The bathroom sink had been wiped down. That much was pretty obvious. There were a few streaks of blood, probably the victim's, around the back edge of the sink. The wastebasket was empty. The toilet flushed. No sanitary strips in this place. And no toothpaste, no toothbrush. You'd have thought Dillard would have wanted to unpack, relax a little. Savor the luxurious surroundings. Enjoy the Nagels. Or at least brush his teeth before he got laid.

"What are you thinking?" he asked me.

"A hooker—"

"Male or female?"

"Does it make a difference?"

"It will to his family," he said.

"Whatever," I said.

"Why a hooker?"

"You don't bring lovers and mistresses to places like this."

"Speaking from experience?"

"You know I'm not," I said.

"Okay, so a hooker—"

"Right, and he, she, it—whatever—had a partner who comes in and robs the guy."

"They take his cash," Brown said, "but skip the watch?"

"No." Shaking my head, thinking it through. "Not working. Why kill the SOB when they could have just hit him over the head, and then robbed him."

"You suggesting a hit?" he asked. "Because that wound don't look like the mark of a pro. Too damn sloppy."

"I don't know what I'm suggesting," I said.

The Scientific Investigation Division unit had arrived. A technician was photographing Dillard's body from every possible angle, while other techies crawled about on all fours, searching for the invisible clues: prints, fibers, and all those bodily fluids we love to discharge. They weren't allowing a single Elm City Motor Lodge carpet fiber to go unturned.

The SID unit was based out of our headquarters in downtown New Haven, as was most of their work. But the division was shared by the neighboring towns: East Haven, North Haven, Harmony, Woodbridge, Orange, and West Haven. The pooled resources bought a lot of man-hours and equipment. They were always ready to jump at a moment's notice. Had to be. Even the Connecticut State Police Major Crimes Unit exploited their expertise from time to time.

"Anything on what caused that wound?" I ask the medical examiner, a small man with thick glasses and a bald spot the size of Fenway Park. His name was Ralph Scissero. I called him Slice.

"Letter opener, ice pick, something long, slender, and sharp," Slice said, poking at the wound with the tip of his Bic. He looked up. "Ask me again at the end of the day."

We turned to the room's lone bureau, a fine piece of classic Americana dating back to the mid-eighties. Black laminated particle board at its best. It went well with the Nagels. There was a leather carry-on bag in the bottom drawer. Hooking my pen through the handles, I lifted it out and placed it on the floor between us.

"Nice bag," Brown said.

"What are you, a fashion consultant all of a sudden?" I asked.

"Just saying, for this place, y'know." he said, nodding at the black leather. "Coach, isn't it?"

I read the stamped logo off the bag's identification tag. "Yeah."

"Bag like that goes for four or five hundred bucks," he said.

"At least," O'Toole said, peeking over our shoulders.

"And it looks new."

"So the guy had better taste in accessories than he did in motels," I said.

I hooked the pen's pocket clip into the zipper and gave it a tug. The bag was more out of place than the crime scene tape. It made it seem pretty obvious that Mr. Dillard had come to the

Elm City Motor Lodge to engage in an illegal coupling. He didn't want to be seen. He didn't want to be known. The old guy just wanted to get laid.

By now we all pretty much expected the same thing: hundred-dollar shirts, thirty-dollar boxers, and twenty-dollar socks. But as I pushed open the sides of the bag, the expected high-ticket items were nowhere to be found. Seeing what was in their place made O'Toole mutter a curse under her breath. Brown began to shake his head and laugh. He went to speak, but it was Slice's voice that came through. "Will you look at this," he said.

We all turned. Slice had Dillard pushed over flat onto his back. He was pointing at something on one of the pillows. Like everything else, it was covered in blood.

"What is it?" I asked.

"A stone," Slice said.

"A stone?"

"A rock," he said. "The kind you'd find in your backyard."

I held on to the ME's amazement, the *what-the-hells?* beginning to churn.

It was my partner who snorted a small laugh as he glanced at Dillard, the used condom not a pretty sight on an old dead man. Then Brown looked up and caught my eye. "Clean, quick, and easy," he said.

I glanced from the bed to the unexpected contents of the carry-on. "Not likely," I said.

FOUR

The New Haven police station was located on Union Avenue, halfway between Union Station and the southeast corner of the Ninth Square. The building looked like it had a migraine. Contemporary in design, made from ruffled cinder blocks—with those ridges for extra flavor. Dirty beige. Four stories, with sheets of windows like space visor eyes.

The homicide division was on the third floor in front, south end of the building. A collection of eight steel desks, about as many four-drawer file cabinets, with lots of broken chairs and ringing telephones. No cubicles. No room dividers. There were two interrogation rooms, only one of which had a two-way mirror. Two bathrooms, neither gender specific. A little veranda with dried-up bushes and a few rusted lawn chairs that no one ever used. Klavan had the only office.

Our division had an administrative assistant named Dora, who did a decent job of getting us our messages. She's a soft-looking, middle-aged woman with bad teeth. But she knows she's appreciated. Every Christmas we chip in and buy her a two-pound box of Godiva chocolates. Dora loves chocolate.

"Anyone see anything?" I asked Mazz as we got our messages. I had one, from my lawyer. It read: "Congratulations!"

I handed it back to Dora with a smile. "File this for me," I said.

Dora returned the smile, crumpling the pink message note into a tight ball and tossing it away.

"Nothing," Mazz said. "The guy checks in alone. No one saw any cars, any people. There were two other visitors at the motel. One was named Smith. Didn't give an address."

"He should be easy to track down," I said.

"The other was named Travolta. John Travolta."

"You're kidding. John Travolta was staying at the Elm City Motor Lodge."

"Yup," Mazz said, shaking his head a little. "Even listed his address as Hollywood, California."

"They should put that in their ads," I said. "When in town, John Travolta sleeps here."

"Let me guess," Brown said. "Dillard gave his real name."

"His real name, address, and a phone number that'll probably check out."

"Not too stupid."

"Maybe he didn't expect them to put him on a mailing list," O'Toole said.

"Or that he's never done this before," I said, "And he thought for sure they'd check his ID."

"I'll buy that one," Brown said.

"Not me," O'Toole said. "He probably did it all the time. You don't use a pro only once, just for the hell of it."

"Would this be ex-husband number one or two you're talking about?" Mazz asked.

"All I'm saying is," she said, "they become habit forming."

"Depriving women like you of your minimum daily requirements," Mazz said.

She gave him the finger.

"You're acting testy, Gracie," Mazz said. "We're gonna start thinking you aren't getting any."

"And you'd be wrong," she said.

I tossed the leather carry-on onto my desk at just about the time Klavan came looking for us. Brown gave him the quick rundown, the lieutenant's eyes growing wearier by the second. I knew he kept thinking about the sixty thousand plus holy rollers coming into town for a weekend get-together at the Yale Bowl. The Sons of God, they were called. I'd been trying to avoid the subject at all cost. But that was near impossible. So I tuned it out. But still—there were headlines all around. The cover of *Newsweek* magazine a few months back. *Time*, just last week. CNN seemed to mention their name once an hour. And that was all off-kilter, at least in my mind. Something frightening about all those men—just men—invoking the Bible and family values and the word of the Lord. Or at least that's what they claimed to invoke. I just knew, deep down, that the town's strip bars and escort services would be in for a record-breaking week. Amen to that. There's something refreshing about hypocrisy in such grand numbers.

"What's in the bag?" Klavan said as he digested the facts my partner presented.

"Fire and brimstone," O'Toole said.

"That's sort of the kicker," I said.

"I thought the kicker was a twelve-thousand-dollar watch in a thirty-dollar room," the lieutenant said.

"This is even better," I said, unloading the contents onto my desk: a King James edition of the Bible, a Sony Mavica digital camera, an unopened box of twenty-five three-and-a-half-inch high-density floppy disks, a roll of duct tape, a box of heavy duty Glad garbage bags, some razor blades, a black rubber enema bag with hose and nozzle, a small bottle of concentrated chloroacetyl chloride—more or less a fancy name for hydrochloric acid—and a pair of acid-resistant rubber gloves.

Klavan stared at the items as we did. "What the hell?" he said finally, rubbing hard at the back of his neck, the visible tension a sure sign he didn't like what he saw, the *clean, quick, and easy* sneaking out the back door.

"Checked the camera," I said. "There wasn't a floppy loaded."

"What kind of contraption is that, anyway?" Klavan asked.

Mazz and I both went to speak at the same time. He bowed to me.

"Takes images you can view on your computer," I explained.

"JPEGs," Mazz said. "Joint Photographics Experts Group. There's also GIFs—graphic interchange format—usually a bigger file with better quality. And BMPs—bit maps—the largest of all, usually used for computer wallpaper."

He was losing the lieutenant. "Most of these cameras can store anywhere from twenty to a hundred pictures on an internal memory chip," I said. "But this Sony stores them right on floppies. You can download these pictures—"

"The JPEGs," Mazz interjected.

"—onto the Net, print them out with a good color printer, manipulate them in any number of ways. A cool toy."

"A best buy according to *Consumer Reports*," Mazz said.

"Kodak worried?" Brown asked.

"Kodak makes them, too," Mazz said.

Putting the camera down, I unzipped a small pocket inside the Coach bag and removed from it a hotel key-card. I slapped it down on the desk.

Klavan stared at the beige plastic card. Credit-card size, with holes punched in some secretive order. "The Omni?" he asked, his voice rising a half octave on the last syllable.

"The Omni," I said.

A high-rise hotel on Temple Street, in the heart of downtown, in the heart of Yale, in the Eighth Square—not that the Eighth Square was ever referred to as such, except perhaps by elders at the Historical Society—one block from the Ninth Square. It was the beginning of the end of the whole revitalization process.

"Shit," Klavan said. "Let's hope he's not in town for this weekend."

"I'd say it was a safe bet," O'Toole said. "Don't the Sons of God have the Omni booked up all week?"

"Wonder if they have the place blessed before they check in?" Mazz said.

We could all picture the gears spinning in the lieutenant's head. The shit clogging up the air-conditioning. The honorable Mayor David S. Pinfield, aka Pinhead, would not be pleased if an SOG bigwig got offed in a sleazy motel while banging a hooker. It wasn't the image New Haven was going for, at least not in an election year. And if the mayor wasn't pleased, the chief of police, Kenneth Zekowski, would piss El Niño torrents on Klavan and the department until everything was cleanly, quickly, and easily wrapped away. The chain of command. The chain of wrath. The piss drips down.

"Can you check it out?" Klavan asked. "I want to know who this guy was and what he was involved in. But—" He paused a beat. "—quietly."

"Yeah," I said, glancing at O'Toole.

She nodded once.

"I think me and O'Toole can look like we're in the Omni on matters other than official police business," I said.

"You okay with that, O'Toole?" Klavan asked.

"A-okay," she said.

The lieutenant stared at her, also nodding once. "Mazz," he said, "check out who sells this . . ."

"Chloroacetyl chloride," Mazz said.

"Right," Klavan said, turning to Brown, "See what you can find out about the victim? He got a sheet? Soliciting. Anything. Family. Work. Maybe he's in town peddling insurance or some such shit. Let's pray."

"We know what he was doing last night," I said, doubting that prayer was the answer—was it ever? Call me a skeptic, but I sure as hell didn't think so.

"Or at least trying to do," O'Toole said.

"What a way to go, huh?" Mazz said, shaking his head, turning away. "You're about to come, and"—he snapped his fingers once—"bang, it's all over. Way too soon."

O'Toole's laugh was about as emasculating a sound as I'd ever heard. "Sounds like most of the sex I've ever had," she said. And when the four of us looked at her, each in our own disturbed way, she added, "You'd have to be a woman to really understand."

S o, how'd you meet her?"

I turned toward O'Toole. She was touching up her lipstick, a deep bloodred that made her mouth appear more full and tempting than I'd ever want to admit. Watching her, I was thinking it was nice change riding with her instead of Brown. A lot easier on the senses, all the way around.

"Reader's Digest, or all the gory details?" I asked.

"Somewhere in between."

"Her car was parked on Chapel," I said, just as we turned left off State onto Chapel—the loveliest stretch of the Ninth Square, especially if you're shopping for porn. "She was about to be towed. I was coming out of a Sam Goody that's long gone. Charlene's crying, begging the operator to put her car down."

"You bought the tears?"

"She was wearing black leggings and belly shirt."

She laughed. "So, you flashed the badge—"

"Right."

"And the smile."

"The driver got the badge," I said. "She got the smile."

"And the big blue eyes."

"The whole enchilada."

"And I'll bet she was very appreciative," O'Toole said.

"Very."

"You saved her a hundred bucks."

"But it ended up costing me plenty," I said, the memory of old Judge Branson's gavel suddenly reverberating in my head.

"How long before the *I dos*?"

"Eighteen months," I explained, pointing out the spot where her car had been, in front of what was now an art supply shop.

"So, you had time to get to know one another?"

"I guess," I said, not very convincingly. We knew what the other liked in bed. But I couldn't help thinking, what did we really know about each other's hopes and dreams? Were our conversations just tailor-made buffer zones between rounds of sex. The arguments seemed just that. Every facet of my life with Charlene began and ended with sex. Was that the attraction? The teenager's dream, to find the insatiable woman? Had that been my teenaged dream? No, I realized now, not even close.

I glanced at O'Toole. "At least we had a healthy sexual relationship," I said.

"You had a completely *un*healthy sexual relationship," O'Toole said, sounding shocked, annoyed even, at the suggestion. "Married couples don't do it five times a week."

"I thought Charlene was romantic," I said, pulling a U-turn and squeezing into a spot just up from where Charlene and I had met.

"There's nothing romantic about screwing," she said. "Y'know the old saying, an erection doesn't count as personal growth."

I just nodded a little. She really wasn't much more of an expert on the subject than I was.

We got out, headed the half block down Chapel and then turned right onto Temple to face the enemy.

"Where'd you"—she softened a lot—"get married?"

"We were down in Aruba," I said, picturing Charlene this morning, looking at me as if I were crazy, as if I were flushing pleasure away. "Decided what the hell. Let's get married. We videotaped the ceremony. Came home, threw the mother of all parties."

"I hear Aruba's nice."

I thought about it for a minute and then turned to face her. "It sucks," I said.

What's up with these guys?" I asked, "The Sons of God?"
O'Toole shrugged. "You know I was supposed to have
been their department liaison for this rally."

"Must have missed that tidbit of information," I said.

"You were busy divorcing your wife."

"My priorities are all messed up," I said. "So, what happened?"

"They requested a man," O'Toole said. "And the mayor suggested Klavan take on the responsibility himself."

"How high?" I said, pulling on the brass handle, swinging
back the gleaming glass door.

"As high as the mayor says," she said.

"Poor Klavan," I said, letting her enter in front of me.

"Not really. It was a piece-of-cake assignment. The Sons of
God brought together a half million followers in D.C. last year.
Zero arrests."

"Christ!" I said, following her inside.

"Close," she said, shooting me a look.

The Omni Hotel's lobby was crowded and noisy on this late
Monday afternoon. There was a feeling of righteous jubilation
in the air. It was like a revival meeting, all Bible-belted, and I
was sure I heard someone speaking in tongues, or at least voices
talking about how to further weaken the first amendment.

We passed the check-in desk and then a sign that shouted
WELCOME SONS OF GOD on our way to the elevators. A lot of
people—men, nothing but more men in suits—were getting off.
But only we got on.

The moment the doors slid shut, she explained, "His name's
James Crawford. An ex-basketball coach from Mississippi State.
His wife was depressed. Borderline alcoholic. His teenaged

daughter had a kid out of wedlock. The usual crap that drives us all to drink."

"But instead of booze, Crawford turned to God?"

"In a big way," she said. "He felt the walls of morality crumbling around him."

"This was?"

"In 1991. He got together a small group of men—"

"White men?"

"White *heterosexual* men."

"Sounds like the religious right to me."

"The embodiment of it," she said.

"Good word."

"Thanks."

"So, you've got a—" I searched for what I felt was another good word. "—cult?"

"Five million members strong," she said.

"A big cult."

"Lots of lonely people out there who want to be closer to God."

"And Crawford's brilliant at slinging the shit."

"He plays on their weaknesses. The broken-hearted divorcé who misses his wife and children."

"Maybe I should join up."

"The man who lost his job to technology or to the quota system."

"Lonely, desperate, grasping at anything," I said. "They think Crawford has the answer?"

"They believe Crawford can return America back to the time when white God-fearing men ruled everything with an iron fist."

"No one's ever called Crawford on this?"

"You'll find very little negative publicity on the Sons of God," she said. "They tend to frown on it."

"Big deal."

"A very big deal. Picture teams of lawyers going after not just the publication, but the editor, the writer, their families and friends."

"But—"

"It's legal intimidation, Will. The *Village Voice* ran a cover story on the group a couple of years ago. Focused on the almost white supremacy thing Crawford had going on. The Sons of Gods claimed libel. They sued everyone involved." She shrugged. "They're just defending themselves."

"So, why risk it?"

"Exactly."

"But the recent cover stories."

"A lot of fluff. *Time* mentioned the *Voice* suit. How it was still pending. But other than that—" Another shrug.

"Okay," I said. "Back to the followers."

"Give me your weak . . ."

"Exactly," I said. "In return for this salvation, this *spiritual* awakening, what does Crawford get?"

"What do you think?" O'Toole said.

I did the math. "A lot of donation dollars."

"Absolutely."

"So, this is big business?"

"It's run just like a corporation. Crawford's the president and CEO."

"Saving souls."

"And pushing their agenda," she said. "They have a lot of clout. The politicians are very friendly. Both Republicans and Democrats."

"That doesn't surprise me," I said.

"Does anything?" she asked.

I thought about it hard for a beat and then shook my head. Nothing I could think of.

SEVEN

The eighteenth was a floor of suites: Presidential, Honeymoon. There was even an official John G. Rowland suite in honor of the Connecticut governor who helped Omni brass remove a couple of bus stops from the immediate downtown area. Can't have people who ride mass transit in view for those upscale Omni guests to see.

O'Toole and I figured a suite was a good bet, what with Dillard's high-priced accessories.

"Okay, I'm a Son of God," I said. "I worship James Crawford, my president and CEO, with all my heart and with all my soul. What does that mean exactly?"

"You honor his twelve commitments," O'Toole said.

"Not commandments?"

"Those, too."

"Can't wait," I said.

"It's exactly what you'd expect, Will," she said. "Honor Jesus."

"Goes without saying."

"Support the church, stomp out promiscuity—oh, yeah, you'll like this one—practice sexual, spiritual, and moral purity."

I couldn't help but laugh.

"You can figure out the rest," she said, smiling. "Build a strong marriage and family through biblical values."

"That's what Charlene and I were missing," I said.

"Fight intolerance."

I laughed again.

"Work toward biblical unity, a greater understanding of God in your community. Blah-blah-blah." She shook her head. "And something about loving God, not Crawford mind you, with all your heart and soul."

"Love the Lord your God with all your heart and with all

your soul and with all your mind and with all your strength," I offered up.

"Yeah," O'Toole said, a lot surprised. "That sounds about right. How'd you—?"

"Sunday school," I said. "There are some things you never forget. No matter how hard you try."

W hat part do women play in all of this Sons of God crap?" I asked. We were walking arm-in-arm down the hall, playing the part of a couple in lust.

"Barefoot, pregnant, and very submissive," O'Toole said.

"Crawford's wife go for that?" I asked.

"He's a recent widow," she said.

"Guess she couldn't take it anymore," I said, shaking my head. "That's got to be the fantasy for these guys. Their fetish."

"What?"

"Barefoot, pregnant, and submissive."

"That's a scary thought," she said. "But it makes sense."

"Wonder if some sort of submissive role-playing had anything to do with Dillard's murder."

"We don't even know he's one of them yet," she said.

"Yeah, and there's always a chance me and Charlene will patch things up."

"What I don't get is, why didn't he just call one of the upscale escort services? There was no need for a cheap motel. For an extra fifty he could have had a girl dressed as a maid, or someone in a business suit. She'd have blended right in. No one would have known."

"Maybe the high-priced girls don't like being lectured on family values."

"Believe me," she said. "A high-priced girl would have not only listened, but she'd also have promised to visit a priest ten minutes after Dillard came. I worked vice long enough to know."

Sure enough, O'Toole had played a large part in the conviction of Saul Rothstein. The Sex King, as he was dubbed by the local media, once ran more than a dozen escort services in Connecticut and western Massachusetts. Once. Not anymore.

"Okay, then," I suggested. "Maybe the Elm City Motor Lodge was part of the fantasy."

She shook her head a little, giving in. "Men have screwed-up fantasies."

W here is everyone?" O'Toole asked. We were at one end of the empty hallway, having already worked the opposite end, and there wasn't a Son of God in sight. I slipped the key-card into the appropriate slot and waited for the little green light to scream *bingo!* It blinked red instead.

"Maybe they're at afternoon prayer," I suggested. "Or taking in the Elm City sights." A shrug. "Or maybe early happy hour."

"No drinking."

"Oh, c'mon," I moaned. "How do they get up the nerve to boss their women around?"

"It's part of God's greater plan," she explained.

"So's Budweiser."

Another door, another rejection. Then one more after that. We passed a glass-topped table with carved legs painted in gold leaf, positioned between two doors at one end of the hall. There was a mirror hung on the wall above it with a matching gold leaf frame. I checked my tie, adjusting the knot with a slight jerk to the left.

"What do you think's really going on here?" O'Toole asked, watching me, then reaching up and jerking the knot on my tie back toward the right, nodding at her adjustment, and tapping the knot a few times, lightly, motherly.

I looked at her. There was a strange and sudden vulnerability in her eyes. Maybe there was something about being in a hotel with a man she found attractive—with a man I thought she *might have* found *reasonably* attractive. Maybe it was the job. No matter how much she might have disagreed with the Sons of God's politics, to see the gaping hole in that poor SOB's throat—

Maybe it was my tie.

"You mean the stuff in the bag, don't you?" I asked.

"All of it," she said. "That. Klavan asking us to sneak in here." She shrugged.

But I didn't have an answer. Not the right answer. Just more questions. Did Dillard have more in mind than an illicit lay? Did he make a fatal mistake by choosing the wrong girl? And what was she doing armed with—whatever it was she stabbed him with—while they screwed? Was this murder really just a case of self-defense?

I tried the next door, and what do you know? The little light that was flashing, was green. I pushed the door open and ushered O'Toole inside. I answered her question finally, though I was pretty certain she already knew.

"I think we're about to enter a depraved new world," I said.

EIGHT

The honeymoon suite. Maid fresh.

"Imagine spending your honeymoon in here," O'Toole said.

"Imagine spending it in New Haven," I countered, relieved that at least there were no Nagels.

We looked around. Everything was untouched, as if we were ourselves just checking in. In the bedroom, I slid back the mirrored closet door. A half dozen dark suits were lined side by side. Next to them, dress shirts, dry-clean fresh. Two pairs of black Italian wingtips, spit polished, stood in formation on the closet floor.

"Got to be twenty grand in clothes here," she said, checking the labels on the suits.

"Were you expecting JC Penney?" I asked.

On the top shelf were two black leather garment bags and a large black leather cabin bag, the now familiar Coach logo pressed into each. A matching set—at least Dillard was consistent. The two garment bags were empty, the cabin bag, as well.

"Look at this."

I turned. O'Toole was standing in front of the open bathroom door. I rushed over, thinking—

But her astonishment was not over a corpse, or a message written in blood on the mirror, but instead over the scope of the room. Marble tiled, with a Jacuzzi, a steam room, a shower large enough to hold eight, with more shower heads than the plumbing aisle at Home Depot. There was a toilet, a bidet, and three sinks. Not to mention a TV and two phones: one by the toilet, the other by the Jacuzzi.

"I could live in here," O'Toole said.

I glanced over Dillard's toiletries: He used an electric razor, baby powder, and toothpaste in a pump dispenser. His cologne was . . .

"Brut?" I said, making a face.

"Old habits die hard," O'Toole said.

Every item, from the towering shampoo bottle down to a nail clipper was lined up according to its height, against the back of the counter, between the first and second sinks. I couldn't help but wonder, when Dillard changed brands, did he reconfigure the lineup?

O'Toole checked the drawers and the cabinets, patting down the towels, looking behind the extra toilet paper and facial tissue. Nothing.

We returned to the bedroom. I went through the drawers of the cherry wood dresser. Stacks of meticulously folded T-shirts, underwear, socks, a sweater, and a copy of the *Celestine Prophecy*.

O'Toole was sitting on the edge of the California king-size bed when I heard her say, "Amen."

"Let me guess, it vibrates for free."

"Will, I can vibrate for free."

I wasn't really sure what she meant, and was distracted from asking as she started pulling items from the nighttable drawer: a wallet, a passport, an organizer, and the one thing that really brought a smile to my face, a laptop computer.

We stared at the face on the Mississippi State driver's license. The thick mass of black hair peppered with gray, over a pockmarked face with bushy, almost crazed eyebrows, thin lips, and unclear eyes. It was our man, our victim, Dillard. But the name: Richard Deegan. The Jackson, Mississippi, address. I grabbed the passport. Same name, and even the same address penciled in. Same initials. Similar photo. Same face. The wallet was filled with other forms of identification, all identifying its owner as Richard Deegan: a platinum American Express card, a platinum Visa card, a platinum MasterCard—I was half expecting a platinum Blockbuster Video card—a Blue Cross health insurance card, a library card.

And there were snapshots. In one, Dillard, Deegan, whatever his name was, posed with a woman about his age—a blonde, a little on the heavy side, with tired eyes. They were sitting by a pool somewhere. On vacation. A honeymoon. A second honeymoon, perhaps. Somewhere.

In the other, he posed with a young woman. The spitting image of the older woman, so much the same face, the same build, but less than half her age. The main difference—the younger woman had shoulder-length dark brown hair. I made the assumption she was their daughter. By their side in the picture, a golden retriever. Deegan and the young woman were out by a lake. The leaves had turned, and both of them wore camouflage jackets. Both also carried hunting rifles.

"Richard Deegan," O'Toole said.

"You have any idea who he is?" I asked her.

She picked up the organizer. A Filofax, butterscotch in color. Holding it in her hands. About to snap it open. But first she started nodding. She looked at me and muttered, "Goddamn," at just about the same time I heard the door to the suite open and shut.

I pulled out my gun, a Glock 21, as I cautiously approached the bedroom door, staying behind it, pressed to the wall, out of sight. O'Toole moved to the other side of the door, her gun also in hand.

"Dick," called an effeminate voice from the other room. "Everyone's waiting for you at lunch." The man rapped lightly against the bedroom door, and when no answer came, he slowly pushed it open, entering. "Dick, what are you—?"

The Glock pressed against the side of his face cut the words short. But it could do nothing to stop the stream of urine that ran down his legs.

"No, please," he cried. "Don't hurt me."

Nauseated, infuriated, I pressed my badge forward only inches from his face. "Identify yourself," I said.

"The police?" he said. "What are you doing here?"

"Identify yourself."

My tone was sharp, and judging from the look on his face, if he had any piss left in him, we'd have been treated to round two. He gulped, and I thought for a moment he had swallowed his tongue. But finally the words came. "Donald Savage," he said.

"Can you prove that?"

He reached into his pocket and retrieved a wallet. He held it out in trembling hands. O'Toole snapped it open, took a quick glance at his Mississippi driver's license, and then nodded in my direction.

I pulled away the Glock, holstering it, but not holstering the attitude. "What are *you* doing here, *Donny*?" I asked.

"I'm Mr. Deegan's executive assistant," he said, relaxing just the slightest bit. Perhaps the slightest bit was all a person could relax after having wet himself.

"And what exactly do you assist him with."

"The day-to-day operations of the Sons of God."

"And Deegan Publishing," O'Toole said.

"Right," Donny said. "Deegan Publishing."

I looked back and forth between them, thinking suddenly about how we were supposed to keep this quiet. About the sixty thousand plus heading our way. About rose-colored glasses. "Day-to-day operations," I said, prodding, "As in?"

"He's the number-two man in the organization," Donny said, as if reading from a press release. "When Mr. Crawford retires at the end of the year, Dick's slotted to take his place. Everyone knows that."

"Not everyone," I said.

When was the last time you saw Mr. Deegan?" I asked. Donny was sitting on the sofa in his boss's suite.

"Look," he said. "I don't know that I should be . . ."

"Answering our questions?" O'Toole said. "You have something to hide?"

He held her look for what seemed like the longest time. I wanted to answer for him: We all have something to hide.

"Last night," he said finally, turning in my direction, "we all—"

"We?" I asked. "Who exactly?"

"Dick, me, Albert Larsen—"

"He is—?"

"Event coordinator," Donny said.

"He was going to be my contact," O'Toole told me.

Donny looked at her. "Albert arranges for hotel rooms," he said. "Transportation, security—"

"Got'cha," I said, cutting him off, thinking Albert came up short on this go-around.

He nodded. "Um, let's see. Tony Sorrentino was there." He answered before I could ask. "He's a vice president in the organization. And, um, Woody Speight—"

"President of Yale," O'Toole said.

Donny nodded, and then said, "And, oh, yeah, how could I forget? Mayor Pinfield."

"*Our* Mayor Pinfield?" I asked.

"Yes," Donny said. "There were just the six of us. Your mayor took us for pizza over on—"

"Wooster Square," I volunteered.

"Yes," Donny said. "How did you know?"

I ignored his question. Out of these three select reasons that

God put New Haven on the map, pizza—real brick-oven pizza—was number one. The Elm City, not Chicago—and certainly not New York—was known the world over as the pizza capital of the world. When ex-Presidents came to town to visit their alma maters, they'd dine at one of three renowned establishments. "Sally's, Pepe's, or Modern?" I asked, naming off the father, son, and holy spirit of pizza joints.

"Russo's," Donny said.

"What?" I asked, a little too loudly, my astonishment getting the better of me. Pinhead was a one-term Republican mayor, with six months to go. Taxes were up, unemployment had doubled, crime was through the roof, *and* he preferred Russo's to Pepe's Pizzeria Napoletana, or Sally's Pizza, or Modern Apizza Place. Armed with that information, I could run against him in an election today and win.

"Russo's," he repeated.

"Yeah, I heard you, it's just—" I was at a loss for words.

O'Toole patted my hand. "Reader's Digest," she said; then, turning back to Donny, she asked, "What did you talk about?"

"I really don't see how . . ."

"What did you talk about, Donny?" I snapped, still pissed about the mayor's lack of taste.

"It's Donald," he said, glaring at me.

I glared right back.

"It was very casual, really," he explained, looking away. "We talked about morality and family values. We talked about God. About what would be happening at the rally on Saturday."

Donny gave us the rundown. My interpretation? Sixty thousand Bible-thumping, misogynistic yahoos praying and crying and begging for forgiveness at the Yale Bowl.

It was an absurd idea brought about when a Sons of God supporter kicked the bucket last year. A billionaire supporter. A graduate of Yale. His dying request was that his prayer boys hold an annual soiree at the Yale Bowl. And Yale alumni are never denied. Especially wealthy Yale alumni. So, a day was set aside. The second Saturday in May. This would be the first of these second Saturdays. Perhaps the one good thing about Deegan's death was that it might also be the last.

As O'Toole accompanied Donny to his room—so that he could change into something a little drier—I rang up Brown to give him the news. That yes, our *victim* was with the Sons of God. The number-two guy. His real name, Richard Deegan.

"Huh," Brown said.

"My feeling exactly," I said.

"I talked to Scissero," he said.

"What's Slice got to say?"

"He estimates the time of death between ten P.M. and midnight."

That was our medical examiner's favorite part of the job. Stick a thermometer under the rib cage, deep into the liver, get a body temperature, and estimate away. How many hours the victim had been dead. Oftentimes there are extenuating circumstances. A body found frozen to death, for instance, or in a hot tub, or in Long Island Sound. But Deegan's should have been a breeze.

"Great," I said. I knew from O'Toole that most agencies stopped doing business around eleven or midnight during the week. Two, three in the morning on weekends. A few did twenty-four/seven, but the pickings were slim. "That opens it up to just about every call girl in the state."

"So does the murder weapon," he said.

"Slice got that already?"

"This one was easy," Brown said. "A pencil."

"You're shittin' me?"

"Uh-uh. The point broke off when it hit bone. Even left a little black dot."

"Like a period."

"Just like one," he said.

I laughed out loud. "All that weird shit in the bag," I said. "A pencil used as a murder weapon."

"Yeah," my partner said, almost as if he could read my mind. "This is just getting more fucked up by the minute."

TEN

The mood was morguelike. Brown and Mazz working the phones, taking notes. They didn't look happy. The door to the lieutenant's office was shut. The blinds shut. Better that way. He probably didn't look happy either.

O'Toole and I led Donny to room one. It was the interrogation room without a cage, without a lockup. It was where parents were often told that their children were dead, where spouses were told that their husbands or wives had been murdered, where relatives were questioned about a loved one who'd gone wrong. It was a room of grief.

I gave him a bottle of spring water. He asked for a slice of lemon, but we were fresh out.

"Donny," I said, leaning against the closest wall. "There's no easy way to say this—"

O'Toole slid one of the Deegan/Dillard Polaroids across the table. It was the least graphic, but still.

"Is that Richard Deegan?" I asked.

The words caught in his throat, but not his tears. They flooded his eyes and flowed freely.

"What—?" he said, making an attempt to say something, but falling way short. His grief seemed immediate. It seemed real.

"Happened last night," O'Toole said. "Mr. Deegan was murdered in a motel room on the other side of town."

"He's dead?" Donny asked.

"Yes," she said.

"I can't believe . . . I mean . . ." He wiped at his eyes. "Who'd want to do this to him? Who?"

"That's what we're trying to find out," she said.

"Did you—" I glanced at O'Toole as I searched for the right words. "—ever provide any special services for Mr. Deegan?"

"Special," he said. The next words came slowly. "I'm not quite sure I follow."

O'Toole reached over the table and touched his hands, looked right into his eyes. "Special, Donny, as in sexual?"

"Sexual?" he said, blushing suddenly. "With Dick? The two of us together?" He pulled his hands away. "He would never—"

"Not the two of you together," I said. "Did you ever acquire the services of a—?"

"Call girl," O'Toole said. "Did you ever hire a professional escort for your boss?"

"No," he said, shaking his head, covering his mouth with the palm of his hand. "Oh, God."

"What?" I asked.

He took a moment. "Dick would—," he said. "Never. I mean—" He took a deep breath, forced it back out. "Why would he want to? He's got a beautiful wife."

"Her name?" I asked.

He looked at me, his eyes confused. He had to shake his head, as if bringing it back from somewhere. "Excuse me."

"What's his wife's name?"

"Margaret," he said, turning back to face O'Toole. "Dick would never use a hooker." He took a sip of water, as if to wash away the taste of the word. "God, no. Why? Why are you asking me this? Do you think a hooker killed him?"

"That's one possibility," I said. Then, thinking about it for a moment, I wondered if perhaps there was another. Perhaps someone like Deegan *would* bring a mistress to the Elm City Motor Lodge. It was worth a shot. "Could he have been having an affair? A younger woman perhaps?"

"No," Donny said, shaking his head almost violently. "No. No. No. Absolutely not." He seemed so sure. "I'd have known. I was with him"—a shrug—"all the time. And when I wasn't there, Margaret was." He placed his hands flat against the tabletop, as if to steady himself. "Detective, Dick Deegan was a great man. A family man. He devoted his life to spreading the Sons of God message. To helping others achieve sexual, spiritual, and moral purity."

I looked over at O'Toole; she was staring right back. What was that? Commitment number eight or nine, or did it really matter?

"And I'm sure that's exactly what Dick was doing in that motel room," I said.

Richard Deegan was an executive. Meetings, phone calls, damage control. Could have been working for IBM, could have been the CEO of Ford. Like O'Toole had said, big business. But instead of selling cars and PCs, Deegan just happened to be pitching morality and that old-time religion. He'd been very proud of the Yale rally. Deegan had been close to the university alumnus who'd made it all possible. "Dick and Kilgore Travers were like brothers," Donny had claimed. I had no reason to doubt him. Travers wasn't a suspect. The billionaire had been dead for almost a year.

But then he added, "They roomed together."

"Roomed?"

"When?"

"At Yale," he explained, shaking his head. "I can't believe he's dead."

"Deegan went to Yale?" I asked.

"Of course," Donny said, as if it were common knowledge. As if every New Haven resident should and would know the name of every Yale graduate. "Class of sixty-four."

"He have many friends in New Haven?" I asked.

"I'm sure he did back then, but—" Donny shrugged.

"No one he's kept in touch with?" O'Toole asked.

He appeared to think about it for a moment. He spoke the words slowly, with effort. "No one that I can recall."

"Old girlfriends, drinking buddies," I said. "Someone he pissed off."

"No, Detective," Donny said sadly. "Dick never mentioned any friends from Yale, other than Kilgore. I'm sorry."

"Any enemies not from Yale?" I asked, my tone perhaps a little too sharp.

"You mean other than the liberal media and pro-choice advocates," he answered angrily.

"You forgot the feminists and gays," I said.

"No," he said, staring hard, his face flushing.

"No, you didn't forget them?" I asked.

"No, Dick had no specific enemies."

I held Donny's look for a long beat. "He had to have pissed someone off," I said.

ELEVEN

Mazz hadn't much luck in tracing the chloroacetyl chloride. "The company that makes this brand is out of business," he explained. "I checked every supplier in this state and in Mississippi. No one has any left on the shelves, can't remember the last time they did."

I turned to my partner. "What about a record?"

"As you can imagine," Brown said. "Dillard was clean as the driven snow. I've been running Deegan through since your call, and he's even cleaner than that."

"He ain't that clean," O'Toole said.

"Okay," Brown read from his notebook, quickly through the facts. "He was born in White Plains, New York. Parents owned Deegan Publishing. Grade A student. High school athlete of the year in 1958." He paused, scanning the page. "But listen to this. Went to Yale. Graduated—" He cleared his throat. "—fourth in his class—"

"Yeah, we got that far, too," I said.

"It's one avenue," Mazz said.

"That's thirty-five years old," O'Toole said. "Doubt many from his graduating class have stuck around."

"Who said they had to be from his graduating class?" Mazz said. "Remember tigers have striped skin, not just striped fur." He shrugged. "The guy obviously liked slumming."

We let that sit; then Brown continued. "After Yale, he did a stint in Nam. Awarded a Medal of Honor for service above and beyond. He went to work for his dad's publishing company after he got out. When his parents passed, Deegan inherited the company, which he ran until ninety-four, at which point he stepped down to join the Sons of God. Today Deegan Publishing is the second largest publisher of Bibles in the world. Deegan still owns it, lock, stock, and barrel."

"Owned it," I corrected.

A nod. "He's an expert marksman," Brown said, "has won numerous hunting awards and was a personal friend to Presidents Reagan and Bush, both father and son."

Didn't exactly make me miss the old guy. Bibles, hunting, Ronald Reagan, and Yale. A snug fit. So where did the hookers come in? The acid, the enema bag? Perhaps they were part of that package as well. "No record?" I asked. "Nothing?"

"Nothing," Brown repeated. "No arrests, no tickets—the guy doesn't even double park."

"A regular saint," Mazz said.

"What gives?" O'Toole asked.

I looked at her, thinking she wanted an answer. But she was looking away. Over my shoulder. I turned and followed her line of sight. We all did. She was staring at the door to the lieutenant's office. It was open now. Mayor Pinfield, Chief Zekowski, Klavan, and two men I'd never seen before were exiting, walking in our direction. Walking except for the chief. He was waddling. A fat man in his sixties, moments away from a massive coronary attack at all times. He smoked too many cigars, drank too much hard liquor, and must have had something good on Pinhead, because none of us could figure out what the hell he was doing on this job. It was an appointment, sure. And he was a lawyer at one time. But never a cop. That irked us.

Klavan called out to us. We stood; then he did the introductions. The two unknowns were Albert Larsen and Tony Sorrentino. Sons of God event coordinator and vice president, respectively. The dinner partners from Russo's. I wanted to tell them to go get some real brick-oven pizza while they were in town, but thought better. Wouldn't want to hurt Pinhead's feelings.

"These are the detectives working the case," Klavan said.

"I just want the person who killed Dick to suffer as much as he did," Sorrentino said, obviously upset. "I just wish I could get my hands on them. Lock me in a room with them for ten minutes, and justice would be served."

Larsen shot him a look. I wondered if he was thinking what I was thinking: not a very Christ-like attitude.

"An eye for an eye," Pinhead said, steepling his fingertips under his chin.

"A life for a life," Sorrentino said. He was looking at O'Toole now, liking what he saw.

"Are there any leads?" Larsen asked. His voice shook a little. I could tell he was doing his best to hold it all together. This wasn't a part of it. Honoring Christ wasn't supposed to leave you dead in a no-tell motel. "Any clues. Do you think you'll catch whoever it is who did this?"

It was Brown who answered. "We're working every angle," he said. He knew the clichés best. He knew how to deal with the suits. All those years buys you something.

"Dick Deegan was a—" His voice caught. "—a friend of mine," Larsen explained. "A good man. A family man. Poor Margaret. And the girls. He had three beautiful daughters. I don't know what they're going to do without him."

"Believe me," Klavan said. "We're putting every effort into solving this terrible crime."

"You'll keep us informed?" Larsen asked. He was watching Sorrentino watch O'Toole.

"Of course they will," Zekowski said.

Klavan nodded, and we watched them leave.

We followed the lieutenant into his office. He told Mazz to shut the door. I went to open the blinds, to let some light in. But Klavan told me to keep those shut for now.

He took a seat behind his desk, a standard steel desk with a good chair. High back and leather. On the desk were the framed photos of his wife and the eight kids. The paperwork, paperweights, and Cross pens. The office supplies that went with the territory.

"What the hell was Deegan doing in that motel room?" Klavan asked.

"That's a multipart question," I said. "The fake ID, the stuff in his bag, the murder weapon, we've got to be thinking—"

"The fake ID can be explained away."

"The pencil can't," I said. "You don't plan on murdering someone with a pencil."

"You're thinking self-defense, Shute?"

"Make that two of us," O'Toole said.

"Three of us," Mazz said.

"It's unanimous," Brown said.

Klavan shook his head. We all knew the look. It wasn't what he wanted to hear. No clean, quick, or easy. "Get anything from the room?"

"A laptop and—," I said, nodding at O'Toole, who pulled Deegan's wallet and organizer from her purse and handed them to Klavan.

"Deegan's assistant, Donald Savage, gave us reluctant permission to take them," she explained. "He thought we were trying to find Deegan at the time—now he knows we're trying to find his killer."

Klavan flipped open the wallet and grunted quietly, still shaking his head. He bounced the organizer in his free hand.

"What the hell kind of leather is this?" he asked.

"Ostrich skin," O'Toole said.

Klavan made a face. I think we all did.

"Anything in here?" he asked.

"Don't know yet." O'Toole said.

He handed it to her. "What about the laptop, Shute? That's your specialty."

"Absolutely," I said, glancing over at Mazz, who was just as handy. He shrugged and smiled. A sign that it was no skin off his back.

"See what you can find," Klavan said.

"Sure," I said, turning back to face him. "Now I've got one for you. What do the suits know about how Deegan died?"

"A lot," Klavan said.

"They have any ideas as to who or why?" Brown asked.

"They think he was set up," Klavan said. "That this is part of a bigger picture. A smear campaign. I don't have to tell you there's a lot of opposition to what these guys believe in. A lot of people have been trying to drag the Sons of God down."

"I thought they fought back in court," I said.

"Which is exactly why they feel their enemies are taking it to the next level," Klavan said.

"The next level?" I said.

"That this is an act of what?" Brown asked. "Anti-religious terrorism?"

I could feel the anger rising. Boiling over. Perhaps it had just been building all day. Then again, no *perhaps* about that. "So, someone killed the son of a bitch," I said. "Then dragged him to the Elm City, undressed him, stuck a rubber on his limp dick, then stabbed him in the throat with a pencil. Is that what Larsen and Sorrentino think, Lieutenant? Cause if that's what they think, they must be the dumbest sons o' bitches to ever walk the face of the earth."

"Calm down," he said, glaring.

I muttered some obscenity, a string of them, one blurring into the next, and turned away.

"Richard Deegan was an important man—," Klavan began.

"Who was obviously doing wrong," O'Toole said.

"Let he who is without sin cast the first stone," Klavan said, forcing the sentiment.

"You're kidding me, right?" I said, turning back. He didn't

glare at me this time. This time he couldn't even look me in the eye.

"C'mon, Lieutenant," Brown said. "This is bullshit, and you know it. If their pockets weren't so deep—"

Klavan didn't let him finish. It was as if Brown had hit the nerve. The lieutenant held up his hand, palm out, then changed the subject. "What about the assistant?"

We all turned away, or shook our heads. Finally O'Toole answered. "I doubt he had anything to do with it. If that's what you're asking. If you're asking, does he know more than he told us?" She shrugged.

"Let's just hope he knows how to keep his mouth shut," Klavan said.

"Why, Lieutenant?" Brown asked. We were all looking at Klavan now, wondering the same thing. "What's all this about? Really? These closed door meetings?"

"I just think—"

"You or the mayor?" Mazz asked.

"All of us," Klavan said, a little too loudly. "This matter needs to be treated with the utmost delicacy."

"What is it, damage control?" O'Toole said. "They don't want anyone to know their number-two guy was banging hookers?"

"Call it what you like," Klavan said.

"How about *commitment number thirteen*?" I said.

TWELVE

It was a nice enough apartment. All by its lonesome, in a free standing brick building on the corner of State and East Streets. Home to Stacy's Unisex Hair Salon on the first floor. Just me up here after dark. After 6 P.M., Tuesday through Saturday. All day Sunday and Monday. It had a monster living room with sixteen-foot ceilings. The bedroom was a loft that overhung the space. The kitchen was small but serviceable. It was more than I needed, really. All I needed was a fridge and a plug for the percolator. The loft bedroom was carpeted; the kitchen, tiled; the rest, hardwood. The walls were painted white and unadorned, except for a four-foot-square poster of the cover of The Clash's London Calling album. Paul Simonon bent over like the Hunchback of Notre Dame smashing the hell out of his Fender bass. The last tenant had left it there. It seemed like a positive sign. I pushed my old sofa underneath it, opposite the TV and stereo. The sofa was beat, from my bachelor days. Had been in hiding in the basement of the condo I shared with Charlene. I didn't have a coffee table or an end table. But I did have plenty of unpacked boxes. A few pushed together did the jobs just fine. An old lamp by the side of the couch gave me enough light to read by. My speakers, fat B&W's, were spread far apart, one to each side of the TV and the rack stereo system. A large table, which doubled as a desk, was set up against the windows, which looked out onto State Street. My view was a Korean market and three restaurants, one specializing in Japanese noodles, another, The Pantry, serving the best breakfast in town—it's where I'd been spending every morning (except Mondays, when they were unreasonably closed, and which was yet another justification for today's mood). The last was Subway. And that's where tonight's dinner came from, the wrapping still crumpled on the far edge of the table, right next to the first empty beer bottle.

I'd been in no rush to unpack. No need to find the things that reminded me of Charlene. The things given to me by Charlene. The things that belonged to Charlene that might have been packed by mistake. I needed only the necessities, really. The stereo, the TV, my computer. All three were plugged in and turned on at this very moment. The stereo loud, five discs in a changer, on shuffle play. The TV tuned to channel eight, the local ABC affiliate. Its volume off. The computer in sleep mode.

The rest could wait. Would wait. Was waiting. Was playing coffee table, or end table. Old clothes, or winter clothes. Pictures and videos and books. Boxes of books, stacked up against one wall. (I had the shelves to put them on. Just hadn't had the time.) And memories. There were a lot of memories in those boxes. My life with Charlene as I thought I knew it. My life as a blind man. My life as a sucker. My life.

Over by the wall that separated the kitchen from the rest of the space—an interior wall where probably a small dining room table should go—was the hardshell case. Pretty well beat after all these years. A replacement for the original tweed-and-brown-leather-trimmed beauty that came with it. But tweed-and-brown-leather-trimmed cases weren't made for life on the road, in a Ford van, with three other guys. And Gloria meant too much to me. That was her name, Gloria. She lived in that case. Hadn't seen her in years. But I knew she was safe up against an interior wall.

She rested behind a Marshall MK II 2 × 12 combo amp. A hundred watts, all tubes, driving two twelve-inch speakers. It wasn't a stack, but when you're a fifteen-year-old dreaming of being Joe Strummer, it was loud enough. I hadn't turned it on since I don't know when. Hadn't plugged Gloria in—not since a little after getting married, anyway. It was dreaming, in Charlene's eyes. A waste of time. Annoying. She had a dozen different names for it. "You're making noise," she'd say. Then, coming to me, taking Gloria from my hands—"Don't you want to play with me, instead?"

After a while, after not that long, I began to believe her. Didn't want to hear it anymore. Didn't want to argue. Didn't want Charlene anywhere near Gloria. So I took Gloria out less and less, until it got to a point where I was afraid to open the case. Afraid of letting my dreams escape. That I'd ignored them for so long, they'd hightail it out the first chance they got.

A s I positioned Deegan's laptop on my desk, the songs shuffled, and I found myself singing along at the top of my lungs as the slightly out-of-tune guitars led into an explosion of sound, "There they go, fucking up the ratio—"

The image on the TV caught my attention. I turned down one volume, replacing it with another. The press conference. Klavan, Pinhead, and the chief. The chief saying, "Our sympathies go out to the Deegan family." Cut to New Haven's Tweed Airport. A Gulfstream jet landing. The Deegan Publishing logo painted brightly on the side of its tail. The woman from the vacation photograph in Deegan's wallet, identified as his wife, Margaret. Her eyes puffy and dark, she exited the plane, accompanied by three young women. The news anchor explained that Deegan is "survived by his wife and their three daughters." He spoke their names as they walked past on the TV. "Anne." His eldest. Not unattractive, just plain. And blonde. Her hair styled, long and wavy, not completely big. Then "Theresa," the middle child, the brunette who looked so much like her mother. She was the girl from the other snapshot in Deegan's wallet, the hunting photo. Her hair was the same as in the picture. Medium length, straight, lifeless, now held back with a headband. And lastly, "Ruth." A large girl, her hair red, a punky unnatural dye-job, a punky cut. All four Deegan women were dressed in black. But only Ruth looked as if she wore the color every day of her life.

I recognized Tony Sorrentino as he met the women, walking them to a Lincoln Town Car, helping Margaret into the front passenger seat. The daughters took the backseat. Sorrentino's arm curled around Ruth. Protective. A look of concern from the brunette, Theresa, as she slipped into the car, and the doors slammed shut.

I wondered if they were close, Deegan and his daughters— there were no pictures of Anne or Ruth in his wallet, only Theresa. Out on that hunting trip. I likewise wondered if Deegan and his wife were close, or was he too busy promoting family values to pay much attention to what was going on at home?

Aiming the remote, I shut off the TV just as the page-two story started up. It was about the groundbreaking for a new apartment building in the Ninth Square.

It was loaded down with all the bells and whistles: a Dell 2.4-gigahertz Pentium 4, with a 15.9-inch active-matrix display, 1026-megabyte of RAM, a 60-gigabyte hard drive, a DVD/CD-ROM drive, a Zip disk drive, and an internal V.90 fax modem. In short, it smoked.

Only thing missing: the AC adapter. I forgot to ask Donny if there was one around; we certainly hadn't come across one in Deegan's room. The identification sticker on the bottom of the computer told me the unit needed fifteen volts of electricity. I checked the AC adapters I had in boxes, one for a portable CD player, another for a rechargeable screwdriver, another for an MXR Phase 90 guitar pedal, and an Ibanez Tube Screamer. Nine volts, twelve, six—anything but fifteen. I starting thinking that maybe the battery would be next to drained, and I'd have to drive back to the Omni. But by now Larsen or Sorrentino or someone had stepped in, talked to Donny. Perhaps they'd want to see what was on Deegan's computer first. Perhaps—Mazz might have one if need be. But, I didn't want to drive, or leave the apartment. So, I popped open another beer, lifted the laptop's cover, pressed the power button, and hoped for the best.

Someone or something must have been feeling sorry for me. First: no password protection. Second: according to the little window indicator, the Dell's battery had about 60 percent of its juice left. All that, *and* the Zip Drive icon in the lower right-hand corner of his desktop—what I had assumed to be a floppy drive, was in fact a removable Zip Drive. I had a dozen Zip disks, mostly backing up what was on my hard drive. I hoped they could hold what seemed interesting on Deegan's.

Accessing his Windows Explorer, I began with his Microsoft Word text files: everything from the subdirectories named LET-TERS, FAXES, and SPEECHES.

I copied his Temporary Internet Files, his bookmarks, and the entire America Online and Internet Explorer folders. I copied his Quicken account files. His Lotus organizer files. And then I hit the jackpot. Under a directory titled MAGDALENE, I found over thirty-five hundred files, close to two hundred megabytes of information. And while every file had an extension of *.jpg*— those computer photographs—it was the JPEG file names that interested me most: *anna001* through *anna147, lola001* through *lola098, mary001* through *mary620*—620 *mary* files—and so forth. Almost always a woman's name, followed by the number *001* through to whatever, followed by that telltale *.jpg*. There were other oddities as well. Files named *ckbd*, and numbered as the others. Or *fxbd*, or *smbd*, or *hs*, or *sch*. Likewise, all JPEGs.

My hands were shaking as I popped Zip disk after Zip disk into the drive, listening to its hum, watching the green light flicker, as it copied Deegan's secrets. I raced against the rapidly dwindling battery power to capture every last one of those

JPEGs, resisting the urge to pull up just one of those files, not willing to waste one extra moment of power. I needed it all to allow me access into Deegan's depraved but hardly new or original world. To tell his story from beyond the slab he now occupied in the morgue.

The warning beep began. Less than 2 percent battery power. But the last of the JPEGs had been copied. I scanned his Windows Explorer directories one last time. There were games and spreadsheets and an anti-virus program. There was Norton Utilities, some communication software—I copied Deegan's list of phone numbers—and the Bible, as God, I'm sure, meant for it to be seen. I downloaded that, as well, in case there was a clue, a collection of favorite passages, something that could be interpreted. Then the beeping became frantic, and the dazzling active-matrix screen became less so, and began to fade.

And the Dell went dead.

THIRTEEN

I started alphabetically with the *anna.jpg* files. Brought them up one at a time with my viewer. She was the teenager next door, if that teenager just happened to be doing porn. There was nothing over the top in these pictures. Nothing violent. Nothing that kinky. Just a pretty blond girl having sex. Perhaps that was enough.

The *dawn.jpg* had platinum hair cut into a bob; *heidi.jpg* had long wavy brown hair; *lola.jpg* was a redheaded bundle of poutiness and pink. What they all shared, besides a seductive innocence, was a similar body type. These were slender girls, but unlike typical centerfolds, none had large breasts—no implants, nothing unnatural. There was a small boob thing going on here. That was obviously the way Deegan liked them.

I opened a few of the other files, the ones with the obscure names. Those ending in the letters *bd* were bondage pictures. Women in handcuffs and restraints, trying to look turned on, but appearing either frightened or bored instead. The *hs* and *sch* files were schoolgirl pictures. Mostly Asian girls, perhaps fourteen to eighteen years old. Posed in their school uniforms. Posed topless, or showing a flash of panties. Nothing more explicit than that.

Bored myself, I started skipping around. One picture here, another there. A sampling. Saving *mary.jpg* for last, or until I couldn't take the variety anymore, as she was obviously Deegan's favorite, 620 times over. I wondered where Deegan had found these pictures? Searching the Web, the newsgroups? Searching *alt.binaries.pictures.erotica.female*, or *alt.binaries.nospam.teenfem*, or there was even a group called: *alt.fan.oksana-bayul.small-tits*. There was a newsgroup for everything. I discovered them all a year or so back, working an Internet child pornography case involving a Yale professor. There were even newsgroups for that. Then I worked them again, when a local gang started using the Net to sell drugs. Orders via e-mail. Delivered to your door in thirty minutes or less. You could buy anything online.

Or perhaps Deegan was dumb enough to pay for them, becoming a member at any of the thousands of Internet porn sites. For anywhere from fifteen to thirty-five dollars a month they promised thousands of photographs, frequent updates, live chats, live girls. What none of these porn-for-pay sites told you was that the photos all came from the same places, a dozen or so warehousing operations. So what you ended up seeing was the same girls in the same poses on hundreds of different sites. If I spent an hour I could probably find Anna, Lola, Heidi, or any of the others being offered *exclusively* at a dozen different Web addresses. It's a small World Wide Web.

Shaking clear my head, I wondered where, if anyplace, these photos would lead. Were they just Deegan's porn of choice? Instead of a magazine, and to paraphrase Klavan, let he who has never purchased *Playboy* cast the first stone. Perhaps this was his little waste of time. Or, right now, perhaps it was mine.

Perhaps this surfing through Deegan's collection was more for my peace of mind. To know that there were other women out there—

The *traci.jpg* was posed on a basement floor in front of a washer and dryer and baskets of about-to-be-washed clothes.

Obviously available women. Women who'd make love to me and do my laundry—

And *rachel.jpg* was an auto mechanic, leaning over the hood of a BWM.

—and fix my car—

The *patty.jpg* was posed on a kitchen counter. She was half-covered in flour, obviously about to bake a cake.

—and cook for me—

The *nina.jpg* was—

I sat back for a moment, and stared at *nina.jpg*. She was a good-looking woman. With long dark brown hair. Perhaps not as young as the others—perhaps the others weren't as young as I thought—but just as slender. Just as firm. She certainly had a small-breast thing going, but her innocence was lost, at least on me. She wasn't posed in *nina001.jpg* as a centerfold, but with a well-endowed male partner. He was lifting her onto a bed. She had her arms around his neck, as she smiled for the camera. Both were naked. Both were—

I moved through her photos with an urgency, a need I hadn't felt in years, or at least three months. There were 186 in all, from a dozen different shoots. Judging from her clothes, from the way she styled her hair, the photos were recent. Taken over the last two or three years. There were six sets of her posed with one male lover—a different man each time. One set with a female lover. One with a couple: a woman and a man. Three sets with two male partners. And lastly, a foursome, in which she was the only female. Eighteen separate lovers, sixteen men, two women.

The woman in the *nina.jpg* would seemingly do anything to please her partners. She was insatiable. It ripped my heart out seeing the joy in her eyes. So real. So hungry. Full of fire. The smile on her face. The arch of her back. So familiar that I could hear the sounds she'd make. The come-on lines. The moans. The breathy hiccup when she came. That I could feel the heat radiating off her skin. The burning, the wetness. Her tightness. The smell of her hair. The taste of her mouth. Strawberries. Her mouth tasted like strawberries. Always like strawberries. It killed me to see the wedding band and engagement ring on her finger. A three-quarter carat diamond, set in platinum. A matching band. Rings that I had purchased in a small jewelry store in downtown Oranjestad, while she took a nap on the beach. Purchased as a surprise. Between the time we decided "Let's do it!"

and the ceremony. Because I was in love. Truly, I thought. Madly, I didn't know. Deeply, it seemed like love. I had nothing to compare it to.

"Fuck you, Charlene," I said, finally turning away.

FOURTEEN

I was on my fourth beer, still staring at my ex-wife. Wondering what could have been going through her mind. How could she? Why would she? Couldn't she at least have taken off the goddamn rings? I wondered what could have been going through my own mind. Are we all that desperate to take love at face value? Commitment at face value? Respect at face value? Are we that afraid to be alone, or are we just blinded by lust? Devoured by lust? Left stupid and dirty.

The buzzer cut through the music, a slow track about dying within one's reach. The buzzer jarred me. The pictures, well, they turned my stomach. They turned me on. They turned me inside out. And still I couldn't see.

I switched off the computer, watching Charlene's face fade. Then I pushed back, rolling the desk chair away from the table. Standing finally, shaking, not with rage, but with confusion, walking to the door, buzzing the person in. Couldn't ask who? The speaker wasn't working. But I didn't give a good goddamn. It was almost midnight, and maybe this was all a dream. Maybe it was her. Lord let me have this, I thought. Let it be Charlene. Let me have her, this one last time. And if not, I wouldn't let it be ruined until the absolute last moment.

Then came the decidedly light rap against the door. I held the breath in my chest, still picturing those images, willing them to life, to have a voice. Her voice. Her smell. Her joy. Insatiable. Strawberries. Stupid and dirty.

I turned the handle.

She didn't say anything at first. Just gave me a look, shrugged, and then brushed past into my apartment.

"Got anything stronger than beer?" she asked, looking around, eyeing the unpacked memories.

I nudged the door shut and went to the cabinet where I kept the whiskey.

"Bourbon?" I said.

She nodded. I poured, handing her the drink. She took a long swig. Then another, finishing it, lowering the glass onto the countertop.

"You're out late," I said, not knowing what else to say. Looking for conversation. For reason. Looking up, down, away. Trying to avoid eye contact at all costs.

She shrugged. "Got something for you," she said, pressing a small package into my hand.

I looked at it. A condom. The gold foil package read RAMSES. Lubricated. Spermicide. An expiration date, handwritten with a fine-point Sharpie: May 6, 2002.

"This expires in a few minutes," I said, looking at her finally.

And Gracie O'Toole smiled. She stared at me for a long beat and then spoke. "Then you better get moving," she said.

FIFTEEN

We crashed into one another, and something hit me. A realization. An answer to O'Toole's question from before, from earlier, in the elevator at the Omni: Does anything surprise me?

Finding it, the answer, as I pushed up the hem of her dress. Knowing the answer for sure as my fingers reached higher. It had been such a long time since—no one other than Charlene. No one. Ever. Despite—

Her panties were silky. I could feel her warmth, her wetness, through the material. I could tell everything about her through the material. And I understood that this was it in a nutshell. Something I'd forgotten—how could I have forgotten? How it felt to put my hand between a woman's legs for the first time.

The answer to her question—the effect it had on me was quite a surprise.

We drank afterwards. More bourbon. More beer. O'Toole had brought information. About the case. About Deegan.

While going through his organizer, while checking a zippered compartment, O'Toole found other fake driver's licenses. Nine in all. The names all different. The states all different. The picture always the same.

I let that sink in, swirl in my head with the booze, the sex. With *nina.jpg*. What was the Son of God son of a bitch up to? Where were the family values in this picture? Those pictures? The pictures of my wife? How in hell did he get pictures of my wife? Were they from a porn warehouse, available to hundreds of sites, millions of paying members? How many people exactly had seen those pictures? Where were they taken? By whom?

And who were her partners? I buried my face in my hands and pictured her in court so many hours before. All this and she had the balls to contest.

I groaned a little too loudly.

"Bad day?" O'Toole asked.

"Something like that," I said.

"I didn't make it even a little better?"

I looked at her, smiled. "You took my mind off everything for a few minutes there." I was being honest.

"That was my intention," she said. She was being honest.

"Right," I said, letting out a long breath. "So—"

"So?"

"What about Deegan's family?" I asked, standing, pacing, thinking of the news clip. The mournful widow, the three daughters. "We have anything on them yet?"

"Nothing earth-shattering," she said. "Except you know his youngest daughter, Ruth, is pregnant?"

It wasn't connecting. I'd just seen the daughters—

"She's the tallest," O'Toole said. "Bright red hair."

It clicked. The punky one. "I thought she was just—" I searched for one of O'Toole's politically correct terms, not sure why on this night I bothered, and coming finally, full circle, where I'd began. "—fat?"

"Eight months in will have that effect."

"And only?"

"Seventeen," O'Toole said. "And from what I've heard, she won't even tell her family who the father is."

The sexual, spiritual, and moral purity of that bounced around inside my skull.

"Must have really pissed Deegan off," I said.

When I awoke, she was gone. We'd managed a second round—and I fell asleep, as was expected. She slipped out in the middle of the night. As was expected. Relieved. Satisfied. Embarrassed, maybe. Running home to a cat that needed feeding. Or a lover that none of us knew of. Or just running home.

I got myself a drink of water, splashing some of it on my face, in my eyes. Then I went downstairs, returning to my computer. Accessing Deegan's collection of JPEGs once again. All of a sudden I found myself wondering about *mary.jpg*. I'd forgotten all about her. Why so many pictures? What did she have on *anna.jpg*, or *lola.jpg*? What did she have on my ex-wife?

The first photograph answered my question, and then some. *mary001.jpg* was a close-up of her face. Huge green eyes. A full, soft, sensual mouth. Straight dark brown hair cut into a perfect chin-length bob. High cheekbones. The perfect chin. Aquiline nose. She was biting down on her bottom lip, playfully. The *mary.jpg* was beautiful in every sense of the word. A young Audrey Hepburn. And for a moment my heart sank. I didn't want to see this girl in pornographic poses.

As I moved through the pictures, as she pulled her bright red sweater over her head, and the tight black pants slid off her very long legs, those feelings only intensified. She transcended innocence, refined it.

Yet as her innocence was stripped naked, I couldn't pull my eyes away. She was Deegan's obsession. She had to be. Staring at her in various poses, with different partners, in different stages of ecstasy—I looked at all 620 pictures—I found myself aching. Brought down by the images of an eighteen-, maybe nineteen-year-old girl on my computer screen. Brought down by this sudden desire. I'd never felt more vulnerable.

And I was left to wonder, if she'd had that effect on me, how she might have played in the mind of a man who, for a living, preached of biblical values, of moral purity, and of loving the Lord your God with all your heart and with all your soul and with all your mind and with all your strength?

SIXTEEN

Closing the last of the files — *mary620.jpg,* another shot of her face, but nothing like the first one—I glanced at the directory heading, and at least one thing made sense. MAGDA-LENE. As in Mary. As in Christ's prostitute friend. Deegan had named the folder in this girl's honor.

Using Windows Explorer, I scanned the various Zips, looking for—I wasn't sure what. Until the connection hit. It had worked for Charlene.

Opening his America Online account, loading in a local access number—no problem getting connected at this time—then attempting to log on. Deegan's screen name was loaded: *Deegan* followed by four numbers most likely assigned by AOL. How original. Then again, my personal screen name was *AudioWhore,* taken from a favorite song. My password: an important birthdate few would ever guess. I thought for a moment. What would Deegan use? I didn't know any of his important birthdays, or anniversaries, or friends. Perhaps the name *Jesus,* or *Lord,* or *Mary*—Christ! No, not *Christ* as a password, but an exclamation. Mary, the mother of Jesus. The virgin. Mary Magdalene, the whore. And *mary.jpg,* the object of his desire. What was going on in this guy's head? What was going on in mine that I was so tuned in? I typed in *Mary,* clicked SIGN ON, and waited.

You've got mail."
    Even the wealthy received junk. Deegan's was no different from what I deleted on a daily basis.

I checked his favorite places. They seemed mostly religious in nature. The Sons of God site, a Dianetics site, another called the Coalition for Family Values. Fourteen in all. Hardly what I was looking for.

I'd had luck before with CHECK MAIL YOU'VE READ and CHECK MAIL YOU'VE SENT. But not this time. All of these e-mails seemed businesslike in nature. Memos to and from other Sons of God members around the globe. His address book like-wise told me nothing, as did his personal filing cabinet.

I was running out of places to visit when I remembered the Internet Explorer, which provided superior Web capabilities, es-pecially when it came to viewing JPEGs, Deegan's favorite pas-time. I minimized the AOL window and then opened the Explorer, first checking Deegan's bookmarks. Nothing. The list was empty.

"Shit!" I muttered, slamming down the mouse with a little too much force. Raising my hand to my face, rubbing at my eyes. Maybe I should take one last look at *nina.jpg*, at my Charlene. Maybe I should take one last look at *mary.jpg*, and call it a night. Maybe I should—

I glanced at the address. His home page: http://www.the-sons-of-god.org.

The downward arrow to the right of that address would hold the browser's recent URL history. It would hold the last sites visited, unless Deegan had the smarts to reconfigure his laptop to delete them every time he shut down.

But I would have bet my badge against working the rest of my days as a street sweeper in the Ninth Square that Richard Deegan couldn't reconfigure the day and date on his gold Pres-idential Rolex, let alone a laptop computer.

He was too busy shopping online for whores.

SEVENTEEN

I t was a beautiful list:

www.thepleasuregarden.com/main.html
www.american-X-corts.com/main.html
www.escorts-4-u.com/escorts/index.html
www.newenglandcoed.com/main.html
www2.girls-4-hire-4-U.com/comeinside/page1.html
sexy.cllgrls.org/private/welcome.htm
www.tri-state-escorts.com/index.html
www1.escorts-2-escorts.com/escort/CT.html

I printed out the URLs, not wanting to take a chance on losing anything. I was too tired and too hyped-up to trust myself not to make a mistake. Double-clicking on the first. Handcuffs appeared, then a whip cracked by a busty blonde in leather underwear. But all was not so promising. The Pleasure Garden was a sex shop. Bondage gear, videotapes, love potions, and stay-hard creams. I didn't notice any bottles of hydrochloric acid or enema bags. All for sale—on sale all the time—to anyone with a credit card.

I tried American-X-corts. The busty blonde in black leather was replaced by a busty blonde in a black evening gown. Her hip bumped against the American Escorts logo, as she waved in a Vanna White flourish at a list of ten pages to visit, ranging from "Escorts" to "Erotic Travel Services."

I double-clicked on "Escorts," to see what sort of girls were represented. I was given a list of states, not all fifty, but damn close. There was only one girl listed in Connecticut:

JAMIE
25 years old, 5'4", 130lbs

Blonde hair, big blue eyes
An all-natural 38-DD/26/36
I've been told I'm a dead ringer for Drew Barrymore.
Call me for an hour you'll never forget.

There was a beeper number—I hated beepers. Never wanted to carry one, just didn't have a choice on this job. I just never understood the people who lived and died by them. Especially the kids. The teenagers who wore them like tattoos. They were offensive. A sign that your ego had taken a wrong turn somewhere. Did anyone really have to be within reach twenty-four/seven? Was anyone that important? Was any news that urgent? It could wait. It used to wait, and we all survived just fine.

But of course an escort would have a beeper: Beepers could be anonymous; perhaps everyone who carried beepers were prostitutes of some sort. Selling themselves short to stay eternally connected. That would explain a lot. There was also an e-mail address, as well as a picture—a little red box next to her name with the word *PIX* in yellow block letters.

I couldn't resist. It took a moment for the JPEG to download, but when it did I was pretty sure there must have been a mistake. Because this Jamie had to be thirty-five if she was a day. She looked more like Lionel Barrymore than like Drew. And she might have been 130 pounds, if one day she dropped fifty. Sure, the double-Ds seemed real enough. But on a woman of this size, they were irrelevant.

Next. Escorts-4-u had no Connecticut listings. But with New England Coeds, I struck pay dirt with one of the six escorts based in the state:

HEATHER
The teenaged girl next door, the one you've always fantasized
about. I'm 19, tall, slender, and very bi. My breasts are small,

*but its quality that counts, isn't it? Not quantity. I don't have
a picture because I'm afraid of who might see it (my real neighbor maybe, and what if he told daddy?). I'm still learning
everything about how to please men . . . and women. What can
you show me? My rates are reasonable, my smile infectious,
and my personality, well . . . give me a beep and find out.*

This was how Deegan heard Mary in his head. These were
the words he wanted her to say as he stared at the pictures on
his computer screen, thinking whatever thoughts I couldn't
imagine.

This was the ad. Her ad. Heather. This was the girl Deegan
called to the Elm City Motor Lodge. The girl who ripped open
his throat with a Faber-Castell. Not a street hooker, but a professional escort. An internet escort. A girl just like *mary.jpg*.

TUESDAY

The phone was ringing as I stepped from the shower. Glancing at the clock, I saw it was a quarter to eight. Never a good sign that early. I wondered immediately if it was O'Toole calling with regrets. Or perhaps she was just calling to plead that no one should ever know. That she left something. That she just wanted to say she had a nice time. Let it be that.

The answering machine was blinking. Usually people hung up. My message worked nicely that way: "This is the Literacy Self-Test Hotline. After the tone, leave your name and number, and recite a sentence using today's vocabulary word. Today's word is *supercilious*."

But not today. Already there were three messages. And I was way off. Not O'Toole, but the station house. My partner's house. The station house again. Christ!

"Yeah," I said, picking up before the machine.

"We got another one." It was Brown, calling from home. Probably out of the shower only a few moments longer than I was. He sounded annoyed, but at least as if he'd gotten a good night's sleep. As if his eyes didn't burn. His throat wasn't a little raw. His head didn't throb. The muscles in his legs weren't tender. His joints weren't fragile. As if he wasn't losing his mind. I sounded like all that and more. He verified that right off.

"Long night," I said.

"Looking for love in all the wrong places?"

I thought about those pictures of my ex-wife on Deegan's laptop. "Seems like I've been doing that all along."

No sleazy motel this time. This poor SOB bought it in the front seat of his car. Armani suit still on. Pants tugged down around his ankles. A puddle of wrinkled navy linen around his black Cole-Haans. His pressed white shirt stained beyond recognition. A puckered condom on his shrunken penis.

His throat had been ripped open. Ripped forward. Wide and violent. Head pressed back against the headrest. Eyes stunned. A lot like Deegan. But this go-around, we wouldn't have to worry about false IDs. We wouldn't need to match a name to the face. No, that was familiar enough. We'd just met this victim the previous afternoon.

"Sorrentino?" I asked. "Right?"

"First name, Anthony," Brown said. "Tony, for short."

"Always Tony for short," I said. "VP."

"Yup," Brown said. "SOG-VP."

The car was almost as familiar as Sorrentino's face. The black Lincoln Town Car from the news video at Tweed Airport. It had a maroon leather interior and was decidedly new. It still had that new car smell, masked only slightly by the sickly sweetness of blood and death and sex gone very wrong. It was parked in a back corner on the third floor of a relatively unused parking garage off State Street, in the Ninth Square. No other cars around, not much of a view in or out. Just a brick wall on both sides and a sweeping panorama of a vacant office building, the Francesconi Building, out back. No apartments, no peepers who just might have been watching.

Sorrentino was found by an assistant manager for the Dunkin' Donuts around the corner on Chapel. She'd originally parked a space away. Saw nothing, heard nothing. Her senses had been turned off. It was time to make the doughnuts. Except for when she glanced into the new Lincoln. She'd noticed that his pants were down, right away. The hole in his throat became apparent shortly thereafter. Then a scream and a 9-1-1 phone call. Then a cruiser, then us.

It didn't take long for Slice and the techies to follow. Roping off, sealing up, leaning in. Slice's rubber-gloved finger probing the wound. Leaning out, turning our way. Snapping off the gloves.

"Another Faber-Castell?" I asked.

"Can't be sure," he said. "But it looks that way."

"How long ago?" Brown asked.

"My guess—middle of the night. Three, four A.M.," the ME said. "Give or take. I'll let you know soon as I can."

Mazz and O'Toole pulled up. They brought the Willoughby's. I kept looking at O'Toole as we filled them in between sips. No sign of a struggle. At least in her head. It was business as usual. The same mild flirt, the same fast mouth. It was almost as if the previous night never happened. Or perhaps, as if it were no big deal.

"What's going through your head?" O'Toole asked me.

"A lot," I said.

She smiled. I felt better.

"I don't like it," Brown said, staring at the Town Car.

"Think how Sorrentino feels," Mazz said.

"He's not feeling much of anything at all," I said, wishing I could have said the same for myself. But it didn't fit. Nothing fit. Not with what had been playing in our heads collectively regarding Richard Deegan. Self-defense. He'd died at the hands of a woman who was defending herself. But where was the self-defense here?

"No rocks this time," I called to Slice.

He shook his head.

No rocks, no leather bags filled with goodies. The trunk was empty except for the spare, the jack, some golf clubs. There was a road map and a Bible in the glove compartment. Cash in Sorrentino's wallet. A lot of cash. Credit cards. The right driver's license—Mississippi, his face, name, age, address. A worn photograph of a woman in a bathing suit. She looked to be in her late twenties. Big hair, big breasts, tight ass. Just the way a man following in the footsteps of Jesus liked his women. There was an Omni key-card in one of his jacket pockets. The keys to the Lincoln still in the ignition, alongside keys to the house and whatever else in his life was worth locking up.

"But we got prints this time," Slice said. "All over the place. The car's covered with them."

"Just as bad as if there weren't any," Mazz said.

"Right," I said. "Now everyone's suspect."

O'Toole cornered me as I was walking the circumference of the garage's third floor. I'd been looking for—I didn't know what I was looking for. Arrows pointing at something other than THIS WAY TO PARK, THIS WAY TO EXIT.

"Ever find anything useful on that computer?" O'Toole asked, reaching for my tie, but just patting the knot lightly. No adjustments. The smile was back. There was a ripeness to her mouth. Maybe it had always been there, and I'd just never noticed before.

"Maybe," I said. "There are girls that advertise online. Escorts."

"I've heard about that," she said.

"There seem to be a lot of Web sites."

"It's free, isn't it?" she asked.

I nodded.

"And discreet?"

"And dangerous."

"It's always dangerous, Will," she said.

We held each other's look for too long a beat, neither turning away. I was wondering what exactly she was talking about. If there were multiple meanings. That all relationships were inherently dangerous. As was the sex. But wasn't that why we bothered in the first place? Wasn't that the joke and the punch line combined? I'd have to ask Charlene. I was pretty sure she'd know.

"Yeah," I managed to say finally, giving in, turning.

"Check any of it out yet?"

"Didn't have much time."

"I took up a lot of your time last night," she said. "Sorry."

"Don't be."

She nodded a few times. "I'm not, really. It was—" She searched for a word. "—What I expected."

"That good or bad?" I asked.

"Guess you'll find out tonight."

I shot her a look. "Tonight?"

She shrugged. "Whether or not I come back for more."

NINETEEN

Bowing out early, I told Brown and the others that they could break it to Klavan that another Son of God met his maker in the Elm City. "There's something I need to do," I said.

"He's not going to like it," my partner said.

I shrugged, got in my car, and drove away.

The condo I had once shared with Charlene was in the Westville section of New Haven. Just off Forest Road. It was a small complex of a half dozen buildings, all painted with royal blue trim. Each housed four units. We had an end unit. Two bedrooms, two baths, finished basement. A one-car garage. Nothing spectacular. But it looked like home. It seemed liked home. It smelled like strawberries. How deceiving.

I punched the doorbell and waited. My hands in and out of my pockets. This was why people smoked. Something to do with their hands. Charlene smoked. Not that judging from those photographs she was lacking for anything to do with her hands.

She opened the door and just looked at me. Leaning against the jamb. She was wearing green shorts and a beige tank top, no bra. She didn't need one. Her long dark brown hair was pulled back into a ponytail. She didn't have any make up on. She didn't need any.

Music was blaring from within. Mariah Carey. Or Whitney Houston. Or one of the divas. Never could tell them apart. That was all Charlene ever played. Perhaps that should have been my first clue to run and hide. That first date when she popped a Replacements tape out of the deck in my car and turned on some Top 40 FM radio station. That was my warning. That was my sign. But did I heed it? No. I probably smiled like an idiot, forgetting the we-are-who-we-listen-to rule, thinking instead about getting into her pants.

"What?" she said. It was the voice she'd used when a fight was just winding down, before one of us would eventually give in. Before the inevitable makeup sex. Charlene loved makeup sex. So did I. At first. Until it started to matter what we were making up from.

"Can I come in?" I asked.

"What for?"

"To talk."

"You talked yesterday morning," she said. "You got your divorce. Nothing more to talk about."

"I saw the pictures," I said.

She stared at me hard and then took a step back, opening the door wider.

You can't go home again, I thought.

E verything had changed in three months. The furniture, the coffee tables—if I'd have known she was throwing it all out, I'd have taken more. There was a lot of black lacquer. I almost expected a Nagel on every wall. The TV was huge. The stereo, a piece of crap.

"How could you throw money away on this thing?" I asked, turning the volume down to nothing. *It couldn't go any lower than that.*

"Did you come here to criticize my stereo?" she asked.

"No," I said, clearing my head. "I came here to ask you"—and maybe my voice did get a little too loud at this point—"what the fuck were you thinking?"

"Don't use that tone."

"Don't use that tone," I repeated. "I find hundreds of pictures on this perp's computer."

"Looking for something to jerk off to?"

"I was working on a case."

A sarcastic laugh. "You spent so much time on that goddamn computer. Either working, or—I never knew what the hell you were doing. You were always working." She sounded hurt, all of a sudden, as if my job had gotten in the way. As if the hours I put in were at fault.

"I love my job," I said.

"More than me."

"It hasn't fucked me over yet. And any time—"

"Here we go," she said. "Bring up your stupid guitar."

"Don't go there."

"Daydreams, Will. They weren't real or realistic."

"Like you ever were."

We stared at one another before both turning away. I recalled one particular fight. Coming home after a double shift. Hungry, tired, depressed. She told me she had a great idea. She was going to list Gloria for sale in the *Bargain News*. "We can probably get a few hundred dollars for it." I looked at her, and in all seriousness told her that if she ever touched Gloria, ever spoke of Gloria again, I'd kill her. Then I went to bed. That was the only night I slept alone in all the time we were married.

Her voice was soft, bringing me back. "It was just me and a girl, the first time," she said. "And another girl who filmed it. It was in a really nice condo on the water. I always wished we could live near the water. I thought you'd—"

"What?" I said. "Get turned on?"

"Yeah," she said. "I was going to tell you. Don't you remember? I asked you about it one night. I asked you if you ever fantasized about making love to two girls at the same time. You said, yeah, sure, all men fantasized about that. But that you'd feel weird. That it'd be like cheating right in front of me. The way you asked me if I'd be jealous, I knew you wanted me to answer yes. So, I did. And I dropped it."

Sure, I remembered. And I thought her even more perfect just for suggesting it. That was all she had to do, suggest it. And it fed my fantasies for months.

"It was an ad," she said, "in the back of the *Advocate*. Y'know, something like, models needed for photography and video sessions. It sounded like fun. It was just with another girl. Not really cheating."

"Of course not."

"I used a fake name," she said.

"Nina?"

"Nina Dion," she said, glancing at her new stereo. "Y'know, after Celine."

I shrugged.

"Like a month later, the girl who ran the camera called me back. She wanted to know if I'd like to do it again, this time with a guy." Her turn to shrug. "One thing led to another."

"More than one guy at a time," I said. "Was that your fantasy?"

"One of them," she said. "I liked doing it. The pay was good."

It took a second for that to sink in. "Pay?" I said.

"They were videotaped for the foreign market," she explained. "I guess amateur porn is huge overseas."

"What if your parents saw one of these tapes?" I asked. Charlene's parents were decent people. Her father, a mechanic. Her mother, a dental assistant who made the second-best eggplant Parmesan I'd ever tasted. They never said much of anything to me about the divorce, except "We're sorry."

"My parents aren't going overseas," Charlene said. Another shrug. "I got a thousand dollars cash every time. For like only a couple of hours work."

"How many times," I asked.

"I'm not doing them anymore. The girl hasn't called in—"

"How many times, Charlene?"

"Exactly?"

"Exactly."

"I don't know—"

"Take a guess."

"Once a week, for the last couple of years," she said.

TWENTY

The phone number was where I'd left it. Where I'd copied it down last night. Her ad playing now in my head. *mary.jpg*'s voice:

> *HEATHER*
> *The teenaged girl next door, the one you've always fantasized about* . . .

Picking up the phone. Dialing. Thinking: Fuck you, Charlene, as I pressed in my number at the beep.

She called back within two minutes. Heather's voice was everything I expected. A soft crumb cake filled with tapioca cream and sprinkled with powered sugar. I wondered if that's how my ex-wife sounded to other men. If that's how she looked as they met for the first time, knowing in a few moments they'd be posing for the cameras. Knowing in a few moments they'd be—

I gave her directions. Heather said she would be there in forty minutes.

Is something wrong?"

It must have been obvious. The look of horror plastered to my face as I opened the door. The dropped jaw. Heather looked to be at least a half dozen years past nineteen, with permed dirty-blond hair, pushed back with barrettes. A bad dye job in serious need of a makeover. A suspect complexion covered by too much makeup. Thin lips shadowing silver braces. And she was chewing gum. Snapping. Snapping. *Snapping.* She was tall—yeah, okay, sure. And her breasts were small. But slender?

Not even close. Her waist was bigger than mine, and she had a back porch big enough to hold an Adirondack chair. All packed into jeans so tight, I half expected to lose an eye to an exploding Levi's rivet.

"You're not exactly what I was expecting," I said, blocking her entrance into my apartment, looking for the right words, thinking this was not Deegan's fantasy. This was NOT *mary.jpg*.

A sudden snap of attitude to go along with the gum. Adjusting the strap of the oversize leather bag slung over her shoulder. And just as suddenly the voice was not so sweet, nowhere near so appetizing, nowhere—no wonder it reminded me of crumb cake and tapioca and powered sugar. And instead of asking for my ID to make sure the name I gave her over the phone was right, like she probably expected to be doing about now, Heather instead had to legitimize the way she looked. "I've never had any complaints."

"No one's ever said that you were"—again I wanted to be kind—"not exactly as you described yourself?"

"I said I was tall, blond—"

"And slender," I said. "A twenty-four-inch waist. That's what you told me on the phone."

"You can tell I don't have a twenty-four-inch waist by looking?" She was insulted, her face flushing, her mouth snarling up at the corners, revealing more of the braces.

All I could think of was the character Jaws from the James Bond flicks. "Look," I said.

"Look, what?" Heather snapped.

She was pissing me off. Kindness flew out the window. "I know the difference between twenty-four inches and thirty-four inches," I said.

Heather's mouth fell open. Perhaps her measurements weren't usually called into question. Maybe the saps who cruised the New England Coeds Web site didn't know any better.

"So, what are you saying?" she said finally. She wasn't getting the hint.

"That I'm not interested."

She tried staring me down. Snapping. Snapping. *Snapping*. Holding out her hand like a rude bellhop. "Gimme some gas money. I drove all the way out here."

She was so unattractive at this point. I felt ashamed just for having called her number. Guilty. In my presence. On my landing. Stupid and dirty.

I went to shut the door in her face, but a well-placed foot held it open. This *had* to have happened before.

"I've got friends," she said, her tone enraged, sharp like the snapping sound of her gum. "Good friends who can get nasty whenever I ask."

I don't take well to threats. I flashed my badge inches from her face.

"So do I."

TWENTY-ONE

Sipping coffee, wishing it was scalding, wishing it could rip clean the roof of my mouth and burn into my brain, burn away my brain *("Once a week for the last couple of years." Christ!)* I waited for my computer to boot up.

Could Heather's flash of anger, that spark when her bluff was called, could that have been what doomed Deegan? That he, too, tried to show Heather the door after she turned out to be nothing like *mary.jpg*? But what about Sorrentino? And the pencil? No, the pencil wasn't right. Nothing was right. Heather and Deegan. He'd have never had sex with her. She wasn't the fantasy. Not if the pictures meant anything. But—maybe Heather was close enough. Maybe Deegan had a deadline. Saturday. The rally at Yale Bowl. But what did one have to do with the other?

Shaking my head. None of it making sense.

Maybe the other online escort agencies would hold a clue. There had to be other girls, closer to *mary.jpg*, closer to Deegan's girl-next-door fantasy—but first I wanted a crack at his Word files. What he wrote. What was going on in his mind in the days and weeks before he died.

I began with his letters. Most were to others in the Sons of God hierarchy, one was to a credit card company disputing a charge, and one was to a man Deegan was sponsoring:

Dear Alex,

Lust is the devil's strongest tool. It is every man's fate to be tempted. We are driven to procreate and propagate the race. Such is our plight. However, if we are to be Christian and are to follow in the footsteps of Jesus, we must resist these urges. Fight off the temptations and the temptresses. I know it seems that women are the cause of our suffering. The fruit they bear on their supple limbs cannot be denied or resisted. Satan lives in their bellies, beckoning us into their sex. He is born with them, teaching them the secrets of seduction from their very conception onward.

You can defeat the agent of evil, Alex. You can drive Satan from the belly of your wife by keeping her at home. By ordering her to be the mother and wife she was predestined to be. Keeping your house in order, and putting three square meals on the table every day. By forcing her to keep you happy, and to obey your every wish.

Lastly, you must remain faithful, by never daring to taste the sweet breath of Satan on another woman's lips. Do this for Jesus, in memory of Jesus, and in the name of Jesus, and when Judgment Day is upon us he will welcome you and your wife into the Kingdom of Heaven. May God be with you, Alex. I will pray for you.

In the Name of the Lord,
Richard Deegan

Letting that sit, and it didn't sit well. Was this simply the pinnacle of hypocrisy—and no one disdained the religious right more than I did, telling us what to watch, what to listen to, whom to fuck, while they watched, listened and/or fucked what or whom they desired, all the while invoking the name of the Lord. Or was Deegan really that twisted? The depraved new world I had warned O'Toole about as we entered his suite. *Satan lives in their bellies, beckoning us into their sex.* Had Deegan been simply unable to resist the woman who came to his door? He'd have never been able to resist *mary.jpg.* Or someone just like her. Would he have been able to resist Charlene?

Shaking my head. Thoughts of Charlene in the motel room

with Deegan. Charlene killing him with a pencil.

I searched for more. Other writings from Deegan. Other thoughts. His faxes, all business related, and what appeared to be the beginnings of a book on the history of the Sons of God. It was called *Delivering On The Commitment*. But nothing explained what might have been going on in his mind.

Opening the SPEECHES file, I hit pay dirt. There were a lot them, close to seventy. They really delivered on the commitment, and then some.

Each was named after a city: *dallas-01*, or *atlanta-01*, or *dc-01*, spanning close to a decade, from that first Dallas file, to one named *new haven-01*, what Deegan planned on saying to the throngs that would fill Yale Bowl on Saturday. The file had been saved this past Sunday, at 8:13 P.M., only a handful of hours before he died.

There were a lot of blank spaces still to be filled in. A work-in-progress. The expected gab up front about families and temptations and Jesus H. Christ, though Deegan inexplicably left out the middle initial. It was the same crap he wrote to Alex, only in long form. Pages of it, as if he were trying to induce a massive sleep-in.

But then the speech took a turn: Deegan wrote about the wave of brutality that seemed to accompany the Sons of God's visit to New Haven. A "series of crimes," he called them, that began "just this past Sunday evening, when a beautiful young woman named"—and here was one of those blanks—"was found murdered. Her body dumped in a parking garage. Bound with tape, gagged, covered with a plastic trash bag. She had been stoned to death. Like all sinners in Biblical times. Her genitalia and breasts had been burned away with acid. Her face, barely recognizable as the beautiful daughter of a family from"—another blank. "A family which never knew their daughter worked as a prostitute. One who advertised her services on the Internet. Using a computer probably given to her by her parents to help

her with schoolwork. Using it as the Devil's tool. Already the
Devil's disciple. You see"—a space—"was just"—a space—
"years old. She studied"—more blanks. "She wanted to be a"—
blank—"but instead ended up a victim of the tool which helped
her die, when pictures of her desecrated body showed up on
that Internet, for anyone, her mother, father, family, friends, for
the whole world to see. But friends,"—a space—"was only the
first. The body of another young woman was found the next
night. And another the night after that. All-in-all"—a space—
"young women have perished this week in New Haven. Each
worked as a prostitute, escort, hooker—call them what you will.
Advertising their services on the World Wide Web. Each was a
student. Beautiful girls full of promise. Suffering the same heinous death at the hands of a man who has thus far eluded the
authorities."

TWENTY-TWO

Outside, chaos. A Berlin wall of sound crumbling under its own weight. A barrage of reporters, the questions, the microphones, the flash of cameras. Not just the usual suspects, but the big guns: CNN, MSNBC, Fox News, the networks. A story like this chumming the oceans.

Inside, war. The questions a lot more specific. Hostile and confused and—Brown, Mazz, and O'Toole surrounded by suits over in our corner. The Federal Bureau of Investigation. Sounds from Klavan's office. A door slamming open. A woman stepping from the room. Tears streaking her mascara, anger twisting her mouth—Margaret Deegan. Donny Savage by her side, helping her walk. Holding her bent elbow. Deegan's three daughters behind them. The brunette, Theresa, helping Donny with her mom. Pulling her into a tight embrace. Donny stepping back, turning to Ruth, leading her to a bench upon which she could rest. Ruth's eyes were bloodshot. A lifetime of tears.

Inside Klavan's office stood Albert Larsen and Police Chief Zekowski, the mayor by Klavan's side. Staring, distressed, disgusted—there were no words. And, Christ help us all, Special Agent Mae Questral, the local bureau chief. Looking like a cinder block in navy blue. Only not so personable.

I felt a hand on my arm, spinning me around. "Where the hell have you been?" my partner was asking, his harsh whisper mostly lost in the confusion.

"Are the Feds taking over?" I asked, not about to tell him about Charlene's photos. Not yet, anyway.

He shot me a look. "They think we've got a serial killer on our hands," Brown said. "These Sons of God sons of bitches pull a lot of weight. Questral was waiting for us when we got back. Didn't even have time to take a leak."

That's what the reporters had been screaming. A serial killer. Is there any truth to the rumor? That's why the Feds had come out of the woodwork like cockroaches. But the real serial killer was dead, I thought. Stopped in his tracks. Stopped before he could claim his first victim.

"They say an ostrich's eye is bigger than its brain," Mazz said, biting at the words, suddenly by our side.

"What'd the prints show?" I asked.

"They won't say," O'Toole said, stepping in.

"We just give up everything we've got, and they give up nothing."

"You know how it works," Brown said.

The images of my ex-wife on Deegan's computer suddenly filled my head. The number of partners, her goddamn wedding ring catching the light in every shot. Glimmering, sparkling. Shaking my head, trying to let go of the images. Trying to let go, period.

The Feds were not going to see those pictures.

No one was.

"Not this time," I said, pulling away from them, stepping toward Klavan's office, pulling him from his stance in the doorway, pulling him inside. My face inches from his. "We've got to talk."

"So, talk." The voice was Questral's. She *tsk*ed a couple of times before saying my name, "Detective William Shute."

"No offense," I said, eyeing her. Thinking back to our first meeting. I was wearing a blue uniform then. Just a cop, ready to serve and protect. A single guy. Charlene wasn't even close to entering the picture. Questral had sent for me. Called my captain and asked for a face-to-face at the local bureau headquarters. I went thinking it might be something good. That she'd noticed me. That she thought I'd make a superb special agent. *G-Man Shute.* Goddamnit, was I wrong.

"None taken," she said, her voice less appealing than her face. "Talk."

I turned to Klavan. Eye-to-eye. Man-to-man. Cop-to-cop. Whatever. "In private. Just for a minute." I was being so god-damn nice it hurt. "Please."

"That's not going to happen now, Shute," he said. "This isn't our case anymore."

I pulled from my inside breast pocket a printout of Deegan's intended speech. "Give me two minutes, Lieutenant," I said.

"I would if I could. You know that."

Did I? I was beginning to wonder.

He closed the door to his office, cutting us off from the rest of the noise. But there were still too many: Questral, the mayor, the chief, Larsen.

Klavan motioned toward the printout. "So, what is that?"

I weighed the options. Keep what I knew, and let them dis-cover it for themselves, only to screw it up somehow, or lose it, or cover it up completely. My partner's voice sounded in my head: *"These Sons of God sons of bitches pull a lot of weight."* No, I couldn't let that happen.

But—looking into the faces, I didn't stand a chance.

"Lieutenant," I said. "I'll ask one more time."

"Now you're getting on my nerves."

"Fine," I said, wondering how to put it. "You're looking for a serial killer, right?"

There was a beat of silence. Then Klavan spoke up. "Possi-bly," he said.

"Well, he's dead," I said, cutting to the chase, slapping the printout of the speech Deegan planned on delivering at Yale Bowl and then giving them paraphrased highlights. "It explains the rock, what we found in his leather bag, it explains—"

"Nothing," Questral said, cutting me off.

Her voice caught me off guard. I stared at her, a little stunned. "Bullshit," I said.

"Watch your tone, Detective," the chief said. He was standing in the far corner of the room, taking up most of the space.

"Two men are dead," Questral said. "Identical MOs."

"How identical?" I asked.

But she wasn't making that mistake. "How does your theory explain that?" she asked.

I gave it a shot. It was what had been running through my head since I read those words. Deegan's words: "All suffering the same heinous death at the hands of a man who has thus far eluded the authorities." That the son of a bitch would kill to further his cause. To practice sexual, spiritual, and moral purity. It still made me laugh. The great protector of morality. "Deegan's murder was self-defense," I said. "He was going to kill that girl at the Elm City Motor Lodge. He was going to do to her the things he mentioned in his speech. Then he was going to dump her body in some parking garage. But she figured out what was going on. Somehow—I don't know. But she stopped him. She saved herself. It was self-defense." That much I was sure of. The rest, well, shrugging, it was the best explanation I had. Okay, perhaps it wasn't an explanation at all, just a guess. But an educated guess, or at least I wanted to think so. A good guess, goddamnit. Did they have anything better?

I took a deep breath and then dived in headfirst, expecting at least a little dissension. "Sorrentino's murder was a copycat."

The explosions of denial and rage were more than I could have ever expected. Zekowski, his face flushing, told me I was full of shit. Mayor Pinfield called me a jackass and then turned away, staring out the window at what I assumed was the press contingent on Union Avenue. Thinking about sound bites, no doubt. Larsen, the event coordinator who hadn't coordinated this event, shook his head angrily and then, throwing up his hands, left. Brushing past me. Not so much as looking me in the eye.

Klavan, my boss, the only other real cop in the room, didn't say a word.

Questral laughed. Then she asked, "Do you believe in what the Sons of God preach?"

"What?" I said, taken aback at the question.

She repeated herself.

I looked away, figuring it didn't matter. "Honestly?" I said.

"Of course," she said.

I looked into the lieutenant's face. His eyes seemed to be telling me to take it easy, but at this point I wasn't about to listen to his silent warnings. I just didn't give a good goddamn. "I think it's hypocritical bullshit."

"Do you see them as a threat to your lifestyle?" she asked.

I laughed. "I see them as a threat to humanity in general," I said.

"So, then," she asked. "How do we know *you* didn't write that speech, Detective? How do we know you don't have your own agenda?"

"What?" I yelled. That was one way of solving the crime I hadn't thought of. Leave it to the FBI. "You've got to be kidding me? Are you on their fucking payroll or something?"

Klavan shot me a look and then turned toward her. "Hold on there, Mae," he said, raising his voice. "Shute's one of the best men I've got. If you're going to make accusations like that, you better well have some strong evidence to back them up."

She swallowed hard; then she smiled. It seemed forced, but any movement of her face seemed forced. "You have Deegan's computer," she said.

I could feel the flush of red crawling up my neck. I could feel my hands balling themselves into fists.

"On who's approval?" she asked.

I jerked my head toward Klavan. "Just doing what I was told, Questral," I said, a lot too loudly. "Just following orders."

"I'm sure that's all you were doing, *Detective*." It was such a dirty word now, four letters instead nine when she said it. "We'd like to take a look at that computer. If you don't mind."

"Why should I mind?" I said, trying to calm down. Trying to focus on anything else. Even Charlene's photo sessions seemed preferable right about now. "I'll go get it now."

"You've got nothing else to do," she said.

"Thanks to you," I said, turning on her. "But try not to mess it up. Try to pull your head out of your ass long enough to get a glimpse of the facts."

"Shute . . . ," Klavan warned.

"Let him talk," Questral said.

"Yeah, let me talk," I said, turning, glaring at the mayor. "At least I'm not blinded by—"

"At least I'm not blind to the evidence," Pinhead said, cutting me off.

"What gives here?" I shouted, the past thirty or so hours crashing around in my head. Crashing down. Crashing. "The evidence is on his fucking computer."

"Shute!" Klavan yelled.

But there was no stopping me. I was so fed up at this point, this point of not giving a good goddamn, this point of if I didn't get something off my chest, I'd explode. "You cover up for these sick whoring hypocrites," I screamed. "That's all Deegan was. Probably Sorrentino, too. Probably all of them. They preach morality and bang hookers. How's that for doling out both ends of the shaft. Christ! And for what? Because they put a little cash in the city coffers? They help with the revitalization? Or the reelection campaign? They buy their way clear of guilt because they hold a Bible in one hand, and their checkbooks in the other—"

"Enough of this shit," Pinfield said. He was speaking directly to Klavan, a finger aimed at the lieutenant's face, and there was no mistaking the mayor's tone. "Lieutenant," he said, "Get this stupid son of a bitch out of my sight."

"Excuse me," I said.

"You heard me, Detective," Pinhead said.

I made sure he heard me, getting in his face, grabbing his lapels, pushing him back hard against a file cabinet, pointing a finger much more threatening than the one he just aimed at Klavan. And there was no mistaking my tone. "Fuck you, sir!" I said.

TWENTY-THREE

It wasn't my destiny to become a cop. I truly believe that. It was never what I wanted out of life. Never what I needed. There's no history. No tradition. No long line of those who served and protected in my family. My parents run a small bakery, Shute's, in North Haven. My father's worked there all his life, as did his father before him.

As a kid, as a teenager, I never dreamed of being a cop. I never played cops and robbers, at least not that I can recall. Never really watched cop shows on TV. I knew the local cops growing up. Guys who'd come by the store for a croissant or muffin. But did I ever stare at their badge or gun in awe? Never once.

No, as a kid, as a teen, I dreamt of rock and roll. I dreamt of guitars. And girls. And more guitars.

I know I'm not alone. Most of us never follow our destinies. Most of us are too frightened. Or unaware. Or there are roadblocks, oftentimes of our own making—Charlene was my end of the road.

Many times we're just not sure what those destinies are. So, I'm in the majority here. I settled. Compromised. Took the easy out, when things like paying the bills, moving on, growing up, getting married, seemed the right thing to do.

And yet, despite all this, I believe I'm good at this chosen profession. There are days when I love being a cop. When I'm proud to be a cop. And most times now, I can't imagine being anything else.

I probably could have gotten away with most of what I'd said. Even the *Fuck you* to the mayor.

It was the shove. Physical confrontation with our city's highest ranking official.

I knew the moment I'd grabbed his lapels. But by then it was too late. There was no turning back.

They took my badge and my Glock—they even took my goddamn beeper—and told me I was on indefinite suspension. I was to speak to no one about this case. If I so much as showed up at any of the crime scenes, I'd be tossed in jail for evidence tampering. Lieutenant Klavan told me he didn't want to see my face around the station house until this thing was over. If then. "Cool the fuck down," he whispered harshly.

I backed out of his office slowly, staring at their faces. At their indifference. Gone was all self-respect. I had expected to be stripped of it in divorce court the previous morning, not here, not like this. Perhaps I never had any to begin with. Judging from the way my ex-wife behaved. Judging from—

"This stinks," I yelled, pointing at them. Accusing. A sound in my head. Gum. Heather chewing her gum. Snapping. Snapping. *Snapping*. "Deegan fucked some girl, and then he tried to kill her. And he'd have done it again and again and again. How does that make him the fucking victim?"

"Get him out of here," Klavan barked at Brown. "Before I haul his ass down to lockup myself."

"Why don't you try," I said, taking a threatening step forward. "If you can pull your lips away from Pinhead's ass for that long."

By now the explosions of sound had stopped, replaced by an agonized silence. Tension creaking. My nerves—it had been my nerves snapping. My stomach churning. My heart asking me what did I go and do this time?

Brown stepped forward. "C'mon, man," he said softly. "Before you say something you'll really regret."

"You mean I haven't already?"

"Let's just get out of here," he said. "They don't need us on this."

I held up both hands, giving up, shutting up. Taking one step back. It was nothing against Brown. I could leave on my own accord. Head held high. I could live that illusion. Illusions were easy.

"Okay, okay, okay," I said, like it was a nervous tic, turning away, shaking my head slightly. "Okay." Turning around, thinking how Deegan never got the chance to elude anyone. Thinking—

Though I never saw the slap coming, I would feel the sting and resentment of Margaret Deegan's hand across my face for the rest of my life.

TWENTY-FOUR

She was sitting against the wall. On a hard-backed bench usually reserved for criminals or victims, or the families thereof. And I guess in a way that's what she was. Her head pressed back. Her eyes clenched shut against the hostilities. Hands folded over her protracted belly. Looking not so much seventeen, as just tired. Ignoring it all, so tuned out, until I walked past—I had to pass her to get outside. On this, a day that would go down in my personal history as the penultimate *one of those days*. Or was it simply one of those weeks? Months? Lifetimes? Should I just give up now and hope to start again? I wondered. Reincarnated as what in my next life?

And then she looked. For one brief moment, on my way out of headquarters, Ruth Deegan's bloodshot eyes—so large and harshly green—met mine, before turning away and closing again. There was no spark of anger, no sadness, no hatred for the things I'd said. Just curiosity. As if she wanted to see the fool who thought someone might care.

They took my badge.
    Perhaps this was the release. The pardon. My chance to be reborn. A free man. Grab Gloria and run. Find out what could have been. The destiny. The dream. Or was that, like so much else in my life, over and done with? And was I just deluding myself again?

I walked home. The keys to my Caprice Classic had been turned in as well. O'Toole offered to drive. She whispered, "C'mon, Will. To hell with them all. I'll drive you home, we'll get a good bottle of wine, and we'll spend the rest of the day in bed." But I shook my head, shook her off. "I'm sorry," I said.

"No." I needed to think, I needed to know—why?

Why cover up for these bastards? Was the organization that frightened by the indiscretions of its members? Didn't anyone ever learn? Admit to the wrong. Apologize. And the people will forgive. God will forgive.

Charlene again. She never admitted to doing wrong. Not with the affair. Not with the porn. She never apologized. She couldn't help herself. And that was supposed to be enough.

But Deegan could help himself. Deegan could—what sort of control could he have over these people, even from the grave? If there were pictures of my wife on his computer, might there be other incriminating shots? Could *mary.jpg* have been a Senator's daughter?

And what did it all have to do with Sorrentino? If he, too, was stabbed in the throat with a pencil, and I believed that to be the case, was there perhaps a woman intent on taking down the Sons of God organization after all? Who else knew about the pencil? Who else knew enough to make it look as if Sorrentino had died at the hands of the same killer? Or was it just the same killer, and I was the one who was blind? Making Questral right on target? Right about a serial killer.

If we hadn't found the items in Deegan's bag. If I hadn't read his speech, then—but I'd seen the two crime scenes. Deegan was intent on killing someone. Sorrentino just got killed. But again, why go to the length of making them seem connected? Why—?

The Feds, Pinhead, the rest of them, didn't care about the speech. They didn't care about *mary.jpg*—they didn't know about *mary.jpg*. About the sort of girl Deegan fantasized about. About the sort of girl who was probably with him in that motel room on Sunday night. They didn't understand the innocence he so wanted to shatter. They didn't have a clue as to the extent of his evil.

I did.

But they took my goddamn badge.

TWENTY-FIVE

Taking the long way. In no hurry now. Just needing to think. Or perhaps needing to purge my mind.

Turning down Crown Street, into the heart of the Ninth Square. The empty streets, the empty buildings, the empty—I stepped into the shadows of the Francesconi Building and smiled.

Named after Albert Francesconi, the architect who designed it in the mid-twenties, it was more art deco than downtown New Haven. Its design certainly had little to do with the grand Gothic and ivy style of Yale. And it probably would have been a happier building if it had been built on Ocean Drive in South Beach, where it could, at least now, bask in the glories of sunshine and supermodels.

The building's construction was completed just days before the Great Depression. Never a very lucky building. The first time I ever took notice of it, was back in the Grotto days. Early to mid-eighties. Located just down the block, closer to the corner of Church Street, The Grotto was the underground club where local punk bands got to play. My band played there once every week or so. My band played a lot of places. Until our drummer, Charlie, became a born-again Christian, one who instantly recognized the inherent evils of rock and roll. It was never the same after that. Not with the replacement drummer, or his replacement after that.

Back then, before Charlie found Jesus, the Francesconi Building was boarded up. Home only to squatters and pigeons. One night I'll never forget. It was freezing out. A Saturday in January. We were headlining. Packing up after the gig. Everything into the Ford van. I caught the lights of a lone camera person standing out in front of the Francesconi Building. She was from the Hartford CBS affiliate. She was standing, shivering. Blowing into her hands. A short girl, but cute, with huge blue eyes. I asked her what was going on, and she told me. A homeless man was found frozen to death in the lobby.

"Was he black or white?" I asked at the time. Not because it mattered, but because I was trying to keep the conversation going.

"He was blue," she said.

The Ninth Square History Rehabilitation Project cost the taxpayers of the city of New Haven $86.6 million. The renovation of the Francesconi Building ate up a hefty chunk of that. It was the project that signaled the Ninth Square renovations had begun. Damn the torpedoes.

The facade was sandblasted and stuccoed, brought back to its original luster. The windows replaced. The lobby refurbished in marble and teak. The elevators bought new. The fixtures and plumbing updated. It was even featured on *Dateline*, a story about second lives for the great buildings of our past.

Yet despite that effort, it's remained vacant. A little under a hundred thousand square feet of space. The asking price: thirty-five dollars per. This in a town where you can lease decent space for one-seventh that amount, and the grateful landlords will be kissing your ass with incentives.

I passed the windows with the gigantic FOR LEASE signs and pulled on one of the Francesconi Building's double front doors, knowing it'd be locked. Knowing—

The door opened.

Stepping inside, I noticed for the first time the plaster angels on the lobby's ceiling. Cherubs playing in a circular garden. Smiling down upon any who'd pass their way. It was like a church, minus the congregation, minus the pews, minus the crosses, minus the stained glass. So grand in every scheme, meant to impress, to inspire. To make you believe.

"Beautiful, isn't it?"

The voice caught me off guard. I spun around, my hand reaching for my weapon. But my Glock wasn't there. It wasn't needed.

"We chose this building because of the lobby," Albert Larsen said, staring at the cherubs.

It took a beat, but then I turned and caught sight of the boxes stacked in one corner. Of the furniture, store-fresh, still covered in plastic. Of the moving van out front—why hadn't I noticed the damn van out front? And suddenly the ass-kissing, the bending over backwards, the hush-hush, it all made sense. Especially in a reelection year.

"The Sons of God are moving to New Haven," I said.

Larsen nodded. "It's been in the works for a while," he said. "We're going to announce it at the rally on Saturday." He looked at me. "But now—" A shrug, a sad laugh. "Mr. Crawford opposed the move. He felt there was nothing wrong with Jackson, Mississippi. But we, the board of directors, approved it. Richard and Tony, especially. They worked so hard for this." He shook his head. "I remember one meeting where things got so heated, Mr. Crawford stormed out, screaming we'd move to New Haven over his dead body."

"But look who turned up dead instead," I said.

TWENTY-SIX

W hat was in the speech, detective?"
Albert Larsen looked as if those words were the hardest he'd ever have to speak. As if he were forcing himself to face
me, to face the evil he knew I'd deliver head-on.

"Do you really want to know?"

"Probably not," he said, turning away. He was a short man,
perhaps fifty, perhaps forty-five. A little stocky, with brown hair,
graying around the edges, thinning on top. He was well dressed,
but not so flashy as Deegan or Sorrentino. His suits were off the
rack, suits I could afford. His accessories likewise. "But—please
don't judge us."

I turned away, shaking my head, angry—not at Larsen, but
at those who came before him. Those who set the stakes. "Aren't
you the ones who judge?" I looked at him. "Everything so black
and white, so right or wrong?"

He nodded, just slightly. "It isn't easy. There are so many
temptations."

"The trick is knowing which ones to give in to," I said.

"But for us, the trick is not giving in at all."

"Not an easy task."

"I see that now."

Klavan's quote from earlier popped into my head: "Let he
who is without sin—"

"I believe that Tony and Richard were good men," Larsen
said. "That their hearts were in the right places."

D eegan's speech set him straight. He wept openly as I
quoted from it as best as I could, as best as memory would
allow. My interpretation of what happened Sunday night in that

motel room left him pallid and short of breath. He sat on one of the plastic covered chairs. Burying his face in his hands.

I stood against the window, my forehead pressed against the glass, catching sight of the old Grotto. Long gone. Its location, now a gay bar. Its exterior, painted white instead of black. I thought of the smoke, the beer, the loud music. The girls. There were a lot of *mary.jpg*s back in those days. All dressed in black. A little stoned. Hanging around after the gig. Wanting to be taken home. Needing—

"When you find her—" Larsen said.

I turned to face him, actually liking that he'd said *when* and not *if*. Giving him his due for knowing I wasn't about to stop now.

"—Tell her, I'm sorry."

TWENTY-SEVEN

A Yale Co-op pit-stop. Forty dollars and change for a generic fifteen-volt adapter, guaranteed to work with Deegan's laptop. Plus another $24.95 and tax for *Son of God: An Unauthorized Biography of James Crawford*. Figured I had some time now. Better catch up on my reading.

At home, I plugged in the Dell and deleted every photograph—of my ex-wife, of *mary.jpg*, of all the others. I defragged and swept clean the hard drive; then I cluttered it up again, with every useless program in my possession. I wanted those pictures gone from this computer. And I wanted them unretrievable, out of technology's reach. I knew of a program that could find and repair long-deleted files. That program wasn't going to work here.

Then I drove back down to the station house, screeching along at the top of my lungs to a song jacked up to eleven on the tape deck of my 1969 Volkswagen Beetle: *"As you tried to forget all the words that were said/To deny all the things that you keep in your head."*

Handing over the Dell to a uniformed officer at the front desk, I asked him to make sure Klavan got it, ASAP.

I was back inside Herbie in time for the second verse.

P opping a beer, I flipped on the tube in time for the six-o'clock news. In time for the press conference. Special Agent Questral, with Pinhead and Zekowski standing right behind her, the Deegan family, his wife and three daughters, behind them.

Questral hit all the right notes: "our sympathies go out to the families," "examining every avenue," "we can't give out that information at this time," and the always popular, "we have many leads, and expect an arrest at any moment." Zekowski spoke about the "concerted effort" between the New Haven Police Department and the FBI to bring a "quick resolution to this crime." Pinhead talked about New Haven as a "community," and the need to come together "in this hour of despair." It was a greatest hits album of clichés.

Despite the many leads, a hotline had been set up. An 800-number. "If you have any information about these murders, please call. All information will remain confidential. Your identity will not be revealed." They were looking for a young woman, who perhaps worked as a prostitute. Her profile was textbook: intelligent, charming, attractive, with a possible axe to grind, with a chip on her shoulder for the Sons of God.

Then came word on Tony Sorrentino. He was forty-one. A widower who'd lost his wife to breast cancer in the late eighties. They had no children. A picture was flashed of his dead wife. She was the big-haired woman from the old photograph in his wallet.

Tony was born and raised in Alexandria, Virginia. He went to Georgetown. A business major. He played football, but never made it to the pros. A conservative from conception. Went right to work for the American Family Association after college. Rose quickly in their ranks, running their Washington, D.C., branch. He was a well-known opponent of abortion and had led a number of protests against clinics in the greater DC area.

There was the video again of Sorrentino meeting Deegan's family at Tweed. A friend in time of grief. Squeezing Margaret's hand. Opening the front door for her. His arm around Ruth's shoulders. It made sense now. She was pregnant, carrying God's greatest gift, in his eyes: the gift of life, the miracle of life. He probably saw her as fragile. The oldest daughter, Anne, slipping in first. The middle daughter, Theresa, watching after her kid sister. The flash of concern. Sorrentino shutting the door for

Ruth. Locking eyes for a second with Theresa before she, too, disappeared into the backseat. The sadness inherent in Sorrentino's eyes as he got into the front seat, behind the wheel, and the Lincoln pulled away.

Next up: images of James Crawford's private jet landing at Tweed International Airport. The big man exiting the plane, a head of frothy white hair, a bulbous nose and clear blue eyes. He looked in his late sixties, at least. Tired, as if New Haven, Connecticut, was the last place on earth he'd want to be. According to Larsen, it was.

He gave a brief statement to the awaiting reporters in the small terminal: "The world has lost two great men," the Sons of God founder began. "Richard Deegan and Anthony Sorrentino were the embodiments of hardworking Christians. Men who loved their families, their God, and their country. And they were my friends. I loved them as brothers. And I will miss them dearly."

Turning to the computer, I logged on and then punched in the first of the four remaining Deegan escort Web addresses: www2.girls-4-hire-4-U.com/comeinside/page1.html.

They offered some of the more specialized services: bondage and domination, things like that. Clicking on OUR ESCORTS, I found none listed in Connecticut.

Next: www.sexy.cllgrls.org/private/welcome.htm.

And with it an error message that the URL did not exist on this server. They were either out of business, had a new Web address, or the address was wrong to begin with. I altered it slightly, just in case: *http://sexy.cllgrls.org/*, but got the same error message.

Next: *www.tri-state-escorts.com/index.html*.

The classiest looking site thus far. A pretty redhead, who looked like a lingerie model you'd find in the Sunday *New York*

Times Magazine, posed over their logo. At the bottom of the page was a button: MEET OUR GIRLS. That took me to a listing of about fifty escorts doing business in our area. I scrolled down their names and descriptions—no pictures "for discretion's sake." There were five who seemed to fit the bill. Another two that might be close. I jotted down their info and moved on.

Last: *www1.escorts-2-escorts.com/escort/CT.html*.

So nice, they named it twice. But Escorts-2-Escorts was just one woman, Yvette, who posted a few snapshot-type JPEGs. A well-tanned forty-something, she was in good shape, except for the wear-and-tear on her skin, which looked the bad side of leather. She could have been a poster girl for the damage ultra-violet exposure can cause. At the bottom of her home page, was a disclaimer:

> *Please note, this is not an offer for prostitution. Money ex-changed is for time and companionship only. Time together may include services such as modeling, sensuous massage, or erotic dancing. Anything else that may occur is a matter of personal choice between two or more consenting adults of legal age, and is not contracted for, nor is it requested to be con-tracted for, or compensated for in any manner.*

TWENTY-EIGHT

Wading through the seven phone numbers:

ASHLEY
I'm 19 and ready to rock your world.

BEAUTIFUL CONNECTICUT GIRL
Available for escort or massage.

CANDI
Heaven is just one sin away with this hot 20-year-old.

JESSICA
Naughty but nice, and just barely legal.

MELANIE
Cute, slender college girl catering to generous executives.

KARA
Beautiful 18 year old, 5'9, 120lb, 35B-23-34. What more do you need to know?

RENEE
Sexy Claire Danes look-a-like ready to be your Juliet.

I grabbed a fresh beer and started dialing. Ashley had voice mail: "Hi, this is Ashley. Leave me your name, phone number, and the town you're calling from at the beep, and I'll call right back." Her voice was sweet, but I wasn't about to fall for those assumptions again. Not after the fiasco this morning with

132 / Gorman Bechard

Heather. "This is William Shute, from New Haven," I said, leaving my number.

Beautiful Connecticut Girl had a disconnected beeper number. Perhaps she'd finally seen the light. Realized the inherent evil in those little chirping boxes. I crossed her off the list. Candi, Jessica, and Melanie also had beepers. Naturally. Theirs were working. I punched in my number.

Kara had voice mail. "Hi, this is Kara," she said, sounding so natural and normal it caught me off guard. "Leave your name and number at the beep." I followed her instructions.

One to go, and thankfully Renee brought it all back to business. She likewise had voice mail, but her message was a sales pitch. "Hi Romeo," she said. "I've been wondering when you were going to call. Leave me your number, and I promise to get right back to you. This Juliet won't make you wait long."

Melanie called back first. She rattled off her statistics at such a breakneck speed, before I could even get out the words, "Tell me about yourself."

"I'm twenty-one, five foot five, a hundred twenty-five pounds, 36D-26-36, short curly red hair, pierced nipples, and shaved. My fee is one-seventy-five an hour."

Her tone was so lackluster and lacking in lust that I thought for a moment I was standing in line at a burger joint and the pimply kid behind the counter was repeating my order, thinking about anything else, wanting to be anywhere else, wishing he or she were someone else.

I thanked her for calling back and said, "I'd think about it." The entire exchange couldn't have taken more than fifteen seconds. I felt winded. And didn't have time to catch my breath before the phone rang again.

"Hi, baby," she said. "Is this William?"

"Sure is."

"This is Renee."

"Juliet?"

"You've got it, baby."

"Tell me about yourself."

"What would you like to know?"

"How tall are you?" I said. "What are your measurements?"

"You get right down to business, don't you, baby?"

"Might as well."

"Might as well," she repeated. "Well, let's see. How's five-four, 36-24-36 sound?"

"Sounds great," I said. "What do you weigh?"

"Well, you are a nosy little one," she said, giggling. "Around one-forty-five."

The figures didn't add up. So, I asked Renee about her cup size.

"A perfect D," she said, proudly.

Call waiting beeped before I could respond. "Be right back," I said. It was Candi. I told her to hold on. Then switched back and informed Claire Danes's twin that I needed to take this call, and would call her again if I was interested.

"Okay, Romeo," she said. "I'll be waiting by the phone."

I pressed the switch hook. "Candi?"

"Hi," she said. "You beeped?"

"Yeah," I said, figuring I'd try another approach. "I'm looking for someone on the slender side."

"Hmmm," she went. "Like waifish."

I guessed that *mary.jpg* would fall into that category. "Sort of," I said, a little embarrassed, as if I were suddenly somehow responsible for millions of anorexic teenaged girls.

"Well," Candi said. "I have a pretty good body, but I'm not that thin. Still a little baby fat, y'know. I'd hate for you to be disappointed."

She seemed so nice, so real by comparison, that I doubted she'd disappoint.

"I'm tall," she continued, "But what you'd probably consider a big girl. Big boobs, big bones, a big smile." She laughed. It was warm and I couldn't help think this girl must be making a fortune.

"Maybe some other time," I said.

"When you're in the mood for a little meat on your bones," she said.

The phone rang again. Kara. Her voice had an intelligent, just slightly sarcastic edge to it. She said her measurements were exactly what her ad promised. She had shoulder-length brown hair. "I look like I could be Julia Roberts's kid sister," she said. Her fee: $250 an hour—"You get what you pay for"—but she didn't punch a clock and liked to take her time and enjoy herself. I told her she sounded perfect—too many of them sounded perfect, but only one of them could be the girl from room 112. I gave her directions. She told me to give her ninety minutes, asking, of course, if that was okay. She'd just gotten back from class and wanted to shower and change. I told her to take her time; then I hung up the phone.

TWENTY-NINE

The buzzer. Loud and clear and—glancing at my watch. Kara was early, about forty minutes or so. Taking a deep breath. Opening the door. A warm smile on my face. Didn't want to scare her away in case she was the one. Didn't want to scare—

Not what I expected.

Not what I expected at all. She was a *he*. In his twenties, tall. Real freakin' tall. Middle linebacker wide. With stylish dark brown hair. Dressed in a dark suit. An expensive suit. Expensive shoes. A gold watch. No person on earth could have been farther from the truth of *mary.jpg*.

"Can I help you?" I asked, my hand reaching for my gun. This time I wished it were there.

"Have you accepted Jesus Christ as your Lord and Savior?" he asked, his voice calm, trustworthy.

I gave him points for actually being able to deliver the line with a straight face. "No," I said as politely as possible. "But I'm expecting company, so if you don't mind." I tried to close the door. He held a huge hand flat against it. It was as if I were applying no pressure at all. He smiled.

"Look," I said, "I'm a cop."

"Detective William Peter Shute," he said, still smiling. Then snapping his fingers a few time. "Shute. Aren't you related to that nice couple who owns the bakery? Sure. I see the resemblance. You must be their son. Real nice folks, your mom and dad. Bet it must have been great growing up in that house as a kid. Crestview Drive in North Haven, right? Your mom baking up all those goodies for you and your friends to eat."

I didn't like where this was going. But I wasn't armed, and this guy looked like he could break me in half without so much as breaking a sweat. Staying calm, considering. "I didn't catch your name," I said.

"I'm your Angel Gabriel," he said. "Bringing you a message from God."

I stared at him hard. He was at the top of the stairs, a small wooden landing. If I hit him right, if I hurt him, and if he fell backwards. A lot too *iffy*. Then, as if he were reading my mind, he put his free hand on his waist, drawing my eyes as he pushed back his expensive jacket, revealing the holster, the gun.

"And that message would be?" I asked, raising my gaze back up to his face. Feeling the blood flushing my face. Feeling the rage.

"Quit while you're ahead, Detective." His voice wasn't nearly so trustworthy now.

"Meaning?"

"Take a vacation," he said. "Get out of town for a few weeks. Enjoy your time off."

"Maybe take a ride to Jackson, Mississippi," I said.

"I really doubt that old VW of yours could make it that far," he said.

"There anything about me you don't know?" I asked.

A big smile. "Have a nice night," he said, stepping back, turning, walking down the stairs. I watched after him, studied the confidence. Never once did he look back. Never once did he think I might come after him. Never once did he doubt the scare he put in me.

She answered on the second ring. I let out a deep breath when I heard her voice. "Mom," I said.

"Will," she answered, her voice as sing-songy as always. "Your father and I were just talking about you. We've been meaning to call, y'know, about yesterday."

"Yesterday?"

"It was finalized, wasn't it? Your divorce?"

"Oh. Yeah. Right," I said. "My divorce."

"We didn't want to pry. Didn't want to invade your space."

"You never pry, Mom," I said. I'd never once told her she was prying. Never told her she was invading my space. I think it was something she saw on TV when I was a teen. A program for parents about being your teenager's best friend.

"Did it go okay, honey?" she asked.

"Yeah, mom," I said. "It was fine."

"Fine?" she said. "Uh-oh. I don't like the sound of that. Is something wrong?"

You could never fool your mom. "No," I lied. "I was—I miss you, that's all. I miss talking to you guys. I miss your cooking. I was thinking—it's something crazy. Why don't the three of us just hop in the car and go away for the week. Someplace fun. I don't know. I want to take you guys to Disney World." I couldn't think of anyplace else off the top of my head.

She laughed. "Florida," she said. I could hear her call to my dad. "Henry, Will wants to take us to Disney World."

He laughed as well. "Tell him I'd prefer to go fishing off the Florida Keys," I heard him say.

"You are the dreamer," my mom said to me. "You'd end up losing your job, and we'd—well, we've been so busy."

"More than usual?"

"Yes," she said. "Just this afternoon we got this huge order."

"Really," I said.

"Yes," she said. "From that religious group that's coming to town. You know, the Sons of God. Those men sure like their pastries."

My old service revolver—before Glocks became standard issue—a Smith & Wesson, model-60, five-shot .38, was in a box with my Nikon camera, a busted Crybaby wah pedal, and some photo albums from before I got married. The bullets were there, as well. I loaded the gun and stuck it into the back waistband of my pants. Untucking my shirt, I covered it over.

Pacing. Another beer. Wondering, Who was this big son of a bitch? A Sons of God flunkie, but who sent him? Larsen—was his despair just a ruse? Deegan's wife, or was her slap enough? His daughters? No. Donny, the assistant? Gabe didn't look the type to hang with Donny. What about the big man himself, James Crawford? It was a message from God, he said. Could Crawford view himself as—but Crawford didn't know me. I was off the case officially before his plane even touched down on Connecticut soil.

How did Gabe know so much about me? About my family? About the house I grew up in? The house where my parents still lived? Was he that connected? Did he come from the mayor? From inside the division? Was there something bigger here, and I hadn't a clue?

Have I accepted Jesus Christ as my Lord and Savior?

Was I that much of a threat? Not me, but Deegan's speech. The pictures on his computer. Did it come down to *mary.jpg*? Would it get in the way of their relocation? Or—was it the girl? Were they after the girl and knew—Larsen knew—I'd get there first?

This wasn't the legal intimidation O'Toole told me about, but perhaps this was the real reason no one ever went after them, no one ever called them on their lies. Gabe was a grade-A hired goon. Smart enough never to mention the Sons of God. Never to make a threat. Sent out to keep me quiet. To put in a little scare.

Staring at the phone, I wondered if I should drag Brown into this? He was my partner, but—they've got to be watching me. And if Brown's involved, he's got kids, a wife. He's still got a job. Christ!

The buzzer again. I reached for my gun and headed toward the door. So be it. I could do it alone. I was ready this time. Ready to tell Gabe that I've accepted Smith & Wesson as my Lord and Savior.

THIRTY

Opening the door a crack, perhaps a little more. Not Gabe, but—

She was tall, slender, with long, wavy brown hair. Huge brown eyes and an Ipana smile, looking as if she stepped off the pages of a magazine. An ad for blue jeans, which she wore a little loose fitting, with a simple black T-shirt. She carried a small black knapsack, a little strange-looking, with the letters *MH* stamped into the nylon. Her nails weren't painted, and she wore no discernible makeup. There was a shine behind her eyes. And a confidence to that smile. To the way she stood, one thumb hooked through a front belt loop.

I'd forgotten all about her. Jamming the gun back into my waistband, trying to recover. To remember what, why, and how. To calm the fuck down.

Opening the door wider.

"Will?" she asked. With her free hand she pushed her hair back behind one ear.

Suddenly I found myself wondering if her picture would have taken up much room on Deegan's hard drive. Would she have outnumbered Mary? Probably not. Her breasts were too full. Her curves too real. This was a woman. The *mary.jpg* was just a girl.

I nodded. "Kara."

She stepped past me, into my apartment, looking around. Taking notice. The unpacked boxes caught her attention right off. "Live here long?" There was just the slightest touch of suspicion in her voice.

"Three months," I said, thinking, then just telling her the truth. "But I've been in no hurry to unpack. My divorce was just finalized on Monday."

Her reaction was like in a daydream. The suspicion vanished, replaced by a softening both soothing and sensual. I hurt inside, but she knew how to make it all better. Whether it was rehearsed or sincere, or whether I'd had one too many beers, it didn't matter much.

"I just need to see your license," she said.

Nodding, closing the door. I pulled out my wallet, and from it my license, handing it to her, noticing what I had originally thought to be a bracelet around her right wrist was really the most intricate of tattoos. Black vines, red roses, faces of cherubs smiling at a woman lying naked amongst the flowers. "I'm a cop," I explained.

"Oh, yeah," she said, speaking the words as a laugh, in jest, in mock disbelief. She glanced at the ID. "I never thought of myself as the cop's type. Y'know, no big hair. No silicone." She smiled. "I'm not a stripper."

I kept going with the truth. "The reason I asked you here."

She cut me off as if there should be only one. "Reason?"

"I need to ask you a few questions."

She looked at me, as if trying to get a read. "Just questions, huh?"

"Yeah," I said. "Sorry."

"Not my loss," she said, nodding a couple of times. No spark of anger. No resentment at the waste of her time. Just a straightforward, "So, where's the badge?"

"Unofficial questions," I said. "This isn't a bust, or anything even remotely related to one."

It took her a couple of seconds, but she handed back the license and said, "Do you like drinking alone, or can I have a beer?"

I s Kara your real name?"

It was almost standard operating procedure. Instead of being at opposite sides of a wooden table in an interrogation room, we were sitting on opposite ends of a sofa in my apartment. Both drinking a microbrew.

She took a deep breath. "What do you think?"

"It's why I'm asking."

She nodded a couple of times. "It's Daphne," she said. "Daphne Schwartz. Makes you hard just hearing me say it, doesn't it?"

"Kara works better?"

"Would you call an escort named Daphne?"

"Sure," I said.

"You ever use an escort?"

"No."

"Exactly," she said.

I smiled. I had to. "Okay, Daphne, where were you on Sunday night, between the hours of ten P.M. and midnight?"

She gave a moment of thought. "Seeing the new Todd Solondz film with a girlfriend. We always do dinner and a movie on Sunday nights. It's playing at the Showcase in Orange. The nine-forty-five showing. And yes, she'll back me up. Her name's Milissa DiFranco."

"She won't wonder why?"

"She's the one person who knows about this," Daphne said. "My safety net. She knows I'm here right now. I called her from my cell phone when I pulled up. If she doesn't hear from me in ninety minutes or so, she calls."

"She's got my number?"

She nodded. "You want hers?"

I shook my head.

"Hmm," she went. "Sunday night, huh? This have anything to do with Richard Deegan?"

The look on my face must have given it away. My surprise at her having read the paper, watched the news. The whole world was focusing on New Haven, and yet here I was surprised. It was a bias against her profession.

"I'm a news hound," she said. Then it dawned. "You didn't think that I'm that girl—aren't you're looking for a serial killer? Someone else was murdered—"

"The Feds are looking for a serial killer," I explained, then figuring it didn't make any difference or that perhaps there was safety in numbers, I told her, "I think the girl who killed Deegan was an escort who did so in self-defense."

"But what about the other guy?"

"Not the same killer."

"That's not what the papers are saying?"

"No," I said. "It's what I'm saying. It's why I'm officially off the case."

"But unofficially—"

"Right."

She thought about it for a few seconds, finishing off the beer. "Why do you think that?" she asked. "That there's more than one killer?"

"You really want to know?"

She nodded her reply and then said, "And I'd like another beer, please."

THIRTY-ONE

Daphne read Deegan's speech. She sat there quietly for a moment afterwards and then looked at me. "I'm glad he's dead," she said sadly.

She read his letter to Alex, actually laughing out loud during and after. Then she glanced through his collection of JPEGs. I had her pay special attention to *mary.jpg*. Did she know any other escorts, anyone, who resembled her in any way?

She shook her head. "A girl like that could make a fortune with some of the sickies out there," she said. "She could pass for fourteen or fifteen. Claim she's a virgin. A thousand a call, no sweat." Daphne turned away from the computer, shaking her head again.

"The clients that gullible?"

"They believe I'm eighteen."

I forgot about her ad. But then age wasn't an issue with this woman. Daphne was timeless. Daphne was—she couldn't have been eighteen. Her act was too together. Nothing like Heather, who I never for a minute believed to be nineteen, but that was due to her physical appearance. Teenagers shouldn't look that haggard.

"How old are you?" I asked.

"I'll be twenty-four next week," she said.

"And that makes you less desirable?"

"To a lot of guys," she said. "They like fresh meat."

The candor caught me a little off guard. "And that doesn't bother you?" I asked.

"Bothers me a lot sometimes. But I figure everyone has their little fetish. Everyone. There are no exceptions to this rule. Your fetish might be that you're into feet, or tickle torture. Or even something like work. Or that you hate sex, or you hate everyone who's the least bit promiscuous. All those Born Agains preaching family values. Their fetish is to stop everyone else from having a good time. But still, that's a fetish in my book." She stood, walking to the fridge, returning with fresh refills. "But yeah, sometimes it bothers me." She sat on the arm of the sofa, handing me one of the beers. "So, why do it, right? What's a girl like me, blah, blah, blah?"

"More or less," I said.

She shrugged and crunched up her face, turning, taking a long sip. She noticed the guitar case then, leaning behind the amp. Not that anyone could really miss it, Marshalls tend to stand out in one-bedroom apartments. Without so much as a word, without asking, Daphne went to the Marshall, pulled the case from behind it, laying it on the floor in front of the amp. She kneeled, a flash of tattoo now visible on her lower back as her top rode up slightly. An angel, standing in a field of flowers, stars raining from her hands.

The case had four latches. She flipped the first two, and the breath caught in my throat. She flipped the next two, and my heart stopped beating. Watching her. Watching as she lifted the lid. The black plush interior. Worn and crushed and—Gloria. The look on Daphne's face. Watching as her hand ran down the neck, over the strings. I got goose bumps. I wondered what it did for Gloria.

Without knowing how I got there, I was kneeling by Daphne's side. Reaching into the case. Touching the old maple neck, darkened and a little fretworn in the cowboy-chord area. Slipping my hand under. Lifting her up a little, just leaning her out of the case. The fingers of my left hand wrapping around her neck unconsciously forming a barred G chord. The strings sharp against my fingertips.

"Her name's Gloria," I said.

"Oh, yeah," she said. "Why's that?"

"Back in the early fifties," I said, "whoever installed the pickups and did the wiring on the guitars at the Fender factory, usually one of four women, Mary, Virginia, Carolyn or—"

"Gloria."

"Right. They'd write their name, and the date the work was done on a small piece of masking tape, and stick it in the control cavity." I tapped the black pickguard. "Under the pickguard, right about here. This one says: 'Gloria September fifteenth 1953.' "

Daphne read the name from the headstock. " 'Fender Telecaster.' Wasn't Springsteen holding one of these on the cover of *Born to Run?*"

I nodded, strumming lightly with my right hand. So out of tune. My Tele was in the original butterscotch blond finish. Worn down, so the grain of the wood bled through. Worn down even more along the edges.

Gloria would have listed for $189.50 in 1953, thirteen years before I was born. She's worth around fifteen grand now, give or take. Not that I'd sell her for a million dollars. Not that I'd sell her for the world. There are some dreams you never let go of. Even if you do keep them buried away.

THIRTY-TWO

F irst off," Daphne said, finally getting around to my question, "The money's great. But that's not why I did it the first time." A shrug. "I was nineteen, had just broken up with my boyfriend. It was a Friday night, and I was feeling really restless and incredibly unattractive."

"Sorry for yourself?" I said.

"Completely. So, I'm looking through the New Haven *Advocate*, y'know for something to do. Like maybe there's a good band at Toad's—"

"Where the tribute bands to the legends play," I said.

"Or Rudy's, Café Nine, wherever. And I notice these adult-employment classifieds in the back of the paper. All these escort services." She made her voice sound like an advertising pitch man's. "Hiring young women with a desire for the finer things in life. Make two thousand dollars a week. Or more." Another shrug. "So I called. And, again, not because of the money, but because, I don't know, I was suddenly turned on by the idea of going to a stranger's house and letting him screw me. He could have handed me ten bucks, twenty, it wouldn't have made any difference. It was a fantasy."

"A revenge fantasy?"

"More like something different. Something exciting," she said. "My sex life was pretty dreary. So, I called, and an hour later I meet this guy in a parking lot. He drove a yellow Ferrari."

I laughed. Saul Rothstein, the man O'Toole worked so hard at busting, currently on the run from federal prosecutors for skipping out on the jail time he'd have received for being found guilty on the charges of promoting prostitution, conspiracy to promote prostitution, and violating the Corrupt Organizations and Racketeering Act.

"The Sex King," I said.

"That's him," Daphne said. "He looked me over, then told me the charge was two-sixty cash for full service, one-fifty for massage, fifty percent of which was mine to keep. Along with whatever I made in tips. He asked if I knew what would be expected of me? I nodded, though I didn't really have a clue. I'd never given a massage in my life. But figured I knew how to screw. He gave me a beeper and told me someone would be in touch." She shook her head. "It went off before I got home."

"Did the first time live up to your fantasy?"

She laughed. It was warm and authentic and—we locked eyes for a moment. A hesitation. Then both of us looked quickly away.

"I was so nervous that first time," she said. "That night. It was pushing midnight. But I called the number on the beeper, and this guy wants me to meet him. He gives me his name, and like, I recognize it. I've read one of his books."

"Who?"

"Let's just say he's a well-published Yale professor."

"That's narrows it down," I said.

"So, I meet him in front of the Sterling Memorial Library. He looks me over, nods a couple of times, and says 'Follow me.'" She took a long sip of beer. "He takes me up to his office. The building's completely empty. No one around. And I'm a little freaked. I mean, what if he's a serial killer or something?"

"Lot of them running around," I said.

"Exactly," she said, smiling. "But I go along, anyway. 'Take a seat,' he says, pointing at a chair opposite his desk. I do. He reaches into his pocket and hands me some cash. Three hundred sixty dollars. An extra hundred for me, and I haven't even done anything yet. But all I can think about now is, what the hell is he going to make me do to earn that extra hundred?" She took a breath. "So, he's leaning back against the front of his desk, and he starts talking to me like I was, I don't know, thirteen years old. He's lecturing me. About sex. About my budding sexuality. About those 'strange feelings' between my legs."

I had to laugh, because she was.

"I don't know how I kept a straight face," she said. "He went on and on, for like a half hour. It was so freaking boring. He kept referring to it in all these flowery terms. My *rosebud*. My *petunia*." She shook her head, still laughing. "Then he sat down behind his desk, and told me it was time for my punishment. That he hates to have to do this, blah, blah, blah." Another sip. "So I go to him. He bends me over his lap and proceeds to spank me. Not hard. I've still got all my clothes on. And I'm thinking this is doing absolutely nothing for me. Absolutely nothing."

"Perhaps that was the point."

"Perhaps." Another sip, "Now he's really getting into it, to the point where it's starting to sting a little. And I'm getting annoyed. And just about when I've had enough, and I'm about to turn around and let him have it, I notice he's mumbling something. But I can't make out what it is. It sounds like maybe he's singing a song. But, no idea. So, anyway, he finishes, and when he's through, he tells me to stand and pay attention. His exact words: 'Pay attention.' So I stand, and my ass is like killing me by this point. I try to look coy, try not to burst out laughing. Or burst out crying. My whole fantasy was, like, shot to hell. And he pulls out a framed picture of Eva Gabor from one of his desk drawers. It's autographed. Y'know, 'from Eva with love.' And I'm thinking, okay, now what? And he whips it out—"

"His bean stalk?" I suggested.

"Exactly. And he begins jerking off onto the picture, as I stand there and—"

"Pay attention."

"Yeah," she said. "And that's when it hits me. The song he was singing as he spanked me. It was the theme from *Green Acres*."

THIRTY-THREE

Daphne advertised exclusively on the Web because it severely limited the number of voice mail messages. "I usually wait until I'm in the mood," she explained, "or if I really like the voice of the guy who's calling." There were no Saul Rothsteins to answer to. No taxes. It was wonderfully anonymous. *And* she got to keep all the money. Self-employment at its finest.

"I used to average, oh, four to five calls a week. Couple of regular customers, mixed in with a couple of new ones. But in the past few months, I don't know, I've been doing it less and less."

"Why tonight?" I asked.

"I was"—she smiled—"in the mood."

"Sorry to disappoint."

"Who said I was disappointed?" she said. Then, "I'm used to guys who spend ninety percent of their time talking. They're lonely, and respectful, and"—a small shrug—"they treat me a hell of a lot better than some guy I'd pick up in a bar."

Daphne was a full-time student, a senior, double majoring in poli-sci and history, at the University of New Haven. Next stop—law school. The money helped with the bills, helped her live beyond the means of any of the other students. She could concentrate on studying and not obsess about a relationship. And she could have sex whenever she wanted—there wasn't a night when she didn't get at least a few voice mails. It kept her fantasies active.

"Lots of people don't understand that aspect of it," she said. "My friend, Milissa, always gives me that lecture, sex without love, blah, blah, blah. But I swear, she's got this dark side that's dying to try it. I think we all have this dark side, dying to come out, to be set free."

"Most people keep theirs in check," I said.

"Their loss," she replied.

At 11:35, she asked if we could watch *Nightline*. I handed her the remote.

"That's a first," she said.

"What," I asked, "watching *Nightline* with a guy you expected to be—?" I let the sentence hang in the air.

"No," she said, smiling. "I've never known a man to ever willingly hand over a remote control."

I took a seat beside her as the familiar theme music started up. Then Ted Koppel's voice. Then the date. Then something to catch up my attention: a shot of James Crawford's jet landing at Tweed. A quick cut to Crawford's press conference as he spoke about the world losing two great men. Pictures of Deegan and Sorrentino dissolving into video from other Sons of God rallies. Thousands of men. Hundreds of thousands. Crying. Holding hands. Saying *amen* in unison. Koppel interrupting. "In New Haven, Connecticut, a person, or persons, is killing off the hierarchy of the Sons of God. Is this cold-blooded murder random and coincidental, or does someone have a deadly grudge against the fastest-growing religious group of all time? Later in our program, we'll be speaking with Sons of God founder, James Crawford, but first, Peter Shugrue, of New Haven ABC affiliate, WTNH, with his report on the killings in the Elm City."

It was a seven-minute package rehashing everything old. There was no mention of escorts or pornography, or the items found in Deegan's overnight bag. There was nothing about the Sons of God's relocation plans. The only new information was on the murder weapon. Peter Shugrue broke the news that both men had been stabbed to death with a Faber-Castell Number Two pencil.

Then it was time for a commercial.

H ow strange," Daphne said. "No other guests."
It was just Koppel and James Crawford. Each sitting in
a studio, New York and New Haven, respectively. One asking
questions, the other answering. No one to rebuff, rebuke. No
one to disagree.

"Probably the only way Crawford would agreed to go on," I
said.

"Thank you for joining us, Mr. Crawford," Koppel said.

"Thank you for having me, Ted," the Sons of God founder
said. "I just wish it could be at a happier time. In celebration of
a goodness, or Godliness. Or of some miracle. Not in this time
of mourning. These were my friends, Ted. Good men. Men who
served God and their country."

"I have to tell you," Koppel said. "That there's been a lot of
vicious rumor and innuendo surrounding these murders. That a
prostitute is suspected—"

Before I could even begin to cheer Ted on, Crawford cut
him off, his voice strong, a little angry. "Preposterous," he said.
"There's nothing to back any of these rumors. That's why they're
rumors. Spread, I might add, by those intent on destroying what
I've created with the Sons of God. There are a lot of people out
to get us—"

"Not too paranoid," Daphne said.

"—the liberal media," Crawford said, listing off some of his
enemies, "the pro-choice minority, AIDS activists, gay activists.
Need I continue?"

"No, sir," Koppel said. "I think your point has been made."

"A woman is suspected in both murders," Crawford said,
"But it's the press which has jumped to the conclusion that she's
a prostitute. There's no proof. Both the police and the Federal
Bureau of Investigation are working around the clock on this
case, and neither have presented me with one scintilla

of evidence suggesting that the murderer was a prostitute. And dear Lord, if that isn't sexist, backwards thinking on the part of the journalists covering this story—that just because the murderer is female, she's a prostitute—well, then I don't know what is."

I wanted so much for Koppel to drop Deegan's leather bag onto his desk and begin pulling out the items. I wanted him to show examples of the photos on Deegan's laptop. Pictures of *mary.jpg*. I wanted him to read from Deegan's intended speech. Asking, "Perhaps then you can explain this, Mr. Crawford."

But Koppel wasn't armed with such evidence. He could only question Crawford as to why someone would want to take his organization down.

"They're frightened of us, Ted," Crawford explained. "We represent morality, old-time family values, church on Sunday, dinner at six, no drinking, no drugs, no abortion, no birth control. No promiscuity, Ted. And I don't just mean sexual promiscuity. There are many types of promiscuity. Careerism. Greed. This need for absolute equality between the sexes. That's the worst sort of promiscuity. We must return the male to the bread-winning position. Making him, once again, the head of the household. Women need to understand the value of staying at home. Caring for their families, their husbands. People are frightened of the Sons of God because we're taking a lot of money out of a lot of pockets. We're putting condom manufacturers out of business. The breweries, the distilleries, out of business. Pornographers, out of business and in jail, where they belong. Prostitutes, perverts, homosexuals—there's no place for them in our America. And Hollywood, the television networks." He shook his head. "We'd start right with your parent company, Ted. Take them to task for that so-called Gay Day at Disney World. Gay Day at Disney World is not my idea of good clean family fun."

"I was led to believe the Sons of God was pro-gay," Koppel said.

"All men are welcome to join," Crawford said. "But once you do, you must abide by our rules. You must follow our commitments."

"The twelve commitments."

"Yes, sir," Crawford said. "Promiscuity is forbidden. And homosexuality is at its root very promiscuous behavior. To be a Son of God, one must renounce his homosexuality, denounce all promiscuousness, and follow in the footsteps of our Lord, Jesus Christ."

Koppel nodded once, looked into the camera, and said, "We'll be right back."

THIRTY-FOUR

The buzzer cut through before the end of the first commercial. I jumped, reaching behind me for my gun. Just checking. Daphne shooting me a look.

"You okay?" she asked.

I was okay. My gun was in reach. She didn't have to know about Angel Gabe. She didn't—

Going to the door, I opened it a crack.

It was O'Toole. Dressed to kill, not from work, but in a slip of a summery gown. Silky light blue. Sultry and made-up. She opened the door wide, taking a step into the apartment, "You're not going to believe the shit those Fed sons o' bitches put us through," she began, reaching up for where my tie ought to be and then stopping, turning, the words fading away, her features growing hard, her eyes trained on the sofa.

Daphne gave a small wave.

"Look, Gracie, it's not—," I said, the words sounding forced and way-too-sleazy in my head. It's not. It wasn't. This was work. What do you want from me? But the look on her face cut short the string of confusion. "Have a drink with us, and I'll explain."

"Fuck you," she said, looking around one last time, stepping back, and then glaring into my eyes. "Just fuck you."

The stomping of her shoes on the wooden steps faded, and the downstairs door slammed shut. I stared into the darkness of the stairwell. I didn't want to piss O'Toole off. I liked O'Toole. I liked what we did last night. Was it just last night? I liked—

Daphne was suddenly by my side, shutting my door, locking it.

"Sorry about that," she said.

"It's not your fault," I said.

"Let's pretend that it is," she said, leaning close, kissing me. "It'll be more fun that way."

WEDNESDAY

Daphne didn't sneak out in the middle of the night. She was still asleep as I dragged myself down to the kitchen, picturing with every step that look on O'Toole's face. I don't know if it was hatred so much as disappointment. In me.

Taking the first sip of coffee, a gulp really. Scalding this time, even a little beyond. Finally. Perhaps I was attempting to burn away the wrongs, burn away Charlene, thinking O'Toole had every right to be disappointed. Every goddamn right. I rubbed a hand at my eyes, over my face, inhaling . . . Daphne, thinking now how good it was, how right—

I felt her arms around me. Her body pressed tight against my back, the side of her face against my shoulder. Her breath past my ear as I turned and our lips met. It was like I remembered from last night, from just hours ago. But it had no right to be. The way we fit, the way we connected should have been a fluke, or a mistake, or—

Everything stopped. Time stopped. Pain, disappointment stood still; they had to. All that remained were the kisses, tender, so natural, a rhythm of small passions. An exploration, and yet familiar, as if we had done this a thousand times before. I pulled her closer—she couldn't be any closer, but still. I needed—not wanted, needed—her closer, I needed to feel her skin melt against mine, as we stood in my kitchen, as my coffee grew cold, as all I *wanted* was to die in her arms.

"I probably should have told you this last night," she said.

Wondering what was in store, what was coming next, I looked at her. She was even more beautiful now, still a little sleepy. She glanced up and our eyes met. "What is it?" I asked.

"I worked a party a few weeks ago out at a condo in East Haven. It was just a"—a shrug—"a one-time thing. I really didn't like the clientele. The money was amazing, but—anyway, it was run by a girl named Barbara Boyle. Rumor had it that she brought in an extra girl, me, because she had been roughed up by a client, and well, couldn't perform."

"How'd she find you?" I asked.

"I'd placed an ad on The Pleasure Garden bulletin board."

I shook my head.

"What?"

"At www.thepleasuregarden.com?"

"Yeah," she said. "Why?"

"I found that address on Deegan's laptop," I said. "It was at the top of his URL list, but I was too tired to ever look for a bulletin board."

"You've got to scroll down to the bottom of the page."

Still shaking my head, I asked, "You didn't happen to get the name of the guy who roughed her up?"

"No," Daphne said. "Just who he worked for."

"Who's that?"

"The Sons of God."

THIRTY-SIX

It was another one of those days when May was pretending to be August. Already sweating. Waving to Daphne as she drove by in her Jeep, taking a long look around, for Gabe or any other angels of his ilk. Crossing the street, the image of a tattooed attorney in a tight power suit suddenly flashing in my head—she'd make a kick-ass lawyer. Smiling, I pulled open the door to the one-story corner brick building and was immediately assaulted by the smell of waffles and sausages and maple syrup and eggs.

I headed to my usual booth, but it was taken, occupied by a big bald black man in a dark suit. I swung into the seat opposite him.

"Wondering when you'd get here," Brown said. He had coffee in front of him and a menu.

"Didn't know we had a date."

"Just figured you'd like to be clued in."

"Might be nice."

"But first you," he said.

"What?" I asked, wondering what was coming.

"What's the deal between you and Questral?" he asked. "Acting like a spurned lover. Isn't she a little old for you?"

"You really want to know this?" I asked.

"Probably not," Brown said. "But give it to me, anyway."

"She's got a daughter from her first marriage."

Brown shook his head. "I thought you said—"

"This was a while ago, Brown," I explained. "I was single, wearing a blue uniform. I hadn't even met Charlene."

"The good ol' days," he said.

"Right," I said. "She picked me up in a bar. Came on strong. I mean really strong. Never told me her last name. How'd I know she was gunning for me all along. Or at least gunning for a cop. Pissed off at dear old Mom. I don't know why. Never got the chance to ask. All I know is that in her mind, revenge was screwing a cop."

"Sleeping with the enemy?"

"Something like that, I guess," I said. "She spilled everything to Questral the next morning. Gave her every sordid detail. Even my freakin' badge number."

"You wore your badge to bed?" he said.

"No, I didn't wear it to bed," I said. "She wanted to see it."

"During?" he asked, laughing.

"Between rounds," I said. "She told me she'd never been with a cop before. Never saw a badge up close and personal."

He laughed even harder. "Sometimes I think you deserved Charlene."

"Now I've got something to ask you," I said.

Maybe it was my tone, maybe the expression on my face. "This is serious," my partner said.

A slight nod, followed by my description of Angel Gabriel.

"Sounds like a white Lawrence Taylor," he said.

"L. T. wishes he could have been this intimidating," I said. "You see anyone in the Sons of God organization who fits that description?"

"Not that I can recall," he said. "But I've just been working the edges of this case. Am I allowed to ask why?"

"He paid me a little visit, asked me if I'd accepted Jesus Christ as my Lord and Savior." I shook my head and laughed. "He knew everything about me. Where my parents worked. Where they lived. Told me I should quit while I was ahead."

"That *is* intimidating," he said. "And this ain't worth getting hurt over."

"I'm not so sure about that," I said.

"There something else you ain't telling me?"

Before I could answer yes or no, or just tell him about the

pictures of my ex-wife on Deegan's laptop. Before I could tell him about *mary.jpg*, a voice interrupted.

"There are only six words in the English language that end in *d-o-u-s*: tremendous, horrendous, stupendous, hazardous, decapodous and palladous. And I don't have a fucking clue as to what the last two mean."

We both turned to face Mazz, who was glancing at the screen of his Palm, then closing it down, putting it away.

"This seat taken?" Mazz asked, squeezing in beside Brown. "I was just reading in the paper," he said, laughing, "about this stupid son of a bitch who broke the windshield of his ex-girlfriend's Taurus. He used a shotgun, swung it like a club. Thing discharged, blew a hole in his gut. He bled to death in the parking lot before anyone found him." He cracked open the menu. "I'm starving. But we better wait for O'Toole, otherwise we'll never hear the end of it."

"I really doubt O'Toole will be joining us," I said.

"Don't tell me," Brown said, shaking his head, giving me a look. A dirty one this time. There must have been something in my tone that gave me away.

"She told me last night she'd meet us here for breakfast," Mazz said.

"What time was that?" I asked.

"Spoke to her around ten," he said.

"She won't be meeting us," I said.

"You sure?"

"Unfortunately, yeah."

"You care to explain?" Mazz said. "I mean, she is my partner."

"Nothing to explain, Mazz," I said. He shot me a dirty look, too. But the guilt trip wasn't necessary, I already felt bad enough. "Just—" And I shrugged.

"Things that go bump in the night," Brown said.

The food came fast. Hot and sizzling and smoky. And coffee, lots of hot coffee. We dug in, talking between mouthfuls.

"What's Slice got to say?" I asked.

"Same murder weapon," Brown said. "For one."

"Exact same?" I asked. "Or are we just talking about another pencil?"

"Just another pencil," he said. "But get this. It was sharpened by a different sharpener than the first. Something about the circular grooves on the point being different."

"So you're looking for a serial killer who owns two pencil sharpeners?" I said.

"A female serial killer with two pencil sharpeners," Mazz said.

"What about vaginal secretions?"

"Present on both condoms," he said.

"But weeks until we know if they match?"

He nodded, and flipped open his Palm. "But we do know that Deegan had on a Ramses brand, ultra-sensitive with nonoxynol-9 spermicide. Y'know, they're named after the great pharaoh Ramses the second, who had over a hundred and sixty kids."

We didn't know.

"Sorrentino was wearing a plain ol' nonlubricated Trojan," he added.

We waited for some bit of trivia about the Trojans. None came.

"Find anything in Sorrentino's room?" I asked.

"Nothing of interest," Mazz said. "The guy was up and up. Well liked by everyone."

"Not everyone," I said. "What about other women? Girlfriends? A secretary? An intern? Anyone serious?"

"Just the ex-wife," Mazz said, shrugging. "She's dead."

"Nothing to lead us to believe this girl wasn't a pro?" I asked.

"Nothing either way," Brown said.

"He didn't call any of the agencies, no beeper numbers?"

"Not from his hotel room phone," Brown said. "And not from his cellular."

"What about all those prints?"

"A who's who of the Sons of God," Mazz said. "From Deegan's wife and daughters to James Crawford, to everyone in between. The guy was a regular chauffeur."

"What were Deegan's wife and daughters doing in the car?"

"He picked them up at Tweed," Brown said.

"The video they keep playing on TV," I said.

"Right."

"They staying at the Omni?" I asked.

"Why?" Brown said. "Feel like getting slapped again."

"I was thinking about talking to the youngest daughter, Ruth."

"I don't recommend that, partner," Brown said.

"Klavan told us if we see you anywhere near the Omni to shoot first, ask what the hell you're doing later," Mazz said.

"But he was kidding," I said.

"Didn't sound like he was kidding to me," Mazz said.

"Just stay away," Brown said. "That girl goes bitching to Pinhead, you can kiss your badge good-bye for good."

"I don't think she'd go bitching to anyone."

"Why's that?"

"She's the rebel, remember?" I said. "Pregnant. Won't tell anyone who the father is."

"Maybe she doesn't know," Mazz said.

"Maybe, and that would make her even more of a rebel," I said. "But just maybe she does."

"You think she can shed a little light on her dad's kinks?" Brown asked.

"Kids usually know all about their parents' secrets," I said. "Maybe one of you can find out what room she's in."

They looked at each other.

"He's your partner," Mazz said.

"Maybe," Brown said.

I nodded, pretty sure he was talking to me, not about me. "Any other leads?"

"I was just about to ask you that," Mazz said. "Gracie said you were working his computer files into the ground."

"Still am."

"The Feds are coming up empty," Mazz said. "Got us talking to every escort agency in the state, every woman that's been arrested for prostitution in the past five years."

"Sounds like a waste of time," I said.

"You know it's a waste of time," Brown said.

"Did you find anything in Deegan's files?" Mazz asked.

I gave them the finer points of his intended speech. It was almost as if I could recite it by this point. As if Deegan's words had burned themselves a permanent home in my memory.

"The same heinous death at the hands of a man who has thus far eluded the authorities," Mazz said, shaking his head in disbelief. "The SOB actually wrote that?"

I answered with a nod.

"He was planning on killing a different girl every night?" Brown asked. There was a hardening disgust to his face.

"It looks that way," I said.

"Was this his fire and brimstone?" Brown said.

"Kill all the sinners," Mazz said. "Eliminate sin."

"Klavan know about this?" Brown asked.

"Remember that little scene yesterday?" I said.

"I thought that was because you shoved the mayor and told him to fuck off," Brown said.

"That's against the rules?" I said. "Now you tell me."

"The rules don't apply here," Mazz said.

"That's good to know," I said.

"They've got us running around in circles," Brown said.

"*They're* running around in circles," I said.

"And in the meantime," Mazz said.

"In the meantime, we eat," Brown said. "Pass the salt."

THIRTY-SEVEN

I planned on hitting up the Sterling Memorial Library at Yale, to see what I might dig up about Deegan's college life, his connection to New Haven. Then Barbara Boyle. In that order. I was pretty sure the library opened for business first.

But before that, before anything, I owed her an apology.

All I could think about right now was the look on O'Toole's face as she backed off and stormed out. Daphne and I looked too comfortable, too drunk. What else was O'Toole supposed to think?

Figured I'd keep it simple. I couldn't exactly tell her it wasn't what she thought, because it became just that. I didn't want to deny what happened, to lie about it. No lies, ever. Again. Just what I was sincerely feeling.

"Gracie," I wrote. "I'm sorry. I feel terrible about what happened. Please give me a chance to explain. Please give me a chance to make it up to you. Will."

She lived in a small condo complex on Whitney. Just ten units, all in one large building—a former mansion divided and remodeled. She and her ex-husband—a professor at Smith who became a professor at Yale—bought it when they moved from Massachusetts. She got it in the divorce settlement. Guess judges aren't fond of professors who have affairs with their students.

There was a small parking lot around back, but no need, I'd only be a minute. Pulling to a stop on Whitney. Running up the walkway. I'd push the note through the mail slot. She'd get it after work, and she'd think about it, then call. Or drop by, and I'd be alone this time.

Eight stairs up to her landing, taking them two at a time. About to knock. About to—

Her door was open. More than a crack. By reflex, pulling out my gun, no time to think, no time to remember. One hand flat against the door. Pushing it open all the way. The breath catching in my throat. No time. Looking around for any movement, for anything other than O'Toole, dressed as she was the night before, lying facedown on the rug in her foyer. A rug once light gray. Not anymore.

THIRTY-EIGHT

Four minutes twenty-six seconds.
     That's how long it took for the paramedics to arrive.
Forever.

Signal four. Officer down. Detective Gracie O'Toole down.
     She still had a pulse, but had been hit pretty hard on the back of the head.

Watching. Paralyzed. Unable to breathe.

A piece of trauma cloth pressed to her head. No neck brace. No time. Onto the gurney. Into the ambulance. An IV set before they could even pull onto Whitney Avenue.

Brown was there first, arriving as they loaded her in. I'd called him. His beeper, a 9-1-1 to O'Toole's home phone. He called back in less than a minute. Was already on his way. Driving faster than any of the squad cars coming in from every direction—an officer down.

I was still holding the note in my hand. Staring after her. Wondering if I should go. Wanting to—Brown took the note. He read it. He told me, "Gracie told Mazz she was spending the night with you. That she was going to help you forget all the crap about being suspended. Obviously she didn't. Mazz is going to know that was your fault. That, for whatever reason, you turned Gracie down. He's going to have a problem with that. I don't blame him one bit. Because I've got a huge problem with it. And with you. You go crying that you're never going to get laid again, and you send someone like Gracie packing. What the fuck is wrong with you, Will?"

THIRTY-NINE

Sitting in the bug. My hands gripping the steering wheel at ten and two o'clock. Gripping. White knuckled. Holding. Holding it straight. Until I could no longer feel my fingertips. Until I was afraid the wheel would break off in my hands. Holding that grip. Getting a grip. Losing my—

The paramedic said she'd lost a lot of blood. She wasn't responding. He couldn't tell me more. They moved so quickly. No time. Taking her away.

There'd been no sign of Angel Gabriel outside my apartment this morning. No reason. He'd found his target. He'd delivered another message from God. O'Toole, the target. Part of the message. The message itself. I hadn't listened. Hadn't taken that vacation. I hadn't taken O'Toole up on that offer. A bottle of wine, an afternoon in bed.

Did Gabe believe O'Toole was Deegan's girl from room 112? She was dressed to kill, still in that slip of silk. Light blue silk turned so horribly crimson. Nothing else look disturbed. Her clothes weren't torn. She was in no other way disheveled. Her purse lay by her side. She'd been coming in. Just coming home. What time? After my place? She couldn't have been lying there for so long. Please. Allow her to have gotten lucky. To have found some good man who washed away my stupidity.

"Get out of here," Brown told me. "Klavan sees you anywhere near this," he added, not finishing, not needing to.

"I don't give a damn about my badge," I said.

"Yeah, you do," he said.

I watched the ambulance pull away. "Yeah, I do," I whispered.

"You have any idea who did this?" Brown asked. He was speaking to me in a tone usually reserved for street thugs who witnessed drive-bys, but can't seem to remember a damn thing. Can't say that I blamed him. "Because if you do, take that son of a bitch down."

I thought for a minute. There were a lot of names, but they were all connected, they were all pointing the accusatory finger. All pointing at, screaming out Richard Deegan's name. "Yeah," I said finally. "But I can't take him down."

"Why's that?"

"He's already dead," I said, walking away.

FORTY

Heading toward Yale's Sterling Memorial Library, on High Street. Trying to stay focused. Trying not to break down. Thinking about anything but—this was where Daphne had met her first client. Daphne. I couldn't think about her, either.

I was looking for an old yearbook, and copies of the school newspaper from 1964. I was looking for Richard Deegan. I would dismantle Richard Deegan, brick by twisted brick until nothing but his soul remained, and that I would feed to the devil himself.

I knew my way around Sterling Memorial. My way to the microfiche. To the archives. I even knew where to find the old yearbooks. Yale yearbooks can be a New Haven detective's best friend.

Except when they're missing.

Annoyedly, I ran a finger across the spines. They were all there. Dating from the middle of the 1900s to the present day. All there, except 1964. The year Deegan graduated.

I called to a librarian who was rushing past with an arm full of books.

"Can I help you?" he said. He was tall and lanky and seemed as if he didn't want to be bothered.

I said sharply, "1964," pointing to the space it should have occupied.

"What about it?"

"It's not here."

He put the books down on the closest table and took a look for himself, scanning the spines—all the spines. And when he was through, he turned to me. "You're right."

I held back every nasty thought running through my head. "Any idea where it might be?" I said instead.

"It's probably been checked out."

"I thought you couldn't check these out."

"Sometimes we make exceptions," he said. "I mean, if Woody Speight requests a book." And he shrugged—what the president of Yale wanted, the president of Yale got. The university had that exact same relationship with the city. "I'll check," he said, walking away.

While he was gone, I cracked open the yearbooks from sixty-one to sixty-three. They each focused on the graduating class of that year. Pictures of the class from freshman year onward. I'd have to check the background of every photo with a magnifying glass hoping for a glimpse of Deegan.

"That's strange," he said, upon returning.

"How's that?" I asked.

"There's no record of it going out."

"Could it have been stolen?"

"I suppose," he said. "But who'd want to steal a yearbook that's thirty-six years old?"

Whoever took the yearbook, if in fact someone did, didn't bother or have time for the *Yale Daily News*, the school's paper. A rag, really. Not much different from or better than any other school newspaper, which always surprised me considering it came from Yale. They had the money to publish the *New York Times* on a daily basis, and yet they instead opted for—well, the equivalent of the *Hooterville Gazette*.

The *Yale Daily News* was, according to its banner, the "Oldest College Daily Newspaper." Founded on January 28, 1878, but I didn't need to go that far back. Just thirty-six years or so to Deegan's graduating year. Pulling up each thin issue on microfiche. Squinting into the ancient viewer. Moving through September 1963, into October, then November, then—

A photo of the Yale hunting club. Seven of its proud members returning from an outing. Rifles in one hand, their game in the other. Wild turkeys. I shook my head, thinking that Butterballs were probably not enough of a challenge. Six men, one woman. I read the names, stopping at the last three: Kilgore Travers, round in face and body; Richard Deegan, looking a lot thinner, and almost handsome in a rugged sort of way; and Leslie Van Cleef, a pretty young woman, short but voluptuous, with dark hair, huge eyes, and a warm smile. The men were all smiling at the camera. But not Leslie. She was standing close to Deegan, very close, looking up at him. Smiling, most definitely at him. If the picture had been in color I was sure she'd have been blushing, as well. And the look in her eyes. I'm not an expert in this field, but I was pretty sure it was love.

There didn't seem to be much else of interest. An editorial from April 1964 in which Deegan criticized our then lack of involvement in Vietnam. And a picture of the graduating class, of which Leslie Van Cleef was *not* a member. I checked June 1965, 1966, 1967, 1968. She never graduated from Yale, at least as far as I could tell.

Travers and two of the other hunting club members also graduated in 1964. They were part of the graduation photo. The other two members graduated the following year. I found their photos in that yearbook. Bradley Lunt and—

I laughed out loud once and caught a nasty glare from a student with her nose buried deep in Tolstoy.

I knew the other guy. His name in the hunting photo had been Buddy Sachs. No one I'd ever heard of. But "Buddy" was a nickname. The name under his yearbook photo: MESTIPEN SACHS.

I'd have never recognized him from either photo. His crew

cut. Square clothes. Horn-rimmed glasses. Nothing like today, with his long gray hair tied back in a ponytail. Sideburns. Killer suits. A wife half his age. He's an animal rights activist now. One of the best criminal attorneys New Haven has to offer. I couldn't help but wonder what he'd have to say about Richard Deegan.

I found my helpful librarian, and had him print up copies of the hunting photo and the shot of the graduating class, with Deegan smiling proudly in the second row. Then I asked, "Where could I find a list of students who attended Yale but never graduated?"

"Gosh," he said. "I don't know." Then, thinking about it, "Maybe from the dean of admissions. He might have transcripts. But"—he looked so confused—"why would you want a list like that anyway?"

"I'm doing a book on the great losers of the twentieth century," I said, stepping away, photocopies in hand, thinking how I probably deserved a chapter all my own.

FORTY-ONE

Walking to Sachs's office, adjacent to the Federal courthouse on Church Street, I stopped first at the Willoughby's across the street.

"Hey, Will," the girl behind the counter said as I approached. She held a cup ready in hand. "Extra large Ethiopian, no room?"

"You're reading my mind," I said, wishing someone could perhaps make sense of what was going on up there.

"I'm psychic," she said, smiling. "Didn't you know that?"

"I think I'm just predictable," I said, wishing now I could return her smile.

"We all are," she said, filling my cup, just as the skinny heavily tattooed kid standing next to her stepped up, and addressed the next person in line.

"What can I get you today, Mr. Sachs?" he said.

We took a seat at one of the few tables, over in the far corner near an overgrown jade plant. Mestipen Sachs was wearing a light gray suit that was probably equal in value to six mortgage payments on my old condo. He drank espresso and had a sesame bagel, lightly toasted with cream cheese.

"This about the suspension?" he asked.

"You've heard about that?" I was a little surprised.

"Word travels," he said, taking a sip. "Small town, y'know? Want to fight it?"

I shook my head. "Not today," I said.

"What, then, can I help you with?"

"Richard Deegan," I said.

He laughed, just slightly. "I hadn't heard that name in years, and then—" A shrug. "What do you want to know, William?"

Sachs and I had a mutual respect dating back a few years to when I caught one of his clients, a hotshot Republican congressman from Harmony and his extremely hot wife getting stoned in a downtown parking garage. I was just walking to my car, Christmas presents neatly tucked under one arm, when I saw them lighting up in the front seat of their Lexus. I didn't arrest them. Just told them to put it out. The next day I got a call from Sachs. We all sat down. I heard the mumbo jumbo on how if this got out a brilliant political career could be jeopardized. I stopped his speech short. I didn't care. It was a joint. One lousy joint. They were adults. Headed to the Shubert to see some play. There were no schoolchildren around. They weren't selling bags. I told them all as much, then stood, warned the Republican congressman and his wife that the next cop who catches them might not be so liberal minded, and left.

"I want to know about his ties to New Haven," I said. "I want to know about Leslie Van Cleef."

"Whew," he went, letting out a long low whistle. "That's a name from my past."

"Your past?"

"The entire male student body, class of sixty-four, anyway." He shook his head, remembering. "She was the first love of my life."

"You dated?"

"Leslie?" he said. "God, I wish. No. She had eyes for Deegan, and no one else."

"Why were you so in love with her?"

He laughed and then leaned in close, lowering his voice. "Her rack."

"Excuse me."

"I'm from Indiana, remember," he said. "Grew up on a farm. I get to Yale. What few women in attendance were hardly head-turners. Then along comes Leslie. She was loud and vulgar. Very sexual, especially for the time. She knew how to play pool. How to play poker. Strip poker with the boys, she'd always win. Well, luckily not always. She'd answer her door nude in the middle of the afternoon and invite you in for a beer. Hell, she even knew how to shoot a gun." He sat back. A small sigh. Back to the real reason. "Goddamnit, they were huge, beautiful. They defied gravity."

It was hard to tell from the hunting photo. "The attraction was mostly physical?" I asked.

"Mostly? I was young, horny. A virgin. It was like Ivory soap, ninety-nine-point-forty-four percent physical."

"Any idea what happened to her?"

"No. She dropped out after Deegan graduated." He shook his head again, remembering. "No."

"What about Deegan? Ever see him again?"

"We, um—some of the guys in the hunting club got together after Deegan got back from Nam. Bradley Lunt, Joe McGuire, me, Deegan. I think it was just the four of us. Adam Ozersky got shot in Nam. Kilgore was already running his father's business by then. He couldn't make it. He was in Europe or something. Sent his regards in the way of a stripper."

"That doesn't exactly gel with Deegan's righteous image," I said.

He shrugged.

I nodded. "What about Leslie? Was she there?"

"I don't even think she was invited," he said. "I asked Deegan about her, though. Why he never married her? We all were curious about what it was like to have sex with Leslie. Deegan just changed the subject. Said he didn't want to talk about Leslie. We busted his ass a little. But he got all flustered. Turned beet red. He'd found God by this point."

"Yet the stripper was okay?"

"I think she wore a small cross on a chain around her neck."

"You haven't seen him since."

"Let's say we didn't exactly see eye-to-eye on things. He went farther right after graduation, I went in the complete opposite direction."

"What about the other guys? Any chance they've seen him, or Leslie?"

"Last I heard, Bradley's a plastic surgeon out in Beverly Hills. McGuire was working for Sony over in Japan. And you know Kilgore died last year."

It was a big news story. Billionaire dies. But beyond catching the headlines, I paid it little attention.

"He'd have been the one who stayed in touch," Sachs said.

"They were close?"

"Roommates all four years. I'm surprised Kilgore didn't enlist with Deegan. Stayed here instead. Took over daddy's insurance company." A shrug. "I didn't go to his funeral. Haven't seen him since—" He thought about it. "—graduation. Y'know, you're young, full of ideas, ideals, dreams. You spend a lot of time together. You live together. Study together. Drink together. Fantasize about women. About the future. About becoming President of the United States, for Christ's sake. And then one day you wake up and realize how full of shit these people are."

FORTY-TWO

Brown answered on the first ring. O'Toole was still in surgery. The doctors were repairing a subdural hemorrhage. A blood vessel had ruptured in her head. The department was treating it as an assault, separate from the Deegan and Sorrentino homicides. Out of the hands of the FBI. Away from Questral.

I asked if she was going to be okay. If there was anything I could do. Anything I could—

"We wait," he said. "And pray."

"What about Mazz?" I asked. "How's he handling it."

All I heard was a dial tone as my reply.

In my car, the radio tuned to a local all-talk station. Ignoring the babble. Thinking about Leslie Van Cleef. Wondering where she'd disappeared to? Or if she disappeared at all. Could she have been Deegan's tie to New Haven? Still, after all these years? The reason he wanted to move the Sons of God headquarters north? Or was it nothing so devious? He simply missed New Haven. His alma mater. He missed the New England winters. Or perhaps the Connecticut turnpike.

Thinking about what I'd told Brown earlier. That the person responsible was dead. Perhaps I was on to something. Not Deegan, but his reason for wanting to come back to New Haven. What or whom was dragging him here? What was it that he could not resist?

Barbara Boyle lived on the other side of the Quinnipiac Bridge—the Q Bridge—in a large condo in the Morris Cove section of New Haven. She probably thought of the place as having an ocean view. To me it was just New Haven Harbor, just Long Island Sound. In a Tudor–meets–Cape Cod style. Pre-weathered browns and beiges on the outside. Made to look like it had been there forever, though it wouldn't last nearly that long. There were three cars parked in the carport: a Mercedes, a BMW, and a Porsche. All candy-apple red, two-seater convertibles. Speedsters. A couple hundred grand' worth of automobile. Inside the reds and browns and beiges were replaced by white. All white walls, bleached pine flooring. Everything about it still so damn new. And sterile. The white sofa, the chrome coffee table. Copies of this month's fashion magazines scattered about. Not a newspaper in sight. She shared the three-bedroom with two girlfriends. I didn't catch their names, but I would have guessed Bambi and Brenda, or something equally breathy. They were all in their early to mid-twenties, tall, with lots of hair. Barbara was a brunette, one of her roommates was blond, the other a redhead. All shapely in a silicone sort of way, I was pretty certain the two roommates traveled similar career paths. If asked, they would have probably answered, "I work in the adult entertainment business." But then so did my ex.

Surprisingly they were up before noon. Already enjoying the sun, they lounged around the living room in their Calvins—underwear, not jeans. Barefoot, long legs stretched out on the coffee table. Munching Doritos and sipping diet soda. Watching bad daytime TV—CNN was probably blocked out by the V-chip.

A good half-dozen beepers were collected in a ceramic bowl, as the centerpiece for the coffee table. Each labeled. One going off after another. Completely ignored.

"How is Kara?" Barbara asked. She wore baggy blue sweatpants and tennis shoes. As if she were covering up on purpose, at least from the waist down. From the waist up, she wore a sports bra.

We'd stepped away from Bambi and Brenda, onto a deck.

The Long Island Sound calm, the mostly sweet salt smells. The seagulls honking in the breeze.

"Good," I said, taking a beat to remember Daphne's professional name.

She smiled knowingly and then said, "So, what, can I do for you, Mr. Shute?"

"Detective Shute," I said. But it had no effect. This was a woman not harassed by police officers, despite her profession. A woman who never for a moment thought she might *not* be a cop's type. That she couldn't win a cop over with a smile or something more, if need be.

"So, what can I help you with, Detective?" she said, the word sounding so much different from when Questral said it. Her smile widening, as if she knew what was coming next.

"Richard Deegan," I said.

The smile disappeared. Barbara's mouth twisted to one side. "What about him?"

I played my hunch. "Kara said she heard something about you getting roughed up. What happened between you two?"

"I thought," she said. She shook her head and started over. "I thought that bastard was going to kill me."

"How long ago was this?"

"Couple of months." She paused for a moment. "First week in March. He, um, said—he said he was here on business. Something about relocating."

"What did he do to you?"

"Why do you want to know?"

I carried the New Haven *Register* with me. Opening it up against the breeze, flapping it once, showing her the front page of yesterday's edition. Her eyes took on a frightened glaze as she stared at his picture. Then she looked away, out at the water. Clearing her throat. Her voice even. "He's really dead?"

"I think a girl, an escort, killed him in self-defense," I said.

"Should have been me who killed that son of a bitch," she

said, turning back, tears coming suddenly to her eyes. "Would have definitely been self-defense."

She led me back inside, into the first-floor bathroom. "He wanted to tie me up," Barbara said. "Looked harmless enough." A small disgusted laugh. "I'll do that sort of thing for my regulars. Usually get a pretty good tip. But this guy was new. It was in-call—he came here, instead of me going to his hotel room—and we were here alone. My roommates weren't around. So, I told him it'd be extra. He didn't care. He slapped six crisp new hundreds onto the bed. Why not, right? Meant I'd be making double my usual fee for an hour's work. I charge three hundred an hour. Advertise on the Web. Me and my roommates are all in the adult entertainment business. Got our own Web page and all. Have you seen it?"

I shook my head, wondering whether Barbara or her roommates had ever made sex films for the European and Asian hardcore market. If she knew Charlene. Any of Charlene's partners. If the whole world was in on it except me.

"It's www.onourknees4u.com," she said, continuing. "The *four* is just the number four, not spelled out. And the *you* is just the letter *u*. Cute, huh?" A small shrug as if she knew better. "So, he ties me up using these leather restraints." She kicked off the sneakers. "Y'know, the kind you can buy at any adult bookstore. They usually come in a set. Bondage in a box. Look like small dog collars." She slid off the sweatpants. She wore loose-fitting boxers underneath. "He goes the spread-eagle route, arms out to each side of the headboard, feet out. Y'know?"

I nodded.

"But instead of climbing all over me, or—" Tears came to her eyes now, and she wiped the back of one hand across her mouth. "The son of a bitch comes out of the bathroom still in his three-piece suit. He's got rubber gloves on, and he's holding this black rubber bag high. I didn't know what it was at first. Then I figured it out. A douche bag. I guess it was in his brief case all along. He jams the nozzle in me. No lubrication. Nothing. Just jams it in." Her hands were balled into fists, slapping against the sides of her thighs. "I screamed at him. Y'know, stop it! What are you doing? He picks up my underwear from the floor and sticks it into my mouth. Then he kneels on the bed by my side. He's holding the bag high in one hand, the little clip that turns the flow on and off in the other, and the son of a bitch starts to pray. 'This is the gate of the Lord through which the righteous may enter.' Or some shit like that. Then he turned the nozzle on." She stopped for a moment, looking away. "Do you want to see what he did to me, Detective?"

I honestly and completely did not. Afraid at how I might react. Afraid of what I might see. But instead of answering, I stared stone-faced into her large wet eyes.

Slipping down the boxers, Barbara sat on the edge of the sink. She looked down, the pain of seeing the damage making the tears subside. Replaced now by an anger that I could never even begin to know.

"This is after two months of doctors and creams and—I won't be able to return to work for at least another two months."

"Chloroacetyl chloride," I said.

"Yes," she said. "The doctor said I was lucky. Do you call this lucky?"

"If he'd used a stronger concentration, it could have killed you."

"The way it burned," she said, shaking her head, looking away. She didn't have to finish.

FORTY-THREE

The car again, the radio. Tuning it out. Hearing Barbara Boyle's voice instead. Her words ringing. *At least another two months before she could return to work*. Why would she want to? What could she possibly be thinking? Other than—

Revenge. How could she not want to kill Deegan? How could she not wish him dead? Self-defense. That's what it would have been. But why have sex with him first? She couldn't have anyway—another two months. But her roommates. Would they have been willing to help? Probably. Barbara could have set Deegan up with one of them.

But that wasn't working. Barbara and her roommates were nothing like *mary.jpg*. There wasn't a scintilla of innocence remaining between the three of them. Could Barbara have been just a practice run? The first escort to return Deegan's page? Who cared what she looked like? Or were looks not an issue, at least at first? Deegan never planned on having sex with his victim—he didn't have sex with Barbara—but then someone like *mary.jpg* shows up at the door to room 112, and suddenly the Son of God can't resist.

I shook my head clear. Leaving. Barbara walking me to the door. Walking past her roommates one last time. The Doritos bag crumpled and empty on the coffee table. *Ricki Lake* on the tube now. I said, "Can I ask you all a question?"

"Sure thing, baby," one of the roommates said. "Shoot."

"Just out of curiosity," I said, "Why?"

The three Bs looked at me.

"Do you at least enjoy the sex?" I asked.

They laughed. One of them almost choked on a mouthful of diet soda.

"You're kidding, right?"

"A visit to the gyno is more enjoyable."

"At least the gyno knows what he's doing."

"I make lists in my head. What I have to pick up at the grocery store. What needs to go to the dry cleaners."

"So, it's just the money?" I asked.

"It's all about money, baby."

"I could flip burgers at Mickey D's and maybe pull in three bills a week, before taxes. Or I can dance three shifts, and escort another three nights a week, and clear ten times that, tax free." A shrug. "What would you do?"

"But what about the risks?" I asked. It was a question I so wanted to pose to Daphne, but somehow couldn't.

"We all take risks every day of our lives."

"I could walk outside, get run over by a car."

"I could get raped in the parking lot of the mall."

"Then think about how it affects your sensibilities," I said.

"To what?"

"Men, for one," I said. "It's got to make you hate us."

They looked at one another as if I didn't have a clue.

"What was there to like in the first place?"

S pecial report."

"Coming to you live."

"Four-alarm fire."

It took a beat for the radio to grab my attention. Turning up the volume. Loud. Drowning out Barbara Boyle's voice in my head. All the voices. All the pictures. O'Toole lying facedown on her carpet. The hardened smirk on Angel Gabriel's face. The sexy smile on Daphne's. The *mary.jpg* biting down on her bottom lip. The joy in Charlene's eyes. Drowning out everything as the bottom of my stomach fell free. As my life bungee-jumped before my eyes. As it all came to a crunching halt.

The DJ stepped in. "To recap. We're speaking with Maya

Prestwood, live in downtown North Haven, where a four-alarm fire has destroyed at least three historic buildings. Maya, are there any casualties?"

"We don't know for certain," Maya reported. "But the damage is extensive. It seems to have started in the kitchen of a bakery shop."

FORTY-FOUR

Exit 11 off Interstate 91. Driving as fast as the bug would go. Nowhere near fast enough. Taking the corner off the exit, hoping it wouldn't flip over. A right at the light onto Washington Avenue. Washington becoming Church Street. North Haven wasn't known for its historic downtown. There were only a handful of buildings to each side of city hall. There was only one bakery.

Church was blocked off. I didn't have a badge. I didn't have a siren or flashing lights. But the cop turning cars away recognized me. "Hey, Shute," he said, blanching suddenly and then letting me pass. Turning, looking away, as if he couldn't face me. As if it suddenly dawned something terrible had happened to me.

I pulled to a stop near the town green. Rushing toward what was left. Flames greedily grabbed at the sky. Roared at the heavens. Four fire trucks, the fire fighters doing their best. But the buildings were so old. Their nineteenth-century brick facades melting away. The wood frames like kindling. Small, two-story buildings. Shute's Bakery in the middle, with an insurance company on the second floor. A small copy shop to one side, a luncheonette to the other.

Nothing was left. Or so very little. A wall of bricks, a charred metal jukebox, the bakery sign, on its side. Blackened and battered and—

Searching the faces, the pained and awestruck looks of many whom I remembered from when I was just a kid. Having all grown old, or older together. Have all grown up on Shute's pastries. A few caught my eye, sharing the pain or just staring in pity.

The ambulances were on the other side of city hall. I moved

toward them now. Searching for any sign. The most familiar of faces. Anything, please. Then, a glimpse of a white apron wrapped around a small woman with short brown hair. She was standing beside an open ambulance door. Holding a hand to her face. She was crying. That son of a bitch Gabe had made my mother cry.

"Mom," I said, coming up behind her.

"Oh, God, Will," she said, turning, stepping into my arms. A hug. She needed a hug. I needed a hug.

"Dad," I said. "Is he?"

Gasping, pointing toward the back of the ambulance. My dad inside, sitting on a gurney. An oxygen mask pressed to his face. A medic taking his blood pressure. Staring out at us. Smiling. Giving us a thumbs-up.

"He's okay?" I asked.

"We're both okay," she said. "I just can't believe—"

"I know. I'm sorry."

"I'm so mad," she said.

"It's okay," I said. "It'll be okay."

"I want to kill your father right now," she said. "He's so goddamn stubborn sometimes."

It took a moment for what she was saying to register. "This isn't his fault, Mom," I said.

"Like hell it isn't," she said. "You know that old oven in the basement? The ancient one? The one we use for extra cookies at Christmastime?"

"Yeah," I said, watching her.

"Your grandfather bought that oven used when he opened the business. I've been trying to get your father to replace that thing for years. 'It's an electrical fire waiting to happen,' I'd tell him. But does he listen? No. Instead, he uses it today, to help us with that big order I told you about. Next thing I know, I hear him screaming in the cellar. I look down. It's full of smoke, and your father's running up the stairs yelling, 'Fire! Fire! Fire!' " She shook her head, and the tears started again. "I could just kill him right now."

FORTY-FIVE

If ever in my life I needed to cry—

Standing with my parents on Church Street, watching as my home away from home as a child—I'd do my homework in the basement of the shop, my band practiced in the basement of the shop. As everything my parents worked for, seemingly lived for. As their hopes and dreams—at least in my heart I believe Shute's Bakery was the embodiment of many of their hopes and dreams—burned to the ground.

But the tears stayed away, saved for some other tragedy, or some other time. My mom and dad were okay. I knew they'd be okay. That was what mattered. It didn't help that my mom kept saying she wished we were in Disney World right now. Because she could never understand how I wished for that, too. How I wished we were anywhere else. How I wished I'd grabbed O'Toole's hand and took her and my parents away. Anywhere, just away. It didn't help knowing that this wasn't a warning from the Sons of God. It made no difference that my Angel Gabriel had not set the fire himself. Because in a way he did, they did. They'd placed the order. And right now, considering everything else, that was enough.

My mom asked if I would come for dinner, but I told her I couldn't. She didn't press, and for that I felt guilty. On this night, of all nights, I should have accepted her invitation. "What about Sunday?" she said. I told her Sunday sounded great. "I'll make eggplant Parmesan," she said, "with garlic bread." She knew that was my favorite.

Heading home. I needed to be home. I needed for this to end. Pulling into an empty space in front of my building. Hurrying to the door. Keys in hand. Remembering Deegan's words. *Suffering the same heinous death at the hands of a man who has thus far eluded the authorities.* But he couldn't elude an escort armed with a pencil. Remembering what he did to Barbara Boyle. His bag of tricks. How he would have used them on the girl in room 112. And the next girl after that.

I never noticed.

Never saw.

Never heard.

I just felt the first blow to the back of my head. It brought me down to my knees. The next was a dead on punch to the jaw. Knocking me over. Then came a kick to the ribs. Once. Twice, for good measure. Then a voice, close to my ear. Not the voice I expected. I expected Gabe.

"Next time you fuck with Heather," the voice said. "I'll kill you."

I tried to think. Heather? Who the hell? What the hell? What freaking planet was I on? Then, all of a sudden, the snapping gum—*snapping, snapping, snapping*—the explosive Levi rivets, the good friends who could get nasty whenever she asked. That Heather. I tried to get a look at her good friend. I tried to turn.

But the only thing I saw was the boot headed toward my face. Not in slow motion like in the movies. But moving at a ferocious clip. Moving like it intended to hurt.

FORTY-SIX

M ust have crawled to the porch. Leaning back against my door. A hand on my shoulder. The familiar voice.

"You okay, partner?" Brown asked. At least he didn't sound as annoyed as before.

Opening my eyes. Focusing. Trying to focus on anything but the pain. He was kneeling in front of me. I saw his Caprice parked alongside my VW. A cruiser, its flashers going, right along side it. A small group of people had gathered, among them Stacy, who owned the hair salon on the first floor. I figured she called the cops. Perhaps she'd seen it all. A witness to payback for me acting a little too rude. For me not coughing up a ten spot for gas.

"Okay is open to a lot of interpretation," I said.

"You're being a wise-ass," he said. "You can't be in that much pain."

"Care to make a wager on that," I said, attempting to stand. My head a little woozy, leaning against the wall for support. Rubbing at my face, some dried blood over my left eye.

"EMTs on the way, Detective." It was a cop standing a few feet behind Brown.

My partner nodded.

"Don't bother," I said. "He didn't hit that hard."

"Who didn't?" Brown asked.

"Didn't get a good enough look," I said.

"So, this wasn't your big friend checking up to see if you'd accepted Jesus?"

"No," I said.

"And this has got absolutely nothing to do with Gracie?"

"Absolutely nothing."

"You sound sure of yourself," Brown said. "Would you like to tell me why."

"Absolutely not," I said.

Sitting on my sofa, a plastic bag of ice pressed to the side of my head. There was a scrape to my forehead. A couple of bruises. The rest of the injuries internal. If you couldn't see them, they couldn't be that bad.

"How's O'Toole?" I asked.

"She's in recovery," Brown said. He was standing at my kitchen counter, fixing me a drink. Fixing one for himself. "Doctor says she's going to pull through. It's just going to take a while for her to get back on her feet. Back up to full speed."

"No permanent damage?" I asked.

"Doctor wouldn't give us a guarantee on that one," he said, walking toward me. He handed me the drink and then took a hard swallow from his.

"Any idea how long she was like that?"

"No," he said, another swallow. "What about you? You okay? I heard about the fire."

A shrug. It hurt to shrug. "My folks are okay," I said. That's when I thought I'd lose it. That's when I thought the tears would come. But—

He must have sensed something. "What's going on here, partner?"

Clearing my throat. That hurt as well. "You want the Reader's Digest," I said, "or all the sordid details."

FORTY-SEVEN

The day fading. Time fading. I sat there for a long while after he left. A handful of Advil killed the physical pain. I took a shower, washing the blood off my forehead. Washing away the taste from my mouth.

Brown was headed back to the station house. His head overloaded. He had it all, from Daphne to Leslie Van Cleef to Barbara Boyle, from the pictures of *mary.jpg* to the order for pastries the Sons of God had placed at my parents' bakery. I asked him for help. To check around. To run Barbara Boyle's name, and Leslie Van Cleef's as well. See what he could find. Then I told him about Charlene, the movies she made. I'm not really sure why, but he said he'd pray for me as well as for Gracie.

"Thanks," I told him. "I can probably use it."

"We all can," he said.

Looking up now. Looking around. The computer. Moving slowly to the table. Taking a seat, just as slowly. Hitting the power button. Staring at the screen as it came to life. Where to start? Where? Goddamnit! Someplace new. Someplace—scanning Deegan's files. The Bible. A computer Bible. Double clicking on its startup file.

The King James edition, complete with illustrations. Complete with a search engine. What to search for? Thinking. Pulling words from Barbara Boyle's lips. Key words. Typing them in. They'd had a ring to them. Something familiar. The things we never forget. There were too many things that I'd never forget. And not enough of them were good.

Psalms 118: 20—
This is the gate of the Lord,

Through which the righteous shall enter.
I will praise You.
For You have answered me,
And have become my salvation.
The stone which the builders rejected
Has become the chief cornerstone.
This was the Lord's doing;
It is marvelous in our eyes.
This is the day which the Lord has made;
We will rejoice and be glad in it.

Scrolling down to the last line—

Oh, give thanks to the Lord, for He is good!
For his mercy endures forever.

I typed three more key words into the search engine: "Sons of God." And came up with Romans 8:14—

For as many as are led by the Spirit of God,
these are the sons of God.

Then the next line—

For you did not receive the spirit of bondage
again to fear, but you received the Spirit of
adoption by whom we cry out, "Abba, Father."

That made as much sense as anything else. As much sense as—closing the Bible program down. Shaking my head. Remembering—the bulletin board Daphne told me about. The Pleasure Garden. Where was the pleasure in any of this?

I logged on, thinking about Barbara Boyle. She told me Deegan never said anything else to her. He finished the psalm, made a cursory examination of the damage, and was gone. Left her there. Left the money as well. One of her roommates finally came home. Found her that way. Helped her clean up, then to the doctor's.

But she hadn't gone to the cops. "Why would the cops care?" A good-looking woman, with the hair and the body and—not a streetwalker. And clean, all three of them. No junkie side-effects, no tracks. Dancers, some of the time. Never knew a cop who didn't like strippers. And when I corrected her. When I told her I was a detective. She didn't blink. But then neither did Daphne. Perhaps none of them cared, cops went with the territory.

"Ever try to get even?" I'd asked. "Tell his wife? The press? His boss? A harassing phone call or two?" No, no, a thousand shakes of her head. Barbara Boyle might have been angry, but she was also scared.

Or so she claimed.

The special of the week at thepleasuregarden.com was a bondage kit. Two leather wrist bracelets, two ankle bracelets, a collar, blindfold, and four leather tie-downs, all for the low, low cost of $89.95, plus shipping and handling.

I scrolled down until I found the ESCORT BBS button. There it was, bold as daylight. Between the triple-X photo gallery and the adult links. I double-clicked. It brought me to an unadorned page. Just typed listings: a subject, a date, a time.

Busty Boston Blonde . . .
Escort needed for fun night at Foxwoods Casino . . .
!!!ON OUR KNEES FOR YOU!!! . . .

I double-clicked on Barbara's and her roommate's listing. Posted just this morning, a little before I called.

"Three hot babes at your service. A blonde, a brunette, and a redhead. Specializing in every fetish, as well as two-girl shows. Come and play in our oceanfront condo, or we'll come to you.

Beep us, or check out our Web site." And there was the address, along with two separate beeper numbers.

Every fetish. Deegan must have known she'd go for the bondage routine. An easy mark. And once she was tied up—

I was shaking my head. Staring at the listing. Something was wrong. It was too bold. Too brash. Not even a disclaimer like on the Escorts-2-Escorts site. There was no doubt as to what the three roommates were selling, and yet they treated it like Tupperware. As if it were legal. As if they could go door-to-door and offer whatever-your-pleasure and no one would mind. Or, more likely, those who might would look the other way.

I hit the BACK button on my browser, thinking they had to be connected. That there was at least one cop, or a detective, or even a police chief, for Christ's sake, or any combination thereof, who knew what Deegan did to Barbara. Who cared about Barbara, about the pain she was in.

Scrolling down. Checking every listing. Barbara Boyle and her roommates posted theirs every morning, like clockwork. Usually around 9 A.M. The wording hadn't changed once in ten days. That was how far back the listings went. When a new post was added, the oldest dropped off. I scanned down the few hundred subjects. About half were from guys looking for escorts or mistresses. A few from women looking for sugar daddies. Some just general information: "How should I behave my first time with an escort?" "How not to get busted." The rest were from escorts, south to New Jersey, north to Boston.

There were two worth copying down. I wrote their names and numbers on the bottom of the list from last night. Only Jessica's and Ashley's names remained, not crossed off. They'd never called back.

FUN COLLEGE COED
Beep Shannon for a trip around the
world. I'm 19, slender and an

expert in all foreign tongues.
Connecticut males only please.

BEAUTIFUL GIRL
Beautiful girl for massage or escort.

The ad from Beautiful Girl was near the bottom of the listings, posted last Monday. It was never repeated, and would soon drop off. Though there was no "area covered" mentioned, I recognized the 203 area code, the 915 New Haven exchange. An exchange reserved exclusively for beepers and cell phones.

I phoned them all, including Jessica and Ashley. Punching in my home phone number, or leaving voice mail, after the appropriate beep. Then I called Barbara Boyle. I left a friendly message, hung up, and began the wait.

FORTY-EIGHT

Shannon, the fun college coed, called back first. Followed only moments later by Ashley. Both were friendly but cautious-sounding girls, who, when pressed, were a little heavier or older than advertised.

This was getting me nowhere. And I wasn't even sure anymore why I bothered. Did I owe the girl one? The girl I pictured in my head as *mary.jpg*? Thinking about what Deegan did to Barbara Boyle. Picturing the same happening to—

Shaking my head. I called Barbara again. This time she picked up. "I was just about to call you," she said. "Just got back from shopping." A short beat. "So, what can I do for you?"

"I have to be honest with you, Barbara," I said. "Even though you weren't completely honest with me."

Silence.

I gave it a shot. "You knew Deegan was dead. You've got a few too many friends on the force not to."

She turned on the coy. "What makes you think that, Detective?"

"I mentioned your name around the station house. You are a very popular girl."

She laughed. "They're supposed to be quiet about it."

"I just got divorced," I explained. "So, the boys were feeling sorry for me."

"Aw, baby, you should have told us," Barbara said, explaining the situation to her roommates, or whoever was in the room. "My roommates weren't doing anything."

I heard one of the roommates say, "He should have said something," in the background.

"If I'd have known there was a deal," I said.

"Didn't take you long to figure it out."

"I'm a detective, remember."

Another laugh. And it didn't even sound forced. "Y'know, I'll bet I can guess who it was who spilled the beans."

"Oh, yeah?" I said.

"Sure thing, baby," she said. "I'll bet it was Brian."

Her roommates in the background laughing. One of them said, "That big-mouth."

"Yup, Brian Luponte," Barbara said. "Studs like that just love to brag."

FORTY-NINE

I should have called in Brown and Mazz, but that didn't seem an option right now. Or at least not the right option. Not with Luponte possibly involved—I could buy that he'd want a piece of Deegan, especially if he was tight with Barbara Boyle, but Sorrentino, what was the connection? And could he possibly have anything to do with O'Toole? I hoped to hell not.

Luponte lived in a small ranch-style house, covered in green vinyl siding, off Quinnipiac Avenue, near the East Haven line. The lawn was well maintained. Fenced in with white picket. Funny, I thought, as I drove past, up the street a quarter mile, and pulled into a parking space in the lot of the Big Kmart. I never thought of Luponte as a white-picket-fence sort of guy.

The security was typical for a cop. Virtually nonexistent. As if everyone on the block knew who lived there. And no one would ever have the balls to break in, to steal anything, to stain the sanctity of his home. It took me all of about fifteen seconds to jimmy the lock on his back door with a Swiss Army pocket knife.

Once inside, I grabbed two beers from the fridge. Budweiser. The King of Beers. Exactly what I'd have expected. I took a cursory look around. The bedroom first. The unmade bed. A couple of ratty issues of *Penthouse* on his night table. The wall-to-wall. The furniture mostly laminated. Made to look good those first few years. But that make-believe warranty on Luponte's bedroom set had long ago expired.

The living room could have been taken from the pages of an *Idiot's Guide to Bachelor Life*. From the *Playboy* wall calendar to the rear projection TV, the black leather La-Z-Boy to the matching black leather sectional, the bowl filled with mint-flavored condoms to the mood lighting a cat couldn't read by. Black venetian blinds covered the windows, all the windows. It was dark and sleazy.

"Classy," I said to no one, taking a seat on one end of the sectional. I waited in darkness. The slight ticking from a battery-powered wall clock pushing forward the time. A dog barked. A car in need of muffler repair drove past. A door somewhere was slammed shut. Then a car pulled into the driveway. The lights went out. The door opened and closed, and he walked to the front door, singing some big-haired eighties power-ballad. Slightly off key, but the enthusiasm made up for his voice. Key in lock, he opened up, flipped on the lights, while absentmindedly flipping through the mail. Giving the door a nudge with his boot, Luponte noticed finally he had company.

"Brian," I said, from my vantage point, toasting him with his own beer.

"What the—"

"Have a seat," I said. He was out of uniform, wearing stonewashed jeans and a muscle shirt. But that didn't mean he wasn't carrying.

"—fuck?" he said, finishing the sentence.

"I just want to talk," I said, tossing him the second beer.

Tell me about Barbara Boyle—"

"What about her?" Luponte said. He was sitting on the La-Z-Boy.

"—and Richard Deegan."

"I don't know him."

"C'mon, Brian, sure you do," I said. "Monday morning. Our victim in room one-twelve. Nothing in the reservoir tip."

He stared at me hard. "It's not like you think," he said.

"I don't know what to think," I said.

"The deal with Barbara and her roommates. We just sort of look the other way, y'know? In exchange for." A shrug. "No one's getting hurt—"

"We?" I asked.

He told me the names of those involved. A long list that surprised even me, even at this point. Half the guys on the force, or so it seemed. He called it a *fraternity*. All Barbara and her roommates required was an hour's notice.

"Those deals are as old as her profession," I said, attempting to dislodge from my brain the image of Barbara and her roommates servicing some of the men in that fraternity. Trying my best not to think about what might have happened at the party Daphne worked. Her one-time thing. "What about Deegan? It's Deegan I want to know about. I saw what that son of a bitch did to her."

"Then you know."

"I know he'd have done it again, only worse, if someone didn't stop him."

"That someone deserves a medal."

"Perhaps," I said. "But right now that someone's public enemy number one."

"Thought you were under the assumption that there was more than one perp," he said.

"Where'd you hear that?"

"Word gets around."

"What do you think of that assumption?" I asked.

"Don't know," he said.

"Takes a lot of heat off you."

"Listen, Shute," Luponte said. "I know you probably don't care much for me. I'm not as well-read. Not as educated. I'll probably be wearing a uniform until the day I retire. But"—and he let every word ring clear—"I did not kill Richard Deegan. Wish I had. That son of a bitch deserved to die. He deserved exactly what he got." He shook his head. "But he didn't get it from me. And neither did Sorrentino. And if you so much as even suggest I had anything to do with Gracie getting knocked on the head, I'll break you in half now." He looked away angrily, his jaw clenched, his fists balled. "You can check the logs on this one," he said. "I've been working nights. Lots of overtime. Did a double-shift, Sunday night into Monday. Sixteen hours straight."

"Where were you exactly on Sunday night between ten P.M. and midnight?"

"A drug bust in Fair Haven," he said, turning back. "There was six of us called in. I was there from just after eight till almost four A.M., cleaning up." He shook his head. "I was grabbing a coffee at the Dunkin' Donuts on Whalley when I got the call. But I didn't know it was the guy, not until later. Barbara never told me his name. Then she saw his picture in the paper. Calls me, tells me. You have any idea how I felt? You have any idea? I've been seeing her for over a year now. At least once a week. You might not approve of what she does, but I like her. I like her a lot. She's a good kid. She didn't deserve that."

H ow do you know Barbara didn't off Deegan?" I asked. "She and her roommates, set him up? Are you telling me that isn't a possibility? There's got to be a lot of anger and resentment. He almost killed her, for Christ's sakes."

"She was busy on Sunday night," Luponte said. "They all were."

"Doing what?" I asked.

"Not what, Shute," he said, "Whom?"

"Okay," I said. "Whom were they doing?"

"You didn't hear this from me."

"I'm not even here right now."

He stared at me, then nodded and mentioned a name he'd

left off the fraternity list. A name he'd obviously left off on purpose. "Lt. Theodore Klavan," he said.

The picture of Klavan's wife, his eight kids. Still ending every conversation with an *I love you*. So clean, so quick, so easy. *Let he who is without sin cast the first stone.*

"If you don't believe me," Luponte said. "Ask him yourself."

FIFTY

The phone was ringing when I got back. Running up the stairs now. Or at least hobbling at a good clip. Still a little sore. The ribs a lot sore. But that would go away. Soon enough. I'd be okay long before O'Toole.

A little after ten now. Starving. Thinking about Barbara Boyle and her roommates with Lieutenant Klavan. She had a reluctant alibi for Sunday night. But—what about Sorrentino? What if he and Deegan were linked by more than just their employer, their beliefs, their commitments? Perhaps Sorrentino also had a speech he was working on. Perhaps he had a bag of goodies somewhere. Or he and Deegan shared. What if Barbara Boyle liked the idea of ridding the world of more than just Deegan. She had the alibi. She knew the MO—how hard really would it have been for her to find out how Deegan died? How hard would it have been for her to find out about the pencil? Kill Sorrentino in exactly the same way.

But what about O'Toole? Could Barbara—or my Angel Gabriel—or anyone have possibly thought O'Toole was the escort who'd been with Deegan? Or that she'd at least be suspected of being the escort? And if she were dead, then all bets were off. The serial killer was found. The case over. If Questral would give in that easy. And seeing that the mayor was in the Sons of God's back pocket, that seemed a distinct possibility. But—nothing was taken from O'Toole's condo, nothing seemed disturbed. Could something have been left? Could evidence linking her to Deegan have been planted? I'd have to call Brown, or Mazz, or—

Unlocking the door. The answering machine blinking one message. I snatched up the receiver before the answering machine got its second chance. "Hello."

The voice was soft and tentative. Almost childlike. "You—"
A pause. "—beeped me earlier."

"Yes," I said, my heart racing faster. There were only two
possibilities. I played my hunches, figuring by now Jessica wasn't
calling back, or Jessica was out of business, or Jessica didn't work
during the week, or Jessica didn't do calls to New Haven ex-
changes, for whatever her reasons. Leaving only one ad left. It
played itself in my head. I recited it to her. "Beautiful girl available for massage or escort."

A small hesitation. A smaller laugh. "That's me."

"Tell me about yourself," I said.

She took a small breath and began, saying the words as if
auditioning for a part. "I have straight dark brown hair which
just brushes my shoulders. My eyes are hazel. I have a very
round face, with full lips. I'm five-ten, a hundred fifteen pounds.
Very, very slender. My measurements are thirty-four, twenty-
two, thirty-four. I wear an A-cup, but I'd be lying if I said I was
overflowing. I'm very flat-chested."

"How old are you?"

"Nineteen."

"What's your name?"

"Midori."

FIFTY-ONE

Midori could meet me in a half hour. But she preferred someplace public. She said she was nervous. That she was new at this and wanted to feel comfortable with me. She wanted me to be happy with her appearance.

I suggested Dempsey's, a restaurant just down the block on State Street. Midori knew where it was. I told her what I looked like, what I'd be wearing. That I'd be sitting at the bar, munching on some salty sweet potato fries. That made her laugh. She told me it was a good detail.

Hanging up the phone, I hit the answering machine's PLAY button. "You have one message," the automated voice told me. Then it gave me the day and time. "Wednesday. Nine-forty-seven P.M."

Then a completely different voice: "Hmmm. Let's see. Okay. A question. 'To what extent does God detest the *supercilious* hypocrisy of men like Richard Deegan?' That's the best I can do on the spur of the moment. It's Daphne. Give me a call."

She left her number.

A North Haven exchange.

I had twenty-eight minutes. I needed to remove Midori from everyone else's game plan. Even if she wasn't the right girl, why risk it? Why risk her?

Turning on my computer, I attempted to log on to America Online using Richard Deegan's account. But instead of "Hello. You've got mail," I received an error message. "Account already logged on. If trouble persists, please call America Online customer service."

Muttering to myself, wondering if it was Feds? Or one of

Deegan's daughters? Or Gabe? Or, who the hell knew? Who the hell—bringing up my AOL account. I needed a new screen name fast. I went through the motions. Trying to come up with something that wouldn't be taken. Something close. I tried: "RDeegan." AOL came back with: "RDeeg9821." I don't think so. I tried: "SonsOfGod." No. "LiarsInGodsName." No. "HypocritesForGod" And what do you know?

As fast as possible to the The Pleasure Garden bulletin board. The "Beautiful Girl" posting was three messages away from disappearing into cyber-eternity. I double-clicked on the button that read: POST NEW MESSAGE, and wrote:

SUBJECT: *Hypocrite Seeks Girl Next Door*
MESSAGE: *If you're young, beautiful and innocent, you can be my next victim. Contact me at the new Sons Of God World Headquarters, located in the resplendently gentrified Ninth Square of New Haven, Connecticut."*

I double-clicked on POST MESSAGE, and waited a beat, until I was returned to the main screen of the bulletin board. I did it again, then once more, varying the subject and message only slightly. When I scrolled down finally to check. The Beautiful Girl posting was gone.

FIFTY-TWO

The kitchen was backed up. No time for that basket of sweet potato fries. I settled for a beer and some peanuts instead. Dempsey's was more of a bar than a restaurant, but it had a better-than-average menu. The walls were covered with the usual memorabilia, the floors with peanut shells. There was an NBA game on the TV over the bar. A bartender who knew me well enough to know my choice of beer watched it with disinterest. The place was filled with neighborhood types looking for something to eat before retiring for the night. They had the time.

Picking up a bar napkin, borrowing the bartender's pen. I made a list. A long list:

1. Deegan's murder
2. Stuff in his bag/true identity
3. Charlene's photos
4. O'Toole stopping by
5. *mary.jpg*
6. Sorrentino dead
7. Heather/snapping gum
8. Deegan's speech
9. FBI/Suspension
10. SOG moving to NH
11. Angel Gabe
12. Daphne
13. O'Toole attacked
14. Leslie Van Cleef
15. Barbara Boyle
16. Bakery
17. Heather's friends

18. Brian Luponte
19. Midori

It took up both sides of the napkin. Crossing out Daphne's name, and the two Heather references. Then anything to do with Charlene. The Bakery. The time O'Toole stopped by. That was before I'd found the speech. Before I could have been a threat. Connecting number two to number eight, it was all one in the same. Reading what remained. Reading. Tapping the tip of the pen against Midori's name. Would I be able to link her to number one? Would she be the link that started it all. Would she— letting a long breath escape. Giving up. Pocketing the napkin, turning, watching the citizens of State Street move past Dempsey's windows. They were an odd bunch, bohemians and students, teachers and waitresses, and those few who just liked being surrounded by such types. Toss in a few neighborly drug dealers. A homeless person or two. And you had the makings of good place to call home. Or at least something resembling that elusive fiction.

I cracked open a peanut shell, dumped the two nuts into my mouth, and took a sip of beer. Lowering the bottle, I caught my first glimpse of her. There was no doubt in my mind when she approached. I knew before she even reached the door. I knew also that I'd been right all along: Deegan wanted a living, breathing *mary.jpg*.

She wore a simple dress, long, almost elegant. A shimmering material. Short sleeves and a V-neck. Her body so slender and long. Her hair, a medium-length bob. Very dark brown. Her green eyes large and looming. Her mouth—such the spitting image of *mary.jpg* in almost every way.

Midori didn't belong on State Street. It seemed to frighten her. The night frightened her. Biting at her bottom lip—a *mary.jpg* trait. Tucking her oversize purse tightly under one arm as she reached for the door.

The bartender called to her as she entered. "I'm gonna need to see some ID, honey."

I stepped in on her behalf. "She's with me."

"Still need to see some ID," he said. "Unless you're her dad."

I shot him a look. But yeah, it was probably close. Walking up to her. "Midori," I said.

She nodded every so slightly, then looked me up and down. Into my face. Eyeing the scrape. Staring into my eyes. But instead of asking about me, she asked about herself.

"Am I okay?" she said.

"Perfect," I said, sure that I heard her laugh a little sadly, as I held open the door and followed her back outside.

FIFTY-THREE

Daphne looked happy to see me. Watching my VW pull to a tentative stop. She was standing in the doorway to her North Haven condo. It was a medium-size complex, perhaps fifty units. Built up a hillside just off Clintonville. She had on black capri pants today, and a sleeveless off-white tanktop. Just a swab of flesh visible between the off-white and black, the slightest peek of belly button. The glint of silver from a small navel ring catching the porch light just right. Her hair was pulled back with a scrunchie. Her mouth pulled back in a wide smile, until she noticed Midori getting out of the passenger side of the bug. I hadn't told her I was bringing company.

The smile faded as she watched me approach. It was quickly replaced by concern. She reached up, touching the scraped skin on my forehead. "Is this the girl you were looking for?" Daphne asked.

Nodding, I made the introductions.

Midori looked a little nervous. "I've never been with a couple before," she said.

I shot her a confused look and Daphne laughed.

"A threesome, Will," Daphne said. "Every man's fantasy, y'know?"

"So I've heard," I said.

Midori took a seat on a sofa in the living room. "I'm a little nervous," she said, looking back and forth between me and Daphne. "But I'm willing to try."

I sat down beside her. "I've got to level with you," I said.

Her eyes opened a little wider, as if expecting to be told she didn't live up to the fantasy. She hadn't passed the audition. "Is something wrong?" she asked.

"I'm a cop," I said. "Detective William Shute, of the New Haven PD."

Her reaction was so vastly different from Daphne's or Barbara's. Or even Heather's, when I had shoved my badge inches from her face. Midori's began with a quivering bottom lip. Tears flooded her eyes next. Crocodile and drowning. A thumbnail, or what was left of it, found its way to her mouth.

"I'm investigating a homicide," I explained.

A sucked-in gasp. Maybe the word no, hardly but a whisper. She didn't ask to see my badge. She didn't seemed to doubt my word for a minute.

"A man was murdered in the Elm City Motor Lodge on Sunday night. Do you happen to know anything about that?"

She tried to get words out, but they caught in her chest. Hyperventilating, searching for a breath. The back of one hand pressed against her mouth. The floodgates down.

Daphne handed her a box of tissues. She grabbed a few, but just held them in her hand. Balling them up. Compacting them. Staring straight ahead. Shivering suddenly. Her arms hugging herself. "I knew I shouldn't have," she said quietly. "I should have never placed that ad."

"Were you in room 112 at the Elm City Motor Lodge on Sunday night?" I asked.

But instead of answering, she asked, "Am I under arrest?"

"That depends," I said.

"On what?" she said, the tears coming in streams now, shaking her voice with convulsions.

"On whether or not I can find out who killed Tony Sorrentino," I said. "Before the Feds find you."

FIFTY-FOUR

After a drink, Midori calmed down a little, believing, at least for the most part, that I wasn't about to harm her. Or immediately arrest her. I got her to tell me most of what happened that night.

"He was"—she made a face—"inside me. I heard him talking. But nothing dirty. Nothing sexual, like I expected. So I opened my eyes, and—" Shaking her head. "He was praying."

"This is the gate of the Lord," I said, "Through which the righteous shall enter."

"Yes," she said, surprised that I knew, staring at me through glassy eyes. "I will praise You. For You have answered me, and have become my salvation. The stone which the builders rejected has become the chief cornerstone. This was the Lord's doing; It is marvelous in our eyes." Clearing her throat. "Psalm one hundred eighteen. I looked it up the next morning. I couldn't get those words out of my head." She was breathing hard again. Catching her breath. "He tried to bash my face in with a rock, Detective." A small exhale. "He missed the first time. I fought him off. Held his arm back." She demonstrated by holding her right arm high. "I, I—" Another exhale. A puff of a breath. "I reached into my purse. It was on the night table. Y'know. I keep it handy. For condoms, and I carry some pepper spray, but—"

"You grabbed a pencil instead."

A hard swallow. "Yes."

She told me how she'd wiped down the room for fingerprints. That was all she had racing through her mind afterwards: fingerprints.

"What have you been doing since?"

"Hiding in my dorm room mostly," she said. "Burying myself

in my schoolwork. Brushing my teeth. I think I've brushed my teeth like a thousand times since Sunday night. It's as if I can't get them clean. I can't get the taste—" She shook her head. "I was so scared, and then I heard about the other murder. They think I killed that guy, don't they?"

"Yes," I said.

She nodded. "I didn't, y'know. I—" A gasp. "—honest, Detective. I, oh, God."

"Why come out tonight?" Daphne asked. "Why answer Will's call?"

Midori looked at her for the longest time before answering. "I couldn't stand it anymore," she said. "I was—I was going nuts. Stir crazy. I turned my beeper on." She turned back to face me. "And there was your number. You were the last person who'd called. And I thought—I don't know what I thought. What the hell, I guess. I didn't care anymore. Maybe you'd be someone beautiful and make love to me and make me forget about all this. Or maybe you'd succeed where he failed. It didn't matter to me. It didn't—" She started crying again. "I don't understand why he tried to do that to me."

Perhaps one day I'd show her the pictures of *mary.jpg*.

FIFTY-FIVE

You could still feel the heat. I was standing on the sidewalk now. Just at about the place where the front door to Shute's Bakery had been. Having just left Midori at Daphne's condo. Having turned down an offer to spend the night. Having turned down a grilled cheese sandwich. "I make great grilled cheese sandwiches," Daphne told me. "I'm worried about you." Thinking back to the last time a woman told me she was worried about me. Perhaps my mom, when she found out I'd married Charlene.

Thinking back to one of my earliest memories of this place. This home away from. I was four. The front door was painted bright red at that time. It was decorated with cut-out Santas and snowflakes. Christmas Eve. Snow was falling at a pretty good clip. It was cold. Yet people were lined up, out the door, waiting to get in. I'd been playing with my friends, sledding, when I noticed. Running toward them, toward the bakery. Wanting to know what was going on. Cutting through the line, up the counter. There in the main display case. A gingerbread house. One I'd never seen before. Larger and so intricate in every detail. A Colonial. The two car garage. It didn't take long. "That's our house," I said. My mom and dad smiling proudly as they stood behind the counter and watched my reaction. "That's right, honey," they said. Everything was there in its gingerbread glory. Even a little boy making a snowman in the front yard. That was me. I was the little boy. The little gingerbread boy. And all those waiting for a glimpse squeezed in beside me. Pressing their face to the glass. They oohed and aahed and pointed and said, "How beautiful." They spoke to my mom and dad, commending them on their handiwork. I tuned out their voices, focusing instead on the little gingerbread boy. I heard him talking to me. His voice sounding just like mine. He was saying just one thing over and over. "You're the luckiest boy in the world," he said.

Stepping back, wiping away the tears that had gathered in the corner of my eyes. Taking one last look, stepping back into the bug. What did gingerbread boys know about anything?

FIFTY-SIX

Driving. I had her now. I had Midori. The woman in room 112 with Deegan on Sunday night. The girl who'd ripped open his throat with a sharpened Faber-Castell. Ripped it open in self-defense.

Now what? I thought. Could I protect her from the Feds? From Angel Gabe or whoever it was who bashed O'Toole's head in? Could I protect her from herself? To serve and protect and—she said she wasn't the one who killed Sorrentino. And I believed her. She didn't seem capable. Though I'd still have to admit what happened to her could leave scars, could leave her damaged. Could leave her seeking revenge or—

I made one stop on the way home. Pulling up on Whitney, right behind Mazz's Caprice, I realized I wouldn't be alone.

He was sitting on the steps leading to her front door. Holding his chin with one hand. He looked as if he'd aged a decade since I'd last seen him. Even the wrinkles in his suit seemed tired.

He stared at me as I approached and took a seat by his side. "I saw her tonight," he said. "She's out of intensive care. Looks like she'll be okay. Eventually. Won't be back on the job for a while."

"But she's okay?"

"Yeah," he said. "She was only awake for a couple of minutes, but still, she was asking for you."

"Probably still pissed at me for the other night," I said.

"I'm pissed at you," he said. "You blame her?"

"Not at all." "Any idea what time it happened?"

"She went straight home after leaving your place."

"Christ!" I said.

He slapped one of his knees, and then brushed it clean. "You can be a real asshole sometimes, Shute."

"So I've been told," I said, then, "What about you, Mazz?"

"I can be an asshole, too."

"No," I said. "You holding up?"

"I, ah, feel like—" He paused for a long minute. "I think I love her more than the wife. Not in any romantic sort of way— we never." He shook his head. "Gracie spilled the beans about you and her the other night before it happened. Said she was gonna go and cheer you up. I knew what that meant for Gracie. And I gotta tell you, I was jealous as hell. Made me wish the wife had divorced me and I needed some cheering up." He looked away. "Goddamn to hell. She makes me laugh, y'know. She's my best friend. She's a good cop."

"No doubt about that," I said.

"Yeah," he said. "Why are you here?"

"I've been thinking a lot about what's been going on," I said.

"That's all we've been doing is thinking," he said. "Running in circles. The Feds got their heads so far up their asses. Y'know what Gracie called it? They suffer from rectal-cranial inversion." He laughed once, shaking his head. "We're looking for hookers. A hooker didn't smash in Gracie's head."

"Do you think it's connected to Deegan and Sorrentino?"

"I don't know what to think," he said. "Yeah, I guess. Something stinks about these Sons of God bastards. They come to our town and everything falls apart. Everything goes to shit. I'm talking about that Crawford. Him, especially. He walks like he's walking on water. Like he's God, Jesus, and the Holy Ghost wrapped into one."

"Promiscuity," I said.

"That's the word," Mazz said. "The way he says it, I'd swear he bought the rights. *Fungulo!* He owns the place now, y'know? Pinhead and Zekowski are eating out of his hands. Questral's kissing his ass. Makes me want to puke."

"Let me ask you something, Mazz."

"What?"

"You find anything strange in her purse, in her pockets. Something that wouldn't fit with Gracie?"

He looked at me hard as if I knew something he didn't. "Why?" he asked.

I told him what I'd been thinking. That maybe someone had followed her from my house thinking she might be the girl who offed Deegan. They planned on planting something that could incriminate, tie her to Sorrentino. With the girl dead and out of the way, case closed. Only the girl turns out to be a cop.

He reached into his pocket and pulled out a beeper. He handed it to me as if I'd understand.

"Her beeper," I said. "So what?"

"Uh-uh," Mazz said, pulling another beeper from his pocket. "This is hers. That other one." He shrugged.

"Where'd you find it?"

"In her purse," he said. "Pocketed it. Took 'em both. It's gone off a couple of times tonight. The numbers don't mean anything to me. I haven't had the balls to call them. I don't want to know."

I went to hand the beeper back. He shook his head. "You keep it," he said. "I can't. I don't want to—" He rubbed at his face. "You're more likely to call those numbers than I am."

"This the only thing you found?" I asked.

A nod. "Yeah. And the only thing that was missing—"

"I thought nothing was missing."

"That's what we thought at first," Mazz said, turning back to face me. "Nothing in the place was touched. Jewelry box in place. TV, VCR, everything untouched. She still had her watch on. Eighty bucks, give or take, in her wallet."

"So, what was missing?"

"Her badge, Will," Mazz said. "They took her freakin' badge."

FIFTY-SEVEN

First thing I did when I got home was check O'Toole's beeper. There were three numbers stored in its memory. I dialed the last one to call. A man's voice answered on the second ring.

"Hello," he said.

"Hi," I said. "Someone at this number beeped me."

"I, ah—"

"About an hour ago."

"—might have dialed the wrong number."

"Y'know," I said in my most pleasant voice. "That's been happening a lot lately. Someone calling for a girl."

"Yeah, um, Pandora," he said, weakly.

"Right," I said. "This has been driving me crazy. Calls at all hours of the night."

"Yeah, well—" He laughed a little nervously.

"How close is her number to mine?" I asked.

"It's, ah—" He recited her 800-number off the top of his head.

"One digit away," I said, writing the beeper number down. Writing down the name Pandora as well.

"Sorry I, um—"

"Don't worry about it," I said. "Just next time make sure your fingers are more careful when they do their walking."

Pandora.

What the hell was going on? Was O'Toole moonlighting as an escort? Or working undercover on her own—she'd spent so much time putting Saul Rothstein away.

Or was this beeper a plant? Someone out for her from the

get-go. The Sex King getting a little revenge. Had someone been following her all along? Waiting for their chance. Waiting—

Could it have been left behind by the same person who took her badge? Evidence to link her to Deegan's and Sorrentino's murder. Dropped in her purse, before noticing the badge. A cop. A mistake. Not the girl who killed Deegan.

The phone rang, interrupting my confusion. It was Brown, calling from home. I could just picture him sitting at the kitchen table, a much needed glass of Scotch in hand.

"Wake you?" he asked.

"Who can sleep?" I said.

"Only the innocent."

"At least I'm not alone," I said. Then, "Saw Mazz. He said O'Toole's doing better."

"That's what the doctors say."

"Yeah," I said. "So, what have you got for me?"

"Nothing on Leslie Van Cleef for one," he said. "Her name's not showing up."

"So she's married, or dead, or—"

"Right," he said. "Barbara Boyle's another story. Two arrests on prostitution. Charges dropped both times."

"That doesn't surprise me," I said, telling him about the fraternity. About her alibi for Sunday night. About Barbara and her roommates playing ring around the lieutenant.

"You're shitting me," he said. Brown's wife, Bernie, was best friends with Klavan's wife. "How do I go to bed now, and not tell Bernie about this? She'll know right off I'm holding something back. She'll tell me I have *lie face* on."

"I don't know," I said. "Tell her it's me who's sleeping with escorts."

"There goes your invitation to Sunday dinner."

"My veins couldn't take it, anyway," I said. "What about Ruth Deegan."

"Room 1715," he said. "Do I have to tell you to be careful?"

"I need reminding every once in a while."

"You need reminding every day."

"Thanks for reminding me," I said.

"Yeah," he said. "Scissero called me a little while ago. Told me they found hair samples that link Gracie's attack with Sorrentino's murder. We're looking for someone with dark brown hair."

"That narrows the field," I said. "He compare them to what they found in room 112?"

"You know he did," he said. "Either that person declined to leave a hair sample in room 112, or was never in room 112 to begin with."

"I've been preaching that all along," I said.

"And I'm already converted."

"So, are the Feds in on O'Toole, as well now. Saying it's linked. That's got to throw a bone into their theory about someone trying to tarnish the Sons of God's name."

"Haven't been privy to their most recent theories," he said, "But I did hear this. Guess who's got herself a new gig lined up as head of worldwide security for the Sons of God?"

"You've got to be kidding me?" I said, guessing what was coming next, knowing what was coming next.

"Uh-uh," he said. "Your pal, Questral."

It was a perfect publicity stunt. How could they be anti-woman when—?

I guess I *had* known all along.

THURSDAY

Ruth Deegan's room was on the seventeenth floor of the Omni Hotel. The junior suites. It was just moments after 9 A.M., when I took a deep breath and then rapped lightly on her door. Twice. Normally I'd have had my badge out.

Ruth Deegan opened the door a crack.

"Ms. Deegan, I'm Detective—"

"I know who you are," she said, cutting me off. She was wearing a black maternity dress that fit her like a sack, and clunky boots. Her red hair was pulled back. She wore no makeup. No accessories.

"Could I possibly have a few minutes of your time?"

She eyed me for a moment, evenly, letting no emotion break through. One hand on her belly, holding it. Up, I would imagine. The other, her left hand, on the edge of the door. No rings, I noticed. Her nails as damaged as Midori's.

Ruth gave the door the slightest push with her fingertips and it swung open.

"You can have as much of it as you want."

My father was a deeply religious man," Ruth Deegan explained. "He believed in the Bible. Every word of it. He believed in Jesus Christ."

She was sitting on a wing-backed chair over by the room's small dining table. She'd already eaten. Her breakfast, finished, covered as in death by a linen napkin, lay on the table in front of her. I sat on the edge of the sofa, facing her.

"And James Crawford?" I asked.

"Father believed in him, as well."

"But why the Sons of God?"

"Do you know anything about my father?" she asked.

"What I've heard on the news," I said.

"Richard Deegan," she said, "came home from serving two years in Vietnam to marry his high school sweetheart. Nine months later, she died delivering a son. Matthew. Who subsequently died of pneumonia a few weeks later. My father was devastated. He buried himself in his work, at his father's publishing company. And though he was already deeply religious, he felt the need to further serve God. He believed that God was displeased with him, and was thus punishing him, first by taking his wife and then his son.

"He began publishing Bibles. Everything from lavish reproductions of the Gutenberg, to small pocket-size paperbacks containing only the most popular passages and psalms. These were a great success. So he published more: different translations, Bible picture books for children, hymnals, prayer books. Deegan Publishing became one of the largest religious publishers in the world. A few years passed before he met my mother. She came in for a job interview, and he was so—" A shrug. "—impressed, he told her to forget about the job and took her out to dinner, instead. They claimed to have fallen in love that first night. They got married. My father felt that God was giving him a second chance. But instead of the son he so desired, someone to carry on the family name and traditions, they had three daughters. Anne first. It took over a year for my mother to get pregnant again, and if you hear them tell it, not for lack of trying. Theresa was born two years after Anne. It took twice as long for mom to get pregnant with me. It was a very difficult delivery. So much so that after I was born the doctors warned my mother against having any more children. So, that was it. My father would never have a son."

"May I ask about your baby," I said.

"It's a boy, Detective," Ruth Deegan said. "I'm going to have a son."

Y ou'll have to understand," she said, "my father's state of
mind when he joined the Sons of God. Our country's morals
had fallen into the sewer. First there was *The Last Temptation
of Christ*, then novels mocking the Second Coming. The National Endowment for the Arts sponsored a crucifix dipped in
urine and called it art. Christians were being ridiculed in the
press, on TV. Christianity was a joke in the eyes of the world.
Families were falling apart. Drug use was rampant. Teen preg-
nancies were at an all-time high. And the number of abortions
performed in the country was growing daily."

"And your family was falling apart," I said.

"There were problems. Yes," she said. "My mother and father
fought quite a lot. They—" She paused. "—I think they both
had affairs. Mother started drinking. And my oldest sister, Anne,
she ran with a rough crowd for a while. It was real bad. Got
pregnant when she was thirteen. Overdosed on sleeping pills—
tried to kill herself. Lost the baby. Got busted for drug possession the next year." She shook her head. "Heroin. She's clean
now. If you don't count the booze and sedatives."

"And Theresa?" I asked.

"Quiet. Independent. Very much her own person. The complete opposite of Anne."

"So, everything's falling apart. Including, I assume, your father's faith?"

"He felt God was punishing him again," she said. "He didn't
know what he was supposed to do."

"My God why have you forsaken me?"

"Something like that."

"Enter James Crawford."

"His group had ordered a Sons of God edition of the Bible
to be given away at their meetings. It was small, mass-market
paperback sized. First printing of two million copies. He and my

232 / Gorman Bechard

father started talking about their beliefs. About what the Sons of God were trying to accomplish." A shrug. "They became friends."

"And the next thing you know."

"Yeah," she said. "Dad stepped away from the day-to-day operation of Deegan Publishing to devote his time to the Sons of God."

I knew the tag line by heart. "To help millions of men practice sexual, spiritual, and moral purity."

"Yeah," she said.

"You must be very proud," I said, for lack of anything better. She sounded sincere. And I didn't want to tell her what was running through my mind.

"You kidding me?" Ruth Deegan said, looking me right in the eyes, dead serious. "I think it's all a crock of shit."

FIFTY-NINE

I beg your pardon."

"Look," Ruth said, "I don't figure you came here for the press release. Which is what I just gave you. You don't exactly seem a religious man, Detective."

"I'm not, really," I said, wondering how she knew—or was it just that obvious? Had the years of watching those in religious power point the blame for society's ills at video games, movies, shock jocks, and, most important, at rock and roll—why did our drummer Charlie have to blame rock and roll?—finally taken a toll on my face? Or was I just tired?

"Tell me first, though," she said. "What do you know about my father's death."

"You want the Reader's Digest?" I asked. "Or all the gory details?"

"Somewhere in between."

That's just what I gave her. And afterwards, Ruth nodded a few times, but didn't flinch. "Why does it not surprise me?" she said.

"Perhaps you knew what he was capable of," I suggested.

"Oh, definitely," she said. "They hide behind the words in a book. That—" Shaking her head, muttering to herself. "—book. I know every passage by heart. To have it drilled into your head from the time you're born. To want to play with your friends—but no, it's time to study the Bible. It's time to pray. You're four or five or six years old, but it's always time to study the Bible. Always time to pray." She took a deep breath, exhaling slowly. "He used acid?"

"Yes."

Ruth turned away. "Bastard," she muttered, biting at her top lip, sniffling back tears. "When we were young, he'd whip us whenever we made the slightest mistake." Shaking her head frantically, her eyes clenched shut now, she took a deep breath. "Is that first girl . . . is she all right?"

"She will be soon."

"And the other."

I lied about Midori. "I haven't found her yet."

"You don't believe she's responsible—"

"I don't believe she's responsible for anything other than bad judgment."

"We're all guilty of that," she said.

"I know I am."

She turned a little to one side, holding her hands at her belly in obvious discomfort. "So, then," she said, "who killed Tony?"

"I don't know," I said. "Anyone come to mind?"

"Tony was a decent guy. A guy's guy, y'know. But nice enough. Real good looking. A sweet talker. I think he believed most of what he was preaching. Not all, though." A sad smile. "But I don't know anyone who'd want him dead."

Staring at her. She smiled as she spoke of Tony. Smiled beautifully. Her father was dead, and yet . . .

"Do you believe in any of this, Ruth?"

"Oh, let's see," she said. "I believe, I believe, huh, y'know it's funny, Detective. I don't know if I believe in anything anymore." She shook her head. "I've run away from home so many times. I'm really just waiting it out. My eighteenth birthday, and I'm gone. Away from all the hypocrisy. Away from Jackson, Mississippi."

"But your father's gone now."

"You think my mother or my sisters are any better? Not Theresa, really. I get along with her well enough. We only have one major disagreement."

I gave it a shot. "Your father?"

Ruth nodded. "Theresa loved him." A small laugh. "I told her she needed to take off her rose-colored glasses, but—she's idealistic. I think she was moved by his passion. Now that he's gone"—she shook her head—"Theresa's pretty upset about everything. Especially those things you said in the station house the other day. She just can't believe they're true."

"They are," I said.

She shrugged. "As for Anne and Mom. It's as if they live the press release now. Only it's submerged in a bottomless pit of Scotch and pills. The words get kind of fuzzy, and they begin to not mean much. They're only words, after all."

"Whose words?" I asked.

"My father's. James Crawford's. They probably worked on it together."

"What about James Crawford?" I asked. "How much do you know about him?"

"Uncle Jimmy," she said. "Truth or press release?"

"What do you think?"

She nodded. "He scares me. Always has. James Crawford is a very strong-willed man. Used to getting his way. It's as if the whole of his existence is the Sons of God. Nothing else matters. Especially since Mrs. Crawford died. He just wants—I don't know, it's like he wants to take over the world."

"So, then, why would he step down?"

"What are you talking about?"

"Your father was going to take over the top slot when Crawford retired at the end of the year."

She looked at me as if I were crazy. "James Crawford isn't retiring," she said. "He was, at one time. A few years ago. He was going to do it for his wife. To take care of her. But when she died." Ruth shook her head. "He'll head the Sons of God until the day he dies."

M ay I ask something personal?"

"Why not?" she said. I could tell from the sudden tightness of her face that she knew what was coming.

"Who's the father?"

"Hmm," she went, exhaling the sound as a breath. Then nodding a few times, she told me. The name came as sort of a jolt.

"Did your father know?"

"I would never tell him," she said. "Would never give him that satisfaction. I wanted him to think the worst. I wanted him to hurt inside. To feel some humiliation when people spoke of his pregnant seventeen-year-old daughter. 'The apple of his eye,' that's what he once called me in an interview." A disgusted laugh.

"Does anyone know?" I asked.

"Just Theresa," she said. "She's about the only person I talk to nowadays. Even though she's gone a little off the deep end recently, she's a good listener. And I think she understands my passions as well as she thought she understood father's."

Ruth walked me to the door. I thanked her for her time. Shook her hand. Her handshake was strong and warm.

"Just one more question," I said. "Why did your father want to move the Sons of God headquarters to New Haven?"

"Have you ever been to Jackson, Mississippi?" she said, smiling.

"No," I said, returning the smile.

"He and Tony believed, or they said they believed, that if they could move the Sons of God out of the deep South, out of the Bible Belt, they could be taken seriously. As an organization, as a religion, as a political force."

"Is that why Crawford went along with it?"

"Crawford didn't want dissension," she said. "No fractures at the top. Fractures would bring public scrutiny. That would bring criticism. Crawford doesn't take well to criticism. And deep down, he probably believed that he could bring his religion to the cities, to the minorities."

"New donation dollars."

"Oh, yeah," she said. "But really, you know why I think father wanted the move? Why he came up with it in the first place? It was so he could be near Leslie."

"Van Cleef?" I asked.

"That was her maiden name," she said. "She was the only woman he ever loved."

"When he was at Yale."

"So, you know?" she said.

"I didn't know she was still around."

"I don't think that in my father's mind she was ever really gone," she said. "And when her husband died, it seemed as if father suddenly spent all of his time up here. Not that he was ever home much to begin with."

"When did her husband die?"

"Um," she said. "Uncle Kilgore died last summer."

The name was like another slap across the face. *Uncle Kilgore*. A boot to the face. In slow-freakin'-motion. "Kilgore Travers?" I said.

"Didn't you know?" she said as the telephone in her room began to ring. She glanced back at it, then looked to me and shrugged. "They got married the day after my father joined the marines."

SIXTY

The hallway was empty. Quiet. What little sound from the TVs and conversations seeping from behind closed doors was quickly absorbed by carpeting and wallpaper. Waiting for the elevator car. The down arrow button bright. Thinking about Leslie Van Cleef. Could she and Deegan have reconnected after all these years?

The elevator doors slid open, and I stepped into the car, pressing the *L* for the lobby. Such an unconscious move. Not paying attention. Wondering instead what it would all add up to.

A large hand snapped me back into reality. It stopped the door on its slide shut. The face familiar, a little more ruddy in person. Topping off a tall frame, large hands, wide shoulders. An expensive suit. Damn expensive. The perfect fit. A perfect black. The watch, the shoes, accessories that could have been traded for a luxury car. And then some. He commanded attention. He commanded space. I stepped back, as he stepped on. As he turned his back to me to see that the *L* was lit. No sense pressing it again. The doors finally shut. And we were on our way.

We hadn't traveled more than two floors—we were between fifteen and sixteen—when the big man reached out and gave a tug on the red emergency stop button. I'd watched his hand pulling it. Now I watched his back.

He began without turning. His voice as familiar as his face. "Have you any idea with whom you're fucking?" James Crawford asked, adding seemingly as a sarcastic afterthought, "Detective Shute?"

He turned then to face me. Ever the preacher, the teacher. Ever the hypocrite in the eyes of God. His mere presence so intimidating that by reflex I reached for my gun. He saw the movement and laughed. "That is the language to which you're accustomed, is it not?" he asked.

"Abso-fucking-lutely," I said, not blinking, not taking my eyes off his. Not taking my hand off my weapon. As if I were waiting for him to twitch. As if I were ready to shoot him dead if he so much as blinked.

"Are you going to shoot me?"

"Give me a reason to," I said.

"In your eyes, haven't I already?" he said. "Isn't my very existence a threat to men like you?"

"Men like me," I said. I knew I was yelling, I could hear the words bounce off the elevator walls. My words pounding at the walls. And the walls not giving an inch. "You don't know the first thing—"

"Then why get so defensive?" he said. Again slowly. Enunciating. Calmly. "Why not just admit that I'm all about depriving you of the one element more important to you than air. Than nutrition. Than water. More important to you than the blood which streams through your veins. I'm here to take away your"— and the word never sounded dirtier than when it slithered off his lips—"*cunt.*"

"She's already gone," I said, not hesitating a beat.

He came right back with, "Not just your wife."

I didn't like that he knew. Exactly how much, I wasn't sure. Had he copies of the same JPEGs on his laptop? Could he connect *nina.jpg* to me?

"Why not start with your employees," I said. "Or do the same rules not apply? It's okay for your men to bang hookers? To burn them with acid. Or is that what you're referring to. Burn away the temptation, and there goes"—and I spit out the word

as he did, enunciating every letter and dotting the goddamn *is*—
"promiscuity. Out the goddamn door."

"You know nothing about my fold," he said.

"Your *fold*," I said, laughing. "You've got to be kidding me.
What does that make you, the shepherd?"

He took a step toward me.

"Uh-uh-uh," I went. My hand still gripped the butt of my
gun. I wasn't the fastest draw, but—"You're not going to give
me a reason to shoot, are you?" I said. "Because if you are, this
must be my lucky day."

"How would that look?" Crawford said. "How would you explain my unfortunate demise to your mayor? How would you
ever get your badge back?"

"Deegan's speech," I said, wondering if there was anything
that escaped him. "When it gets out—"

"It never will," he said, so matter-of-factly.

"I'd say that would be up to me."

"Would it now?"

"Or do you have one of your hired goons take me out next?"

He acted so damn surprised. "What are you talking about?
Hired goon? I don't—"

"Like what happened to Gracie O'Toole."

"If you think I had anything to do with that whore's—"

My breaking point. I drew my gun with one hand, grabbed
his throat with the other. Using all my weight, using everything,
I slammed him back against the elevator doors, pressing the
muzzle under his chin. Pressing it hard. Raising his face toward
the heavens. Let him face his God. Let him look God in the eye
and try to explain.

"You son of a bitch," I muttered.

He said nothing more and made only one move. Quick and
very much to the point. Slapping the flat of his palm against the
emergency stop button, pushing it back in. All the while staring

down at me. His eyes never leaving mine. They were cold, dark, deep. Nightmare eyes.

The car started to move. My time was limited. But I didn't have anything to say short of pulling the trigger. And all I could think of, what if the son of a bitch had something on Gracie? That goddamn beeper.

The *ding* caught me a little off guard. I backed off and holstered the gun as the elevator doors slid open. Crawford straightened his tie. He straightened his jacket. He smirked, ever so slightly and then turned and disappeared into the lobby. I followed eventually, burning inside.

SIXTY-ONE

Two steps into the open, trying to breathe, trying to think, trying to ignore the mumbling, the buzz. What were people saying? People. Suits. Men in suits. "Thank God," seemed to be the prevailing theme. I just wanted out of there. Rushing through the lobby, past the suits. Rushing—

"Detective Shute," Special Agent Mae Questral called out.

I stopped dead in my tracks.

"Not a surprise at all."

Turning to face her. She had a grin on her face the size of a Dumpster. And just as pretty. I looked for words, for an explanation. But nothing came. "I was just leaving," I said.

"Not here on any official business, I hope."

"Of course not," I said, snapping, suddenly annoyed. "Just banging someone's daughter. Now that I'm single again, I plan on making it a habit." The words were loud. The volume startled even me.

Her smile faded just a bit.

"Speaking of which," I said. "How is Lisa?" Her daughter's name was Lori, but she knew who I meant. "She seeing anyone?"

I saw the slap coming this time, but stood still, taking it, not giving a good goddamn. Someone not too far off said, "Ouch." But it didn't hurt that bad.

"You through?" I said.

"All through," Questral said.

But there was something different about her tone now. Or maybe I just hadn't noticed it before. Something going on that I didn't like. "Meaning?"

"The case is closed," she said. "We've got our girl."

The look on my face must have given away my cluelessness.

"The whore," Questral explained. "Oh, excuse me, I believe

you like to think of them as professional escorts. She did have your name and number in her purse."

"What?" The words weren't connecting. She was speaking but I couldn't make sense of it.

"We got the girl who killed Deegan and Sorrentino," she said, "and put Detective O'Toole in the hospital."

"What do you mean, got her?" I asked.

"Followed up on a tip. She was staying at a friend's house. Not answering her beeper. But she made the mistake of calling her roommate for messages. She told her roommate where she was. When we showed up at her door asking questions, the roommate gave her up."

Staring at Questral in disbelief, the implications running through my head. Midori had told me she'd paid cash for the beeper. Three months in advance. That she'd given a fake name. Could that have just been a lie? Could she have forgotten? Was Daphne okay? Was I capable of protecting anyone?

"Has—" A hard swallow interrupted my words. "—anyone talked to her?"

"That's going to be hard, Detective," Questral said. "She went for a weapon and had to be put down." Questral spoke about her like a sick animal. She *tsk*ed a few times. So blatant. So bold. "Such a shame," she continued. "Pretty thing. And only nineteen."

Running now. Pushing away. Getting away. Through the lobby. Past this convention of hypocrites. I couldn't catch my breath. Couldn't breathe. Faster. Through the glass doorway. Into the open. Faster. Still, I needed to breathe.

A phone. I needed a phone. One halfway down the block in front of the Temple Medical building. In use. Someone on it. Someone talking. "A police emergency," I said, no badge to flash, no—"I need the phone."

"In a minute." The kid was big and baggy and full of attitude.

I grabbed him by his shoulders and pushed him aside, catching the receiver, slamming it against the switch hook.

His words: "Motherfucking pig bastard."

Grabbing his collar. My Smith & Wesson pressed against the side of his forehead. "Back off. Or you're going to be making your next call from the morgue."

He fell backwards, tears suddenly in the tough guy's eyes. Turning, I pulled a slip of paper from my wallet. A coin, a quarter in the slot. Dialing. The click. The connection. Footsteps. Turning again. Watching the tough guy run away now. Run away. A ring. My heart skipping a beat. Another ring. Another. Again, Christ! Picturing Midori from just the night before. Picturing Daphne. Another. "Please answer the goddamn phone." Another ring. Another.

And another.

SIXTY-TWO

You couldn't drive on Union Avenue. You couldn't move. There were steel dams on black rubber soles holding off the traffic, directing the pedestrians downstream. The satellite news gathering trucks parked every this way and that, blocking off most of the street in front of the station house. The fourth estate towers of babble in their sharp suits. Holding their silver microphones high. Holding their heads high. Their hair hard. Their expressions serious and tight. They were always as much the story.

I went in the back way, a series of short blocks lined with apartment complexes that had seen better days. Parking wherever. It didn't matter. Nothing mattered right now beyond getting to her. Seeing her. Confirming the guilt slamming around inside my head. Slam dancing with misery. There was a goddamn party going on up there. Moving toward the basement. Morgues were always in the basement. They were closer to hell that way.

Rushing, running now, past Feds and our guys in blue. Through the door. The smell making me think twice. Slice, turning around. Snapping off his rubber gloves. A look on his face like I'd never seen before. Disgust or perhaps he was just tired of it all.

"Where is she?" I asked.

"Thought this was off-limits to you," he said.

"It is."

He nodded and then pointed. "She's over there." I guess it wasn't as rude to point at the dead. "One bullet to the head, one to the chest," he said. "Don't know which killed her yet. Looks like either or." He dropped the rubber gloves into a waste basket for just such materials. "Trigger happy jackasses." He shook his head. "She wasn't even armed."

"Show her to me," I said. I had to see for myself what they did to her, so when I broke the face of the Fed bastard who pulled the trigger, I'd have a picture in my head to hold on to.

She was lying on a stainless steel table, a bloodstained sheet pulled over her body. The wounds seemed contained. But they were more than enough. One bullet would have been enough to rip Midori in half.

Slice led me over, pulling back the sheet from her face.

I gasped. And the feelings retreated. The rage fell into relief. And I felt miserable for that. More guilty than before.

She looked peaceful now, almost beautiful. More so than in life. Standing in my kitchen. The too-tight jeans. The attitude. The lies. The snapping gum. Snapping. Snapping. *Snapping.* I really didn't believe she was nineteen. She didn't look nineteen. But thinking back, Heather certainly acted nineteen.

S lice told me how it went down. The Feds had been working every independent escort, every escort service in the tri-state area, including those who advertised on the Web. Two dozen special agents meeting every girl. Tracing down any and every phone number, beeper number, e-mail address. But they were getting nowhere. And then came a tip. An anonymous tip from a pay phone. "Here's the phone number of the girl you're look-ing for," Slice explained. "Or something close. The guy on the other end of the line said this girl had been bragging on how she was famous. In the papers."

"You've got to be kidding me," I said.

"I'm just telling you what I heard."

"They didn't think that was a little too easy?"

"They didn't think, period," he said. "They wanted this over, done with. There are sixty thousand tourists coming to town."

Heather had been staying with a girlfriend. When the Feds showed up to ask some questions, she got cocky. I could picture that easy enough. She threatened them. Reached into her purse. And when they told her to freeze—

"They found—"

"Let me guess," I said, "O'Toole's badge."

"Touché," Slice said. "In her pocketbook."

"Any prints on it?" I asked.

"Haven't matched them up yet."

"Hair's probably not going to match up, either."

"The peroxide would have shown up."

"Anything else?"

"Your name and number," Slice said.

"So Questral said."

"And the number to the Omni."

"She probably did half her calls at the Omni."

"But right under it was Sorrentino's name and room number," he said. "And the words, 'black Lincoln Town Car.'"

Walking out, not convinced. Not buying into it. I knew now that Heather's last name was Karg. Louise Heather Karg. It was on her license. And her school ID. She'd been going to Southern Connecticut State University. A liberal arts major with a 3.7 GPA. A sophomore. An escort. They'd call her a prostitute on the nightly news. Ted Koppel would tell the story of her life at 11:35. But he'd leave out one important detail. What she'd been thinking when the Feds showed up at her door. About the cop on State Street. A guy who'd pissed her off. Who wouldn't even give her gas money. Who'd wasted her time. But she'd gotten even. A friend had roughed him up. He'd been warned. And he'd warned her back. These were probably his friends now. They were showing their badges. Telling her to freeze. Not to move. They were pointing their guns. Screaming at her as she moved. As she put a hand inside her purse. Pulling the trigger.

She died thinking that I'd set her up. Thinking that this was payback. I might as well have pulled the trigger myself.

SIXTY-THREE

I sneaked out the back, going as I came. Driving the fastest route. That same local all-news station on in the car. Promises of a news conference. "We'll take you there live."

They came to the door laughing. Casual. Jeans and T-shirts. Daphne's clothes a little baggy on Midori's slight frame. Daphne seemed a little surprised. But it was good surprise. The smile began with her eyes. Midori was standing behind her. Smiling as well. A picture of innocence. An Andrew Wyeth painting: beautiful women through a screen door on a beautiful spring day.

Except for the gauze wrapped around Midori's wrist. The blood spotting through. One of those eternal slaps against the back of my head, ringing from ear to ear. I opened the screen door in a hurry and took her hand.

"What happened," I said. "Why did you do this?" My voice was angry. Loud. I couldn't even begin to comprehend.

Tears immediately came to her eyes. Like a child, being scolded for the very first time. "I'm sorry," she said, biting at her bottom lip. Bringing any remaining fingernail to her mouth. "I didn't mean—"

That's when I felt Daphne's hands on me. Spinning me around. One hand holding my face. Just strong enough to get my attention.

"It's a tattoo," Daphne said. "Like the one I have on my wrist."

"I've always wanted one," Midori said.

"I thought it would take her mind off things," Daphne said.

I had time for a quick lunch. There was Chinese takeout across the street. There was also a pay phone attached to the side of the building. Daphne came with me. I needed a favor. Displaying the black beeper, handing it to her, explaining how it had been found in O'Toole's purse. She figured out the rest from there.

"You want me to call back one of these numbers?" she asked, glancing at the readout.

The beeper had gone off three times since last night. "The last one to call," I said, nodding. "Tell them you're Pandora. Find out where she advertised."

"No problem," she said. Dialing the number. A short wait. "Hi, you beeped me. Yes, this is Pandora. My calls?" A shrug. "Two hundred an hour." A warm laugh. "Thirty-four-B, and I'm in very good shape. Right." Another laugh. "Can I ask you something now? Where did you see my ad? That's right. You know the old saying. Half your advertising works, the other half doesn't. I like to keep track of which half works." A pause. "Yeah, I've gotten a lot of calls from that board. Where are you?" Another pause. "Oh, no. I'm so sorry, baby. I can't. Not there. I've had some trouble with the police in Harmony. Yeah. I can't take that risk. I hope you find someone you like, though. Bye, now."

She hung up the phone and turned to me. "The Pleasure Garden bulletin board," she said. "The ad reads, 'Are you man enough to open Pandora's box?' " And when I didn't respond, she said, "Now let's get food. I'm starving."

Nodding, I followed after her, hearing her voice echo in my head. The ease with which she'd dealt with the caller. So naturally. Just doing her job. And I realized I wasn't all that hungry anymore.

SIXTY-FOUR

Fifty-seven miles an hour, and the gas pedal was floored. West Hartford a quick thirty minutes north from Daphne's. Thinking now about what she said when I asked her about the people at party she worked at Barbara Boyle's.

"Why didn't you tell me?" I asked, after the Chinese, as she walked me out to the bug.

"It's like lawyer-client privilege," she said. "It's like the sanctity of confession."

The street was easy enough to find. Thornton Circle. A millionaire's mile. A mile and a half, actually. But who was really keeping track of such things? Lined with estates and landscaped lawns. With in-ground pools and tennis courts. Rolls-Royces and Bentleys. Butlers and maids and chauffeurs. The VW never felt sillier as I pulled into the Travers driveway. I felt a step below it.

Ringing the bell. Taking in the pantheons of excess. One of the aforementioned butlers doing the honor.

"I'm here to see Mrs. Travers," I said.

"Is she expecting you?"

"I certainly hope not," I said.

She'd aged thirty-five years since that hunting club photograph had appeared in the *Yale Daily News*, but still Leslie Van Cleef, now Leslie Travers, was a beautiful woman. A voluptuous woman. As if time and gravity had given her a free ride. She wore a simple black dress, as if in mourning. Her eyes appeared weary and sad. As if she'd been crying, or holding back tears for much too long. Her brown hair was peppered very lightly with gray. She agreed to see me without an appointment, shaking my hand, not asking to see my badge. Asking instead, "What can I help you with, Detective?"

I got right to the point. "Do you have any idea why Richard Deegan wanted to move the Sons Of God headquarters to Connecticut?"

She stared at me. Her hands folded in front of her. She went "Huh," making it sound like a laugh. "James Crawford warned me about you," she said.

"Really," I said. "When?"

"An hour ago," she said. "He told me you were a trouble-maker. Said you were trying to sully the group's reputation."

"Do you believe him?"

"I believe the Sons of God do plenty to sully their own reputations," Leslie Travers said. "I don't think they need any help from you."

SIXTY-FIVE

L et's sit."
  She led me through the mansion, to a patio overlooking
a pool that reminded me of the pool at the hotel in Aruba where
Charlene and I got married. Only this one was twice as large.
We sat at a glass-topped table. She offered me lemonade, which
I graciously accepted. She had a glass, as well.

  "They're silly men, Detective," she said. "All of them, my
Kilgore, and my Richard included. Lovable, but very silly. I
doubt that any of them, with the possible exception being James
Crawford himself, believes a word of that nonsense. The twelve
commitments." She laughed loudly now. Nothing like before.
Hers was a big, bold, beautiful laugh. Contagious, sexy. I could
see why Deegan had fallen for her. I could understand why he
still probably loved her. "The only thing those men were committed to was sex. Lots of sex. It was as if they discovered the
secret. Condemn promiscuity, and I must admit to hate that
word and all that baggage Crawford has attached to it. Condemn
promiscuity, and the most promiscuous will fall at your feet.
Strange, isn't it? I always wondered who was trying to convert
whom?"

  "So, why put up with the other women?"

  "Oh, I put up with many things during my years with Kilgore," she said, smiling, "but other women was most certainly
not one of them."

  "How can you be so sure?"

  "Simple, Detective," she said. "Kilgore was a homosexual. He
loved Richard as much as I did."

  "But—" I was at a loss for words. "—your family. Your children."

  "Four beautiful sons," she said. "Richard's sons. The three

eldest are married. We have a few grandchildren. And one more on the way." A sad smile. "My youngest boy. He's the believer. Was heartbroken when he found out what happened to his dad. Just heartbroken." She made a small gesture, touching one hand to her mouth for a moment. "Richard just wanted to be closer to his family. And with Kilgore gone"—she shrugged—"I didn't see any harm."

Leslie Travers must have sensed my confusion. "Let me explain. I was two months pregnant with Richard's child when he enlisted. Such a crazy gesture on his part. So macho. So stupid. Both Kilgore and I were devastated. Richard was my life. Only Kilgore knew about the baby. He said, 'Marry me, and we'll say it's mine.' It was the perfect arrangement. Kilgore's parents couldn't have been happier. Prouder. Or more relieved, I should add. I think they were beginning to suspect. When Richard returned from Vietnam, we explained. He stayed with us that first weekend. It was a wild time. Kenneth, our second son, was conceived. Then Richard went back home to the business of Bibles. He married some girl that he'd dated in high school. We saw each other two, three times a year that first year. I honestly don't think she ever liked me. And I can't say that I liked her much, but still, I felt so bad for him when she died. When his son died. Richard changed a lot then. Became wild— wilder, I should say. Very carefree. He spent a lot of time with us. Even spent a lot of time alone with Kilgore. I don't know what happened between them. I never asked. Though I think mainly it had to do with their little hobby."

"Hobby," I asked.

"Their collections," she said. "Pornography, Detective. What began as a mild addiction grew into a twenty-five-year fixation. Everyone needs a hobby, I guess, but my God, were they ob-sessed. And I don't mean skin magazines you can buy off the street. But private, one-of-a-kind things. They'd have it commissioned. Specifically to their liking. Kilgore and Richard were always talking about their latest star. About the newest girl or boy they'd find to—" A shrug. "—you know. I didn't pay attention, just tuned it out after a while, so I don't know that much about it. And I don't want to. I don't want to know how much money they spent. How many millions they wasted. I'm sure it was a lot. Not that it mattered, but—when Kilgore died, Richard kept it up for a while. Then, I don't know—he seemed to lose interest."

"When was this?" I asked.

"A few months ago," she said. "I felt it was because he no longer had Kilgore to plan them out with, to watch them with." She paused, taking a small sip of lemonade. "I'd watch them on occasion with Richard. It would make him happy. But they did nothing for me. I don't need movies to become aroused. Just Richard, but—I believe we all have our little kinks, Detective. As long as we can afford them." A shrug. "I was in love with one man, having his children, while being married to another. Who was I to judge?"

"Where is the collection now?" I asked.

"Exactly where Richard left it," she said. "Would you like to see?"

SIXTY-SIX

Leslie Travers led me back inside and then upstairs. Up a grand circular staircase, two flights to a third-floor hallway. At the end of the hall we entered a bedroom. Small, considering the vastness of everything else. "This is the guest room which no one ever uses," she explained, with a wry smile. "It's much too cramped." She went to what I suspected was a closet, opening the door. "Are you coming?" she asked.

I followed her through the closet door. It opened onto a room that had to have been fifty feet long by at least that wide. There were no windows. Its walls were lined instead from floor to ceiling by glass panels, behind which were shelves, the shelves lined with books and magazines, but mainly with videotapes. A large-screen high-definition television filled one corner of the room. In front of it, a leather sofa and a coffee table. In the opposite corner, a desk. A computer. A thirty-five-inch monitor. A phone. An answering machine.

"Their den," Leslie said. "They could stay in here for hours."

Going to the desk. The answering machine was switched off. I wanted to pick up the telephone receiver and press the redial button. But what could I say to whomever answered on the other end? Looking instead at the computer. Alongside it was a small wooden cabinet. Hand-crafted, I assumed. It had sixteen drawers, four up by four down, each approximately four and a half inches square, and about a foot and a half deep. I pulled one of the drawers open. It was labeled A–B. Inside were Zip disks. Alphabetically filed. I flipped through the discs, reading the labels: ALISON, ANNA, BARBARA—I couldn't help but wonder, Barbara Boyle, or some other Barbara? She certainly wasn't Deegan's type. But then, perhaps that was why he'd downloaded none of her pictures onto his laptop.

Opening the next drawer. A random sampling of labels: CINDY, DARIA, DEBI. The *L* drawer, LANA, LISA, lots of LOLA. There were two *M* drawers. One contained just disks labeled MARY—always his favorite. The other contained MAGGIE, MARTHA, MEGAN, and so on. There were other names in the *N* drawer, but only one caught my attention: NINA. A dozen disks in all, with each able to hold on average five hundred to a thousand JPEGs. I must have stared into that drawer for a long while, astounded by the numbers dancing in my head. The sheer multitude. Wondering if they contained everything. Charlene's every little indiscretion made for order for only Richard Deegan and Kilgore Travers to see. She'd answered an ad in the goddamn *Advocate*.

"Perhaps you'd like me to leave you alone for a while, Detective?" she asked.

"No," I said. "I, um—who made these videos?"

"I believe they used a lot of different people over the years. Kilgore had his connections, and Richard likewise. I guess the people who do these things specialize. I believe Richard was using just one source lately, though. A woman, if I remember correctly. But there were so many names, I can't say that I remember hers specifically."

I nodded a few times, staring at the name NINA on the Zip disk label.

"If you need to take anything for evidence," she said. "Please, help yourself."

"Are you sure?"

"I have no use for it, Detective," she said. "I've always felt I've owed something to the people on these videos. That I was responsible for opening Richard up. Perhaps a little too far." A shrug. "And I don't see how anything in this room can hurt Richard now."

"What about Crawford? Aren't you afraid of what he might do if he finds out?"

"I have too much money to be frightened of James Craw-ford," she said. "My children already know who their father is. We all have an understanding."

"Your sons understand what was going on between you and Kilgore and Deegan?" I asked.

"There's too much money involved for them not to," she said. "I didn't say they approved. But I don't necessarily approve of their chosen lifestyles, either. It's a two-way street. The money buys a lot of looking the other way." She shrugged. "As to whether or not Margaret Deegan or her daughters know, I don't mean to sound callous, but I really don't care."

I picked up one of the Nina Zip disks. Bouncing it in my hand. Rubbing the flat of my thumb over her name as if I could erase it. As if I could erase Charlene from my life.

"Do you care about how Richard died?" I asked. "Do you know why he was murdered?"

"No," she said. "And I prefer to keep it that way."

There are a number of things I'd like to take," I said, pulling out the one Zip labeled BARBARA, the drawer full of Zips labeled MARY, and the dozen disks labeled NINA. Making a pile on the edge of the desk. My *evidence*. Walking toward the television then. The shelves behind it were stacked from floor to ceiling with videos labeled with similar names. Except there were more of them. A staggering amount. If Charlene had been paid a thousand dollars per tape—millions had been invested here. Thrown away here.

They were in alphabetical order. Perfect order. Named, numbered, and dated. I ran a fingertip over the titles. The ear-liest tape was from 1981. It was of a girl named Lisa. There were four Lisa tapes in all. I pulled the first one down from the shelf and started a stack. There were twenty-six tapes labeled BARBARA. They went back almost five years to just a few months ago. I pulled those down from the shelf. I counted 106 Nina tapes—one a week for the last couple of years, just as Charlene had said. And 479 Mary tapes, dating back almost three years. Deegan couldn't get enough of her. I did some quick math. She averaged over three videos a week. At a grand per session, and something told me she was making more, this young woman was living well. If she could indeed, live with herself.

I was thinking I'd need a truck when some other videos caught my attention. They began after Zoë, the last name in this female alphabetical listing. These were labeled ADAM, or BRAD, or CHARLES, or DONALD.

I turned toward Leslie Travers. "Do you know Richard's assistant, Donny?"

A small, warm laugh this time. "Know him?" she asked. "He was Kilgore's assistant for five years." She pointed at the tapes. "I believe that's how they met. When Kilgore died, well, I was the one who got him the job with Richard. Though I doubt he was doing for Richard what he did for my husband."

SIXTY-SEVEN

The back- and passenger's seats were loaded. The butler had helped. Pulled a few wooden boxes from the wine cellar. Boxes that had once held bottles of a two-hundred-dollar Bordeaux now held videos and photographs that cost well beyond that.

Something Leslie Travers had said was playing in my head as I drove. It was as I thanked her, asking one last question. One last name entering the equation. The second man to die. "Did you know Tony Sorrentino?"

"Not really," she said. "Shook his hand a few times at functions, but—" A shrug. "—I just have to assume he wasn't a very bright man."

"Why's that?"

"To call an escort the day after a friend is supposedly murdered by one."

"True," I said, the words coming out before I could even digest their meaning, "Unless the girl he called came highly recommended."

Stopping at the first pay phone, I made two calls. Charlene first. The line busy. Brown next.

"Need a favor," I said when he picked up.

"Shoot."

"Need you to pick up Donny Savage at the Omni."

"What do you want me to do with him?" he asked.

"Bring him someplace where we can all talk."

"What if he doesn't want to go?" Brown asked.

"Convince him," I said. "In your own special way."

C harlene picked up on the second ring. "Hello," she answered.

"It's Will."

Silence.

"Hello."

"Why were you so mean to me?"

"Charlene."

A long pause. Finally, "What?"

"Got a question."

Silence.

"I need to know the name of the woman who made your videos."

"Why?"

"Cause I'm thinking of getting into the business."

"I hate it when you're sarcastic."

"I know you do."

"I—Shit! You don't know how badly I wanted you the other day."

My turn to be quiet.

A small laugh. "Her name's Barbara," she said. "Okay? I haven't heard from her in a few months, though. I think she's stopped making them."

SIXTY-EIGHT

Brown's Caprice was parked in front of my building. Donny Savage was sitting in the backseat. My partner was behind the wheel. Neither man seemed to be saying much.

I rapped on Brown's window. "Where do you want to do this?" he asked.

"Upstairs," I said. "But first I need a little muscle."

It took two trips, but the boxes of videos were now resting against one of the walls in my living room. They looked at home.

"Excellent wine," Donny said, at first glance. Then he picked one of the boxes up. "What's inside?" he asked, making a face.

"Stuff," I told him, answering his face with one of my own.

I played host for a moment. Getting myself a beer. Donny had some water. Brown said he wasn't thirsty.

"Have a seat, Donny," I said, pointing at the sofa.

He made another face. "I was just about to phone you, Willie," he said, sitting.

Brown snorted a laugh, perhaps despite it all.

Shooting my partner a look, I rolled my desk chair from its place in front of the computer table, taking a seat opposite Donny. Brown remained standing. "Oh, yeah," I said.

"I didn't know where else to turn," he said. "I tried talking to Special Agent Questral, but she brushed me off."

"She's got other things on her mind," Brown said.

"I figured you, well—it's—it's about Dick."

"Deegan?" I asked, just to be sure.

"Yes," Donny said. "And, well, this woman."

"What woman?" I asked.

"A complete—excuse the phrase, Detective—cunt."

"You're excused," I said.

"I doubt that you've heard of her," Donny continued, "but she'd been causing all sorts of heartache for Dick. Threats of blackmail, and—and worse."

"Worse than blackmail?"

"She said she was going to kill him."

"Why didn't you tell us this before, Donny?"

"Didn't think it was important?" Brown asked.

"Because," he said, exhaling a little puff of air, tears suddenly clouding his eyes. "I didn't want to soil his reputation. Dick was an important man. A very religious man."

"Um-huh," I went. "So, why bring it up now?"

"She called again. Last night."

"Who, Donny?" I asked. "What's her name?"

"She's a professional escort, Detective," Donny said, the words obviously painful to his own ears, his own sensibilities. The name music to mine. "Her name's Barbara Boyle."

Blackmail?" I said, letting the notion sink in. Barbara Boyle. Brunette Barbara Boyle. So many lies. She'd never talked to Deegan again. Never tried to contact him. Christ! She'd been working for him for years.

"Yes," he said. "She talked to me because Dick stopped taking her calls. She told me he'd pay for what he did to her."

"And you really didn't think this might have helped us three days ago?"

"I wasn't thinking on Monday," Donny said. "I mean. I can't be arrested as an accessory, can I?"

"To what?" I asked.

"Prostitution," he said.

Brown laughed again.

I shook my head. "No," I said. "No." Shook it some more.

"Did Barbara Boyle ever tell you what Deegan did to her?"

"Did to *her*?"

"What pissed her off?"

"No," Donny said, "But I—I think she was just jealous."

"Of what?" I asked.

"He stopped seeing her."

"How long had they been *seeing* one another?" I asked.

"Ever since, well. The Sons of God have been talking about this relocation for a while now. Almost a year."

"About the time Kilgore Travers died," I said.

He looked at me. "Well, yes. I think it started then. The thing with him and Barbara."

"Not earlier?" I asked.

"I'm not sure," he said. "I've only worked for him since last summer."

"There was nothing more to their relationship?" I asked. "Photographs, videos?"

He blushed. "How do you know?"

"A few thousand pictures on his laptop gave him away."

"That was his—that was personal. I didn't interfere." He became suddenly quiet. "I don't really know."

"How involved were he and Barbara?"

"Very. For a while. He'd see her whenever he visited New Haven. Up until a few months ago anyway, when Dick just seemed to lose interest."

"How often did he pass through town?"

"Often," he said. "A couple of times a month. Sometimes more. It seemed recently as if he'd already moved here. I was so pleased when he broke it off. I told him she'd fall in love with him. And then what would he do? What if she got pregnant? He couldn't afford to take that risk. But he told me she satisfied a need I would never understand."

"We're in the same boat there, Donny," I said.

SIXTY-NINE

God's curse on New Haven wasn't so much Yale, or Yal-
ies—they came in a close second, or the damn Ninth Square
did. It wasn't the lack of public parking, the ratio of two tow
trucks for every car registered in the city. Or even the fact that
New Haven was birthplace to Michael Bolton's musical career.
No, the curse—and anyone who's ever driven it would know—
was the Q Bridge. A massive curving monstrosity. The second
biggest parking lot in the world, after the Long Island Express-
way. A junkyard dog of concrete and steel that soared over the
mouth of the Quinnipiac River. Sometimes you could just sail
past, as I did yesterday morning on my first visit to Barbara
Boyle's *oceanfront* condo. But most times it was bumper-to-
bumper steel-caged road rage. As it was right now.

We were in Brown's Caprice. Having dropped Donny back
at the Omni, and taking the Route 34 connector that would put
us right on the bridge. The radio was on, tuned to the continuing
coverage. "Crisis in the Elm City." A reporter talked about the
sixty thousand plus Sons of God heading in from all parts. There
were interviews with men from as far away as Alaska. Busloads
from the Bible Belt, from the Great Plains, from Seattle, and
Miami. The rally was getting national attention now. It was a
call for unity in the face of tragedy. Held now in memory of
their fallen leaders, Deegan and Sorrentino. Margaret Deegan
would be addressing the crowd. The first time ever a woman
would address a Sons of God gathering.

"I wonder if she'll be giving her husband's speech," Brown
said.

"I wonder if she'd like to read it sometime," I replied.

"Sometimes it's better not to know," Brown said. "That's
what Bernie said to me when I went to bed last night. She knew

something was up. I told her it involved you and one of the prostitutes we were investigating. She stopped me right there."

"She believed you?"

"I guess."

"See, you're not that bad a liar after all."

"It's just that I can't keep anything from her," he said. "She's knows right off."

I nodded as Barbara Boyle's face flashed in my head. The prostitute we were investigating. She and her roommates. What did these women want? What did they dream of? I knew my dreams were soaked into Gloria's maple neck, locked away most of the time—all of the time—in a hardshell case. But what else? Or was that it for me? I'd dreamt of family once. Small, just Charlene and me, but it would have been enough. I wasn't a sucker enough to try to bring children into this world. I wasn't about to inflict that pain, the pain of just getting by, on my son or daughter. But even those dreams seemed like so long ago. Bruised now. And shattered. Left for dead on Aruba's south shore. Mostly—the past months, anyway—I dreamt of just getting through the day. A halfway decent meal. A few cold beers. Pretty pathetic, when I thought about it. I could go to a local pizza joint and live my goddamn dream. No, there had to be more. Or did Charlene get them in the divorce settlement? But she got nothing. We both got nothing. Perhaps that was it. Perhaps it was the reason I married her in the first place. Force myself to grow up, to kill off the dream.

But Barbara Boyle and her roommates. Could their dreams be similar? Or was it a case of *what you see is what you get*? That that was it. Their possessions? Could they all three have been little girls dreaming of red convertibles and waterfront condos, and sucking money from the pockets of men who didn't know any better? Was that what they talked to their mothers about, at night, getting tucked in? Mommy, when I grow up I want to be a high-class call girl. *That's nice, sweetheart. Remem-*

ber to say your prayers. Nighty-night. Or were they just beyond dreams? Jaded and used. And seeking revenge. *High-class call girl seeks unattractive, middle-aged johns into very rough sex.* Were they just tired of it all? No, not tired. Especially the roommates. They were too bubbly, too perky. Perhaps they had silicone implants to their brains.

Or a girl like Heather. Louise Heather Karg. Was her dream to be a whore with a bad attitude? To screw for money and not give a damn? Was it just to be high? To talk about *one of these days*? Or maybe something simple. To graduate with honors. Not that that was simple, a 3.7 GPA. What was a girl with brains doing as an escort? But Daphne was studying to be a lawyer. Perhaps brains had nothing to do with it. I couldn't imagine a reason. I wished I'd asked Heather. I wished now I could get the chance to.

Or Deegan. What could he have possibly dreamt of? Before the perversion. Before Leslie. She'd opened him up. Going way back. A simple life, loving God, his country, his family. Could that have been all he'd wanted out of his stay here? Could that have been it? Or had the demons always been present? And Leslie had just unlocked them? Opened his Pandora's box. Set them free? Had he always not dreamt but fantasized about what he'd do to someone like Barbara Boyle? What he'd do to Midori? And if so, how long had he kept those dreams locked away? Could they have turned out differently? Had he once locked them away in a guitar case all his own, fresh and innocent? Beautiful, with a polished gleam. So in tune. A desire for a fruitful, healthy life. Only to discover they'd gone bad. They'd gone rotten on the vine. When he finally had the courage to unlock the case and set them free.

And where did the fault lie? The perversions begin and end? Did the Barbara Boyles of the world—the Leslie Van Cleefs of the world—corrupt the Richard Deegans? And if so, wasn't it then our fault for creating the Barbara Boyles? Could it have been? Mine? Luponte's? Every guy who ever got a hard-on by looking at *Playboy* or *Penthouse*? Did we create the monster? Supply and fucking demand. Supply and a demand for fucking. It must be what we want. And if it is, obviously we'll pay for it. Pay for it. And keep paying for it. They're just business women, the three of them, Barbara and her roommates. Bored as if they were selling shoes or life insurance, instead of bursts of ecstasy. No matter how false. Everything about them fake: the breasts, the smiles, the laughs. Perhaps we were all the same. The fake pickup lines. Anything for the score. Any difference really from just slapping down a couple of hundred bucks? The end results. Wasn't that all that mattered? To Luponte? To Klavan? Christ! Lt. Theodore Klavan and the three of them. Sunday night. I couldn't picture it. Didn't want to.

And wasn't that all that mattered to Deegan?

No, Deegan had other results in mind. I couldn't forget that. I couldn't forget what he'd done to Barbara Boyle. What he tried to do to Midori.

"This where we get off?" Brown asked, as the exit approached.

"Not me and you, partner," I said. "Just everyone else."

SEVENTY

The three red convertibles were in the carport. It was probably a little early on a Thursday for a call, or a shift at one of the area's strip bars. Perhaps Thursday was their day off. Perhaps it was the day they used to shoot videos for hire. And now the snap and pose was gone, replaced perhaps by a little female bonding to wash away the stench.

I rang the doorbell. Nothing. Pressed it again. Hoping we wouldn't disturb a two-girl show. Or a client coming to play in their oceanfront condo. But there were no other cars parked out front, and would I care, really? Would Brown? Glancing around—the street was quiet, empty. The lawyers and doctors who could afford these condos were working their normal nine-to-fives.

"I wonder if the neighbors know what goes on here?" I said.

"Neighbors usually know everything," Brown said. "Or nothing at all."

"Probably most of them have little deals worked out with the girls to look the other way."

Brown knocked hard against the door. He banged on it, but nothing. No one was home, or at least no one was answering. All three cars were in the carport.

"There another entrance?" Brown asked.

I nodded, remembering the deck.

We stepped off the front stoop and walked around back. The deck had stairs that led to a small beach area. It was hard to think of New Haven Harbor as having beaches. This one looked man-made. We stepped onto the deck, to the sliding glass door that led inside. The screen was shut, but the door itself wide open. Letting in what little breeze there was.

Calling into the house. "Barbara. It's Detective Shute. Are you home?"

Brown's cupped his hands around his eyes as he tried to get a glimpse inside, the sunlight bright against our backs. "Shit," he said, reaching for his gun, for the screen door, sliding it back. I was right there with him, gun drawn, not sure why.

Entering their living room with the sunlight streaming through the windows, casting monstrous shadows against the walls of white, the floors bleached white, the white leather sofa. The brightness playing tricks. The TV on. Too loud. But barely visible in the glare. A commercial for a laundry detergent. No stain too tough. The glass coffee table. No Doritos today. Or perhaps they'd cleaned up after breakfast. The bowl of beepers alive. Like a nest of just hatched birds. Crying for attention.

Barbara Boyle was home.

As were her roommates.

SEVENTY-ONE

I stood, leaning against the hood of my partner's Caprice. The flashing reds, and whites, and blues. The lights burning against the homes. Against the supposed sanctity. Unspooling the crime scene tape. The yellow-and-black warning. To stay back. To keep back. To just go away. Listening. The words, the terminologies. The opening and closing of doors. The slap of a gurney's wheels against concrete. The locking of its joints in place. Slice and the techies. Moving, in slow motion, fast motion. Or not moving at all. The SID van. The unmarked cars. Brown by my side. Mazz joining us. The scratching of heads. The looks of frustration, ineptitude.

The two roommates—their real names had been Susan Bianchi and Tatiana Lamoureux—had both been shot dead. A .38 single-action revolver would be my guess. No casings on the bleached pine floors. No casings anywhere. Susan first, taking one bullet to the back of her head. Tatiana turning, probably reacting in horror, taking a bullet to the side of her face and another to the chest. They were sitting on the couch, almost the same way I'd last seen them. Almost. Still in their underwear, but something a little more dressy than Calvins now. A fancy English lace in which to meet their Maker.

Barbara Boyle wore a dress, as if she were about to go out. Or as if she were expecting a customer. But she couldn't work for another two months. Or perhaps, she could work—another lie—did work, but in a limited capacity. I'd brought myself to the point where I almost believed she was working with Tony Sorrentino the night he died. The hair color was right. And in a dark car parked in a dark garage—the same garage where Deegan would have dumped Midori's body. Sorrentino wouldn't have noticed. Barbara would have dealt with the pain in the name of revenge.

I'd found her in the bathroom, cowering near the toilet. She took one bullet to the forehead. That was all that was needed.

Upstairs in one of the bedrooms we found the video equipment. Upstairs, all three bedrooms had been the backdrops, rooms where *mary.jpg*, where Charlene, where the others, had made videos for hire. The wallpaper, the bedspreads, all sickeningly familiar. But nowhere, upstairs or down, could we find the numbers. A date book, an address book, an electronic organizer, a Filofax, a laptop computer, a cellular phone. If Barbara Boyle had one—and I was sure she needed something to keep track of the actors and actresses, I was sure she needed something to access the Web—it was gone.

"Y'know," Mazz said. "If Barbie were life size, her measurements would be 39-23-33."

Not so far off, I thought.

He shrugged then and scratched at the top of his head. "Any ideas, Will? Any clue as to what's going on?"

There were too many running through my head, and not a one making much sense. These were my main suspects. Barbara Boyle had reason to go after Deegan. And if so, she probably had reason to go after the entire organization. She'd been working for him for so long. So long—Why kill these girls? Because they knew too much? Because they were servicing the rich, the powerful? City officials, perhaps? Donny Savage spoke of some blackmail threats, but would he want to get even in the name of his boss? I doubted he had the stomach for triple-murder. I doubted he could pull a trigger once, much less four times. Or what about James Crawford? The character of his organization hanging on the tip of a professional escort's tongue. Could Barbara Boyle have turned to Crawford as well? Figuring he'd cough up something to keep her quiet. To stop her from telling the world what Richard Deegan had done. To stop her from telling everyone about Deegan's big kink. To keep the Sons of God from tumbling down. And Crawford in turn sent the Angel Gabriel to make another house call. But where was Gabe? Did he exist, or was he just a part of my imagination, to be filed alongside the love of my wife?

"No," I said. "Except that I don't think it's over yet."

"So, who falls next?" Brown asked.

Shaking my head. "I do."

I glanced over at Brian Luponte. He'd been next on the scene. As if breaking the sound barrier to get there. He stared at Barbara for the longest time, unable to touch her. Unable to talk. I asked if he was okay. He didn't answer. He didn't move until finally Slice asked him to make room. Luponte turned to me then. "She had this one customer," he said. "One of us. Who'd line those little dark-green toy soldiers up and down his bare chest. He'd string Christmas tree lights around them. Then he'd have Barbara walk on his chest in these four inch heels, grinding the little men and the Christmas tree lights into his flesh." He paused, "I really thought I could get her away from that," he said, leaving the bathroom.

Luponte sat now on the front steps to their condo. Holding his face in his hands. Running his fingers through the buzz-cut sheen. Looking pale and confused, and just a little nauseated. Despite everything, I knew that Luponte liked the girls a lot. That he actually believed they liked him in return. They laughed at his jokes. Probably told him what a great lover he was. I didn't doubt for a moment that he wanted to save them. That he truly believed he'd let them down. Perhaps he was right. Perhaps we all had.

SEVENTY-TWO

Brown dropped me off at the station house. Then I gave him an address. Daphne's. I told him who he'd find there. And that perhaps someone should be watching out for them tonight.

"I think you're right," he said.

This time there was no arguing. There was no Questral. No mayor. No bullshit. No time to waste. I walked into Klavan's office. He was just coming out of the john, dressed sharply, straightening his tie. I would have thought he'd be long due to pack it in for the night. It had been a week of long days into long nights. No more Barbara Boyles to ease the tension. To make the workload seem a little less so. He saw me and followed me inside, slamming the door shut after us.

"What the hell are you doing here, Shute?" Klavan said, stomping toward his desk. "I warned you to stay away, but all I keep hearing is how you're showing up—"

Cutting him off. "Who else was part of this little fraternity?" I asked, not even giving him time to sit.

He didn't answer at first.

"Barbara Boyle and her roommates." In case there was any mistaking the question in his mind.

"I don't have time for this," he said.

"Who?"

"These are things you don't need to—"

"Bullshit!" I yelled it loud enough for everyone outside to hear. Then lowering my voice, leaning close, over his desk, not too far from getting in his face, said, *"Pinfield*. Is he a member?"

"Shute," he said. "I like my job."

"Look, Lieutenant, I don't give a rat's ass if the mayor is getting some. I just need to know if he had access. If he gave it away as a perk. If he was the one who sent Deegan to see those girls. Or if he sent Sorrentino. Or Crawford. Or any of the others."

Klavan eyed me hard. "Yeah," he said, "the mayor *was* well acquainted with Barbara Boyle. They, um—Barbara, Susan, and Tatiana—were—" He looked away. It was as if he suddenly couldn't say the goddamn words.

But I knew where he was going. Barbara and her roommates had been there to serve, not protect, but as much on the city payroll as I probably was. As much a city employee. Minus the usual benefits, of course. A little help with the reelection campaign. A thank-you for the serious contributor. A perk for businessmen moving their headquarters to New Haven. A big boys' club to keep New Haven running and happy and so very well fucked.

"Never mind," I said, straightening up. "I just figured it out for myself."

SEVENTY-THREE

Cutting through the Ninth Square. Always taking the long way home, as if to torture myself. The For Lease signs had been removed from the windows of the Francesconi Building. The windows washed, the glass gleaming. I wondered who'd had the time to pull them down since Tuesday evening? Who would have bothered. Perhaps Crawford himself. Or Albert Larsen. Or an assistant. Donny.

There was a truck parked out front. One of the big van lines. It had a Mississippi license plate. But no driver, and this time the doors to the building were locked. Pressing my face to the glass, I saw that the sofas were uncovered now, under the watchful eye of playful cherubs. A large sign was mounted on the wall over the built-in marble reception desk. It read SONS OF GOD.

Stepping back, heading to Church Street. I could stop at the Dunkin' Donuts for a coffee, or—glancing at my watch—Willoughby's was open for another five minutes. Walking at a brisk pace, trying to rationalize their move. Not so much what the Sons of God were thinking, but what we, as a city, were thinking? Asking myself if these were people I wanted to serve and protect?

There was a crowd at the steps to city hall. The media. So much media, that sudden influx of celebrities that had descended upon the Elm City. Brought here by the violence and the religion. Tom Brokaw and Peter Jennings and Dan Rather, all broadcasting their nightly network newscasts live from somewhere in town as of last night. They weren't on Church Street, but their news siblings were. All the letters of the alphabet strung out in small groups of threes and fours, and painted to the sides of satellite news trucks and handheld microphones.

Their attention was focused on a podium, behind which

stood Mayor Pinfield and James Crawford. Klavan—that explained the sharp suit, Zakowski, Larsen, Margaret Deegan, her daughters Anne and Theresa, stood off to one side. Ruth must have thought better of attending.

Spotting Officer Juanita Pérez on the perimeter, I asked, "What's going on?"

"The apocalypse, Detective," she said. "The Sons of God are moving to town."

"God help us all, Pérez," I said.

"I think these guys scare even *Him*," she said.

The speeches must have been over, because it was question-and-answer time. Someone asked if this was a wise move in the face of such tragedy. Shaking my head, turning, ignoring the answer—then—something. *Snapping—snapping—snapping!* I don't know what? But it was in that split second between the time Pinhead stopped talking and the reporters present could spit out their next questions. I filled that space. Loudly. My voice shaking with rage. Or perhaps I was shaking and my voice was just the end product.

"How do you explain having three prostitutes on the city payroll?" I yelled.

That split second expanded. Everything stopped. The reporters turned. Some turned their microphones toward me. Some started babbling in my direction. From behind the podium, the mayor covered the microphone with his hand, but still spoke loud enough for everyone to hear. "Get that son of a bitch out of here," he said. From behind the podium, James Crawford glared.

"Were they one of the perks the city promised the Sons of God?" I continued.

Klavan came toward me. I'd seen him pissed before, but never like this. His fists balled, his face tight. "I warned you, Shute, to stay away," he said.

"In a quick, clean, and easy world I might have," I said, not paying him as much attention as I was Crawford, who never moved. Not a twitch. Not a swallow. Just that look. But it was more unnerving than having Klavan charging.

He was a couple yards away when I heard, "Don't even think about it, Lieutenant." Both Klavan and I turned just as Brian Luponte stepped between us. He was in uniform. In one hand a billy club. He looked ready to use it. He didn't seem to be joking around.

"This has got nothing to do with you, Luponte," Klavan said.

"Bullshit," Luponte said, staring him down. The two men locking eyes—Luponte probably knew a lot more about what went on at Barbara Boyle's condo than I did. He probably knew all the names and the kinks that could be attached to them. His testimony could probably bring down the administration and half the division.

"Arrest that man," Chief Zekowski screamed.

Ignoring the chief, Klavan turned to me finally, with a look of such disappointment. "Go home, Shute," he said. Not waiting for my response, he turned on his heel and headed back toward the podium.

Nodding, I backed away slowly. Away from the reporters. Away from the scene. Away from Crawford, who hadn't blinked. I couldn't get far enough away from Crawford.

Luponte turned to look at me then. We also locked eyes, but just for a beat. Only for a look. And in that silent moment, in that desperate look, I thanked him. He said: It was okay. Then he muttered something just loud enough for me to hear.

"Watch your back," he said.

SEVENTY-FOUR

Starting with the Barbara videos, I pushed one into the VCR. Pressing PLAY, standing back. I didn't need to get comfortable. I didn't plan on watching much. The picture blinking on. Barbara Boyle sitting on the edge of a bed in one of her condo's bedrooms. Looking up at the camera. "Are we on?" she asked, her voice bored and uninterested. "We're on," came a voice from somewhere else in the room. And so, suddenly, was Barbara. The boredom replaced by a seductive smile. A come-hither look. The perfect pose. An exact arch to her back. The beginnings of a slow striptease. A man came into the frame. Joining her on the bed. Saying, "You sure look fine, baby." I had to laugh. Not at the dialogue. Not at the inept delivery of the line. Not at the look of stunned stupidity plastered to his face. But because I recognized the guy. Not like he needed the extra grand on the side. If he was even paid. He must have known who'd be watching. He must have been in on it? A favor? A reward? A little showing off? Either way, let's face it, as Barbara did her thing, the notion that this video would fall into the hands of a New Haven police officer, was probably the farthest thing from Tony Sorrentino's mind.

I scanned the beginning of every Barbara tape. Of every Nina tape. Checking for partners. For *mary.jpg*, or someone else that I might know. Sorrentino hadn't been with my wife, as least on video. I recognized no one else, except that the first woman Charlene had made love to was Susan Bianchi. The first woman to die in the condo today. She'd had black hair then. She'd died a redhead.

S he answered on the second ring.
"Any new tattoos?" I asked.

"You still haven't found all the old ones," Daphne said.

I wondered if I'd ever allow myself a chance. Knowing what she did for a living. "I sent a friend to watch your back."

"I know," she said. "He's in here now, eating a grilled cheese sandwich. Want to talk to him?"

I told her yes, and she handed the phone over to Brown. I heard him swallow hard.

"You made the evening news," he said.

"My fifteen minutes," I said. "Hope they got my good side."

"They didn't," he said, then, "Gracie's—"

"What?" I asked, not giving him a chance.

"She's doing good," he said. "Talking. Eating. Mazz brought her a Pepe's clam pizza. She don't remember much, though, from the other night, other than storming out of your place."

"She didn't see who hit her?"

"No idea."

"But she's going to be okay?"

"Absolutely," he said.

"Good," I said. "Anything else?"

"Everything's cool here," he said, then lowering his voice, "I just can't believe how much Midori looks like the girl on Deegan's computer."

"I doubt that Deegan could, either," I said.

SEVENTY-FIVE

The *mary.jpg* videos.

I started at the beginning. Scanning through each. Looking for—I wasn't sure what I was looking for. Deegan. Sorrentino. I already expected Barbara Boyle. What I got was *mary.jpg* talking to the camera, posing, flashing parts of her body, taking a shower, taking a bath, brushing her teeth. I watched her sleeping, eating, masturbating, making love with one partner, two partners, three partners, four partners. Men, women, it didn't seem to matter. Because unlike Barbara, *mary.jpg* was always on. Never did the camera seem to catch her bored. To catch her when she wasn't playful or in the mood. And I was left to wonder if Deegan had found his perfect playmate? Or was he just paying her that much? Was he setting her up for life? Or was he just setting her up?

I watched her look of desire as she took on each partner. A look as if there were nothing more she wanted from this world. Charlene had had the same look in her Nina videos. And I was left to wonder about Daphne. The phone call from this afternoon still haunted me. What look filled Daphne's eyes when she made love to strangers for money? What was going through her mind as they touched her body? As they kissed her?

More important, what was going through her mind when she kissed me?

Pressing PLAY.

The tape was labeled number 63. It was dated March 12, two years ago. It opened on a close-up of *mary.jpg*'s face. They all opened on a close-up of her face. She was sitting in Barbara Boyle's living room. On the leather sofa. She wore a white tank top and white panties. It was question-and-answer time.

"What's your name?" a voice I recognized as Barbara Boyle's said off-camera.

"Mary," *mary.jpg* answered.

"How old are you, Mary?"

"I'll be nineteen in two weeks."

"You go to college?"

"No," she said, giggling. "Why would I need to, I'm a movie star."

"Do you have a boyfriend?"

"I've got lots of boyfriends."

"Tell me about—"

Pressing FORWARD SCAN, I cut Barbara off. The images moved past fast and fuzzy. But I got the point, if indeed there was one: *mary.jpg* eventually removed the tank top and panties. Then she walked through the living room, all the while talking or giggling or—

She went into the bathroom, where I'd found Barbara, where Barbara had shown me what Deegan had done to her. Mary opened a cabinet door under the sink, pulling from it—

I pressed PLAY.

Mary was standing in front of the sink. In her hand was a red rubber enema bag, or a douche bag, as Barbara had called it. She turned the faucet on and then filled the bag.

"What are you going to do with that?" Barbara asked.

"You'll see."

Hanging the bag from a towel rack, *mary.jpg* got down on all fours.

"That turn you on?" Barbara asked.

"Everything turns me on," she said.

I hit STOP before she had a chance to say or do anything else.

SEVENTY-SIX

Taking a seat in front of my computer. Wondering if *mary.jpg*'s little kink had sealed Barbara Boyle's fate? Was it what fueled Deegan? Inspired him? Was it what drove him over the brink?

Moving onto the next tape and the ones after that. Scanning through. Looking for a hint, another clue. But finding nothing. My eyes tired and burning. Feeling dirty and stupid. Needing—

The last tape, number 469, dated March 7. The first week of March. The week Deegan almost killed Barbara Boyle. But Barbara was fine at this point. I heard her voice behind the camera. She spoke to *mary.jpg*, who was seated on the edge of a bed. "We've got a surprise for you today, Mary," Barbara said.

"I like surprises," *mary.jpg* said. What else would she say?

Barbara appeared in front of the camera. She walked over to the bed.

"You gonna play?" *mary.jpg* asked.

"I'm just going to get you ready," Barbara said. Telling her then to take off her clothes and lie back. Making small talk, Barbara Boyle tied *mary.jpg* spread eagle down onto the four-poster bed.

"Sure you don't wanna play?" *mary.jpg* asked.

"I'm sure, honey," Barbara said. Then she called out, "You ready?"

A man answered from the bathroom. "Absolutely," he said, opening the bathroom door, stepping into the room. He carried a familiar black rubber bag, held high. He was fully clothed, wearing a dark suit and dress shirt. A perfectly knotted tie. Sitting on the edge of the bed, he said, "Hello."

"Hi," *mary.jpg* said. "You're cute. What's your name?"

The man smiled a little sheepishly, as if embarrassed. He ran the fingers of his free hand through his spiky hair. His arms so thick, massive next to someone *mary.jpg*'s size. He cleared his throat and then spoke finally. "I'm Gabriel," he said.

SEVENTY-SEVEN

Gabriel didn't kill *mary.jpg*, at least not then, not on tape. She reacted as she always did. She reacted in ecstasy. It was the shortest of all the videos. No sex afterwards. Gabe never took off his clothes. He never once touched her in any way even remotely sexual. He left once the job was done.

Barbara Boyle came back again at the end, questioning *mary.jpg*. Asking her, how did that feel? Were you turned on having a stranger do that to you? Her answers were what I had come to expect. Everything felt great to *mary.jpg*. Everything turned her on.

As Barbara got back behind the camera, zooming in for some final close-ups, I wondered if she knew she was making a training film? If she knew what Deegan had in store for her in the coming days?

But mostly I wondered if *mary.jpg* was still alive.

The videos off, away. There was nothing more the videos could tell me. I started thinking about Donny Savage. He'd talked to Barbara Boyle, but did he know about the acid douche? About *mary.jpg*? About Gabe? And if so, who else knew? Who else could he have told about Barbara's blackmail threat? About Deegan's obsessions?

Grabbing the phone. Someone at the Omni's front desk picked up on the second ring. "Donald Savage, please," I said. But no one picked up in his room. Not after two rings. Not after twelve. Finally a hotel operator interrupted the ringing. Would I like to leave a message? I hung up instead.

Pounding my fists now against the top of the kitchen counter. Crawford. Mr. Promiscuity. He probably knew. He knew everything. He just stood behind that podium and glared. Probably getting as much from Barbara and Susan and Tatiana as the rest of them. What were they getting in return? Dumb question, Shute. A Mercedes, a BMW, a Porsche. A condo worth at least three hundred grand, and who knew how much cash they had stashed away. The girls were getting something called *set-for-life*. That was enough for some people.

But Crawford didn't want to relocate. Despite the free sex. The mayor in one back pocket, the police department in the other. Questral keeping it all clean. All playing the same game. Crawford was—

Leslie Travers told me he was probably the only one who believed in what they preached. So, he was clean? I had a problem buying that after the face-to-face in the elevator. I wouldn't—she also told me he wanted to bring his message to the cities. Those new donation dollars. All those untouched, lonely, desperate souls needing to grasp at something, anything. Shepherd Crawford taking them into his fold. He probably wanted the move as badly as—perhaps he *needed* the move. Perhaps he needed those new donation dollars.

Sitting at the computer table. Turning, spinning in my chair. Spinning in my head. Out of the corner of my eye. The book. *Son of God: An Unauthorized Biography of James Crawford.* Unauthorized. Snatching it from the table. Pulling it onto my lap. Falling open to a page. Reading aloud:

"One former Sons of God employee, who agreed to be interviewed only if promised anonymity, confirmed Crawford's narcissism. "Crawford takes everything he does seriously. And he expects everyone else to, as well. I mean, every word he speaks. Every breath he takes. He holds himself above everyone else, above all else. He believes he is here to save mankind. I do not doubt for a moment that he believes himself holy. That James Crawford believes himself to be not just godlike, but an actual God. As if Jesus Christ were his brother, and it was his turn now to not lead us, but force us all into the holy land. Except unlike Christ, I believe James Crawford would use any means possible to achieve his goal. Threats. Blackmail. Violence. Sometimes I felt as if I were working for the devil himself."

SEVENTY-EIGHT

Religious fanaticism is not a victimless crime. Perhaps there were no victimless crimes. Perhaps there was a victim for every action. Every reaction. We were all victims. We were all criminal.

I groaned, and couldn't help but wonder if I wouldn't be next? The next victim. The next criminal.

Looking around, catching sight of the napkin. My list. On the floor in front of my sofa, where I probably dropped it last night. Picking it up. Staring at it now. I'd added Crawford's name and the words: "brown hair."

Sitting, leaning back on the couch, shaking my head, picking up the remote control, turning the volume on the TV way up. The local news was over. I missed my chance to see what sort of coverage my little commotion had caused.

The date appeared first as it always did, then Ted Koppel's face filled the screen. "I was to have started tonight's program by saying the killing had finally come to an end in New Haven, Connecticut. But such is not the case."

It was the same old, all over again. Something fresh from outside Barbara Boyle's condo. A mention of an allegation that the city used prostitutes as perks to lure the Sons of God to New Haven. And O'Toole's attack, now linked. But otherwise . . . I stared at it nonetheless. Deegan's murder, the start of it all. And poor Tony Sorrentino. Perhaps someone needed a copy of his other videos, otherwise he'd be forever thought of as a chauffeur. Meeting Deegan's family at Tweed. Squeezing Margaret Deegan's hand. Opening the front door for her. Putting his arm around Ruth's shoulders.

I sat up suddenly. Watching the concern in Sorrentino's eyes. Made sense. Now. The oldest daughter, Anne, slipping in first.

The middle daughter, Theresa, watching after her kid sister. The brunette, Theresa. The look in her eyes. The—Christ! Not like a big sister at all.

I yelled at the TV. I wanted it to stop. I wanted to go back. Where was instant replay when you needed it most? Grabbing one of the Nina videos. A little Scotch tape over hole that prevented it from being erased. Into the VCR. RECORD. And I would wait. At the top of the hour. At midnight, CNN would be sure to run it again. Or Headline News. Or MSNBC. One of them. And I'd catch it this time. But until then—

"The proud papa," I said, remembering the look in Sorrentino's eyes as he put his arm around Ruth's shoulder. Ruth Deegan was carrying *his* child. Tony Sorrentino's child. She thought he was cute. And she liked the idea of, to put it in her words, "Doing one of father's buds." She seduced him, not the other way around. She made that perfectly clear to me. "Tony was a good guy," she had said. "He just didn't believe in rubbers. But then, what guy does?"

The apple of Richard Deegan's eye acting up. And when she got pregnant, what a slap in the face to her father. She told Sorrentino, obviously. And just as obviously, the Son of God, the anti-abortionist, suggested an abortion. He must have thought it a sacrament now.

Ruth found this amusing. She coyly invoked the Bible, as Richard Deegan's little girl should. Sorrentino told her he'd support her decision, no matter what. He was relieved when she didn't tell her dad. He probably thought she'd told no one. But Sorrentino was wrong. Ruth spilled the beans to at least one other person. Her sister, Theresa. Theresa with brown hair. Ruth told her everything. Her words came to me as I waited to see the look in Theresa's eyes again. Not a flash of concern. It wasn't looking out for her kid sister. And Sorrentino locking eyes with Theresa, before she, too, disappeared into the backseat. He seemed guilty. As guilty as all hell. And she—I needed to see the video again, but it was a look I recognized now. One I knew all too well. Charlene had given me the same look as I left the courtroom Monday morning.

It was a look that said "Go to hell."

FRIDAY

In her arms. Holding her. Close. My face buried against her neck. Smelling. Kissing. Noticing. A tattoo. Small, on the back of her neck. A drawing of a guitar. A drawing of Gloria. Smiling. Whispering into her ear, "When'd you get that?"

"Just the other day," she says, "Do you like it?"

Pulling back so I could kiss her, so I could tell her yes, and how much so. Her face, her—not Daphne. But Charlene. Charlene kissing me. Devouring me. Riding me.

"We all have our dark sides, Will," she says, "We all have our little fetishes. Remember what you did that night to Lori Questral? Remember what you had her do to you? She was drunk. You knew she'd do anything. You're no better than the rest of us, Will. You're just as much a whore deep down."

Movement behind her then. A camera. Barbara Boyle saying, "Let's move in for the money shot."

Then a beeping, the camera started beeping. Charlene turning around. Barbara turning, too. Asking, "What is that?"

But it just kept getting louder. The beeping, or ringing, or just a sound rattling around. Something in my head. Something—

Snapping open my eyes. The beeping. On the couch. Still—but too hot. Too—the TV on. Must have fallen asleep. Fallen—couldn't breathe. Smoke. Beeping. The fire alarm. A crash through one of my windows. A bottle. Gas. Flames. The Goddamn *beeping*. Standing. Shaky legs. Some sort of bearing. Holding a hand over my mouth. Trying to breathe. Trying. Stumbling to the door. Pulling it open. The flames knocking me back. The heat. The stairs engulfed. Looking around. Panic. I couldn't panic. There was no time for panic. Thinking. What did I need?

What could I not live without? The word snapping in my head. Revenge. Revenge. *Revenge.*

Another crash. Another explosion of flames. Turning. The case. Gloria's hardshell case. What I couldn't live without. Snatching it up. That was enough. That was all. The rest was just memories gone bad. Memories rotting on the vine.

Running up the stairs. Three at a time. To the bedroom. The air heavy with smoke. Glancing back. The fire moving swiftly. Eating at the hardwood floors. At the cardboard boxes. At my couch. Looking to the windows, looking to—the skylight. Pulling a bureau from the wall. Climbing up. Using Gloria's case as a battering ram. Smashing it. Once. Twice. The third time the charm. Through the glass.

Gloria first. Then lifting myself. Up. Through. The roof not so steep. Not so—finding some footing. Looking to both sides. The office building, so close. A flat roof. A three-foot jump at best. The adrenaline taking me, carrying me. Saving me and Gloria. Landing. Rolling. Lying still. Lying flat. Breathing. Breathing. *Breathing.* Watching the street. Searching for the son of a bitch. Searching. Waiting. Nothing. Just sirens in the distance. Then a fire escape. Climbing down. To the street. Crossing the street. A pay phone. Some pocket change. The slip of paper where I'd placed it last. Brown answering this time on the second ring.

"Brown," I said.

Perhaps it was something in my voice. Perhaps he could just tell. Perhaps the whole world knew. Perhaps that's what partners were for.

"I'll be right there," he said.

EIGHTY

I watched it burn from across the street. Waiting for the sirens to come crashing down. Waiting for Brown. Waiting for the sun to rise. All three would be here in no time.

Burning inside. This fire wasn't the fault of an old bakery oven. This fire had a purpose. But I was still standing. I was still—remembering. Just a few hours back. A little after one. The Sorrentino clip, taping it finally off Fox News. Playing it over, freeze framing the look Theresa Deegan gave Tony Sorrentino, before she slid into the backseat. Playing it in slow-motion. Was it disgust in her face? Was that disappointment? Maybe. Perhaps. I didn't know for sure. I couldn't tell. Then just letting it play. Letting the tape roll. Sitting on the sofa. Aiming the remote. Hitting the STOP button. Back to live television. Still Fox News. They were replaying as well. The first Questral press conference. The mayor and the chief behind her. The Deegan family in the background behind them. Margaret, standing between Anne and Ruth. Ruth, so visible because of her hair. Theresa, alone. Theresa the brunette. Off to one side. Not anywhere near her mother or sisters. Not talking. But glaring. Glaring at Ruth. Then turning away. Not able to face any of them. There was the disgust and disappointment, so evident on Theresa's face. On the face of Deegan's little girl. The favorite daughter. The photo in the wallet. The girl with the hunting rifle. With the brown hair. The only one her pregnant sister could talk to. The only one who understood.

Brown pulled up in the Caprice. Daphne and Midori were in the backseat. They joined me, they joined the crowd that was forming. Standing on the sidewalk in front of the Pantry.

The Pantry would be open for business soon. Watching what might have been. My cremation. My funeral. My great send-off.

Daphne took my hand. Midori started to cry. Brown asked what he could do.

I handed him Gloria's case. "Put this where no one can get to it," I said, backing away.

"Where you going?" he asked.

"To finish this," I said.

EIGHTY-ONE

I'd make up for lost breakfasts next week. I'd make up for missed opportunities. I'd make up for everything. Lost time. Lost mind. The music that was never played.

Heading down State Street. Grove Street. Church Street. Slowly. Glancing at my watch. What time was it now? A little after eight. There'd be nothing left of my building when I returned.

The traffic was heavy for the time of day. Traffic jams already around the courthouse, around the green. Blanking out, thinking, not noticing at first. The out of states. The license plates from Massachusetts, New York, Rhode Island, New Jersey. And everywhere else. A lot of cars from down south—Alabama, Arkansas, Louisiana. Not lone riders, but car pools. Cars filled with men. A lot of cars from Mississippi. And it dawned. Cars filled with the Sons of God. The tie-ups would only get worse from here, as the sixty thousand plus strangers got lost down New Haven's one ways. A lot of one-way streets. A lot of no right turns. No left turns. No turns, period.

Across the green—the fifth square. Down Temple. I was probably quite the sight walking through the Omni lobby. Soot covered, drenching in my own sweat. My shirtsleeve torn from climbing out the skylight. But no one stopped me. Perhaps it was the gun strapped under one arm. Perhaps I was the frightening one now.

Donny Savage opened the door to his seventeenth floor hotel room after one knock. His eyes puffy. His clothes slept in. "Detective Shute," he said, surprised.

"Donny," I said. I just needed to ask him one question. I just needed the confirmation.

"I can't believe you're seeing me like this," he said, stepping back into the room. He didn't look that bad or different really, except that it was pretty obvious he'd been crying, and that he'd had a long night. "I couldn't sleep. I spent the whole night just walking and thinking." He looked at me finally. "Oh, my God. What happened to you?"

"I was born again," I said, following him inside, closing the door behind me.

"I don't quite under—"

"A question for you, Donny," I said, cutting him off.

He sat down on the edge of his bed, the covers of which had never been pulled back, just rumpled in places. "Whatever you want, Detective."

"You tell anyone else about Barbara Boyle?" I asked. "About her blackmail threats?"

"I heard what happened," he said, suddenly teary eyed. "Saw it on the news. Oh, God. On *Nightline*. That's why I couldn't sleep. I thought that maybe it was my fault these girls got killed. That if I hadn't blabbed. If I'd kept my big mouth—"

"Who'd you tell, Donny," I said.

"Oh, God," he said, crying harder now.

I yelled, "Talk to me!"

He did. It wasn't the name I wanted, the name I expected, but—

"Mr. Crawford asked me about them the other day," he said.

"James Crawford asked about Barbara?"

"And her roommates," Donny said, "Mr. Crawford knew their names. Susan and Tatiana. Which surprised me. So, I figured he and Dick, well, y'know, they were familiar with the girls. So, I told him."

"About the blackmail threats?"

He looked at me, the words coming hard, as if admitting finally to the greater evil. "About everything," he said.

EIGHTY-TWO

Hiking it up the fire stairs, three at a time, just that one flight. To the eighteenth. Pulling open the door. The rookie cop on duty jumped through his skin.

"Crawford's room?" I said. "Where is it?"

"What?" he said.

"Crawford. Where?"

"Eighteen-oh-one. End of the hall?" he said. "Why?"

"I'm delivering room service," I said.

My gun out, I rapped lightly against the door. There was no answer. Not so much as a peep from inside. I tried the handle. Locked. I was about to knock again when the door swung slowly open.

I watched James Crawford walk back toward the sofa. He took a seat. He had reading glasses on, a printout in his hands. I could tell from twenty feet, I could tell from the look on his face. *Suffering the same heinous death at the hands of a man who has thus far eluded the authorities.* Deegan's intended speech.

He didn't look up from the pages, he didn't have to.

I went to speak, but he held up a large hand, silencing me. He removed the glasses, folded and pocketed them. He placed the printout neatly on the coffee table in front of him. Still he wouldn't look at me.

"Richard Deegan was my friend, Detective," Crawford said. "I loved him like a brother. And you always want to believe the best of those you hold dear to your heart. That they would never be capable of anything so—" He seemed to have a problem with the word. "—vile. If for no other reason than to justify the decision which brought you together in the first place. We choose our friends." He cleared his throat. "We had a lot in common, Richard and I—"

"Did you?" I asked.

He turned to me then. Nothing like in the elevator. Or the stare from in front of city hall. Perhaps that was his moment of enlightenment. An epiphany. One that aged instead of invigorated. He looked old now. Tired. And there were tears in his eyes. "Not this," he said, wiping at them seemingly out of frustration. "I knew nothing of this, Detective. You might think—I know you think—I have no tolerance for—"

"Promiscuity."

"Yes, promiscuity. But promiscuity is merely a disease. A symptom. It can be cured."

"Wasn't that Deegan's goal?"

"Not if everything I've learned in the past few days is true."

"It is," I told him.

He nodded. "It's made me wonder if I knew him at all. All those years working so closely toward the same goal. What I thought was the same goal. To murder these young women in the name of—"

"You mean *whores*, don't you?"

He shook his head and laughed once, seemingly in spite of everything. "Perhaps," he said.

"Let me ask you something, Crawford," I said. "As Deegan's friend, did you at least recognize what he was capable of?"

"Had I a clue," he said, "and I know you might not believe me when I tell you this, I would have killed Richard myself, before he ever had a chance to hurt anyone."

Perhaps it was his tone, or something about the look on his face, but I didn't doubt his sincerity for a second.

EIGHTY-THREE

Finding Donny where I'd left him. The door to his room still open. He was sitting on the edge of his bed, staring at the TV, which wasn't on.

"Who else knew about Barbara Boyle?" I asked from the doorway, beginning to feel as tired and old as James Crawford.

"No one, Detective," he said softly, and then looking up, "I swear to God."

"Does that really mean anything around here?"

"It does to me," he said sincerely, looking away. Ashamed, frightened, frustrated, angry. I didn't know. And at this point—

"Okay, Donny," I said, playing my hunch. Ruth's comment: *a little off the deep end recently.* "What about Theresa Deegan?"

He looked back at me for a second as if I'd completely lost it. I expected him to say, Why on earth would I ever tell Theresa about her father's whore? But instead, he sniffled once loudly and said, "Well, yeah, of course Theresa knew," he said. "She knew everything." A small laugh. "She's the only one around here I can talk to. She's the only one who always understands."

EIGHTY-FOUR

There was only one life in the hotel worth saving. Knocking on Ruth's door. No answer. Pounding on the door. Still no answer. Stepping back. Ready to kick it in. Ready to finally serve and protect someone.

"She's not here," came an annoyed, hungover voice.

Turning. Margaret Deegan standing across the hall. Dressed in black. Ready to face another day as a widow. It was the first time I'd seen her since the slap. She looked at me, but didn't remember. She had no clue who I was. I doubted that she remembered much. A step closer. Already the smell of gin.

"Where'd she go?" I asked.

"I don't know," she said, snapping the words. "They—"

"Who?" I said it too loud.

"Don't raise your voice to me."

"Please," I said. "This is important. Her life might be in danger."

"Oh, please," Margaret Deegan said. Rubbing at her blood-shot eyes. Smiling condescendingly. It was as if she'd forgotten her husband had just been murdered. "She and her sister are eating breakfast with their cousin. Then they said something about stopping over at the new building."

Just then Anne, opening her door. Just as bleary-eyed. Just as hung over. "Is everything okay, Mom?"

I didn't stick around for Margaret's answer.

EIGHTY-FIVE

The Ninth Square wasn't as dead today.

It wasn't being ignored, or vandalized, or—

There were people gathered in the streets. People from office buildings. From banks. From city hall. People stopping their cars to take a look. Not admiring, but—

The police were doing their best to keep them back. Barricades set up around the perimeter. Far enough back. To give the firefighters room.

You could feel the heat from a block away. Flames already melting the stucco facade. The ornate lintel forming the name *Francesconi* blackened and ruined. The windows giving way, popping from the sheer forced of the blaze. Popping, popping, *popping*.

Even the firefighters pulled back. Rushing from the building, axes in hand. Doing their best to contain, to fight. It looked no easier than having to serve, to protect. It looked a hell of a lot harder, in fact.

Pushing through the crowd. Looking for a face I might recognize. A fireman. A cop. Some info. Anything. Then—Luponte.

"Was there anyone inside?" I asked.

"I hope not," he said, sounding dead inside. Another victim of Richard Deegan.

A roar pushed us back, something inside the building. A floor collapsing, the building's lung. Too weak for one final breath.

Stepping away, knowing I was too late. Not even a question in my mind. Ruth Deegan was dead. They would find Ruth Deegan in the Francesconi Building. Or at least what remained of her. Ashes to ashes, dust to dust.

Now it was up to me to find Theresa, before someone else—

Turning. Catching the corner of my eye. The glare was the

giveaway. The dead giveaway. I'd recognize her scowl anywhere now.

Following. Staying far enough back. The noise, the commotion, the crowd, a perfect cover. Watching her cut through a courtyard. The parking garage where Midori's body would have been dumped, where Sorrentino's was found, casting a looming shadow upon which the flames could dance.

EIGHTY-SIX

The garage was mostly empty. Perhaps even the assistant manager for the Dunkin' Donuts had found someplace else to park. Few cars, and no people. Not a soul. Just the echoes of sounds trapped and bouncing against the concrete. Yet somehow Theresa Deegan had vanished into the smoky air.

Cautious, pulling a 360. My gun out. Senses on overdrive. She had to be somewhere. Rounding the corner to the second floor. She—

That's when I spotted her, staring out at the blaze, watching, admiring her handiwork. Her back to me as I approached. Her dark brown hair catching the dry hot wind.

"Blame my sister, Ruth, Detective," Theresa said without turning. "She drove my father to this."

"Would he really have wanted her dead?" I asked, knowing the answer. After what Deegan had planned. After what he tried to do to Midori in that motel room.

"If he knew about Tony?" she said.

"And Tony, as well?"

"Of course."

How easy was it for Theresa to arrange a rendevous with Sorrentino? Perhaps he fantasized about scoring with more than one of Deegan's daughters. And she would most definitely be in need of a little consoling.

"And Barbara Boyle and her roommates, and—," I said, not finishing, not needing to. How easy to see Barbara Boyle? Anyone with cash could make an appointment.

"Yes," she said, her voice shaking just a little. "My father was set to take over this organization. To deliver his message to the world. But they destroyed him first. They crucified him."

I wanted to shoot her now and get it over with. To put an

end to her delusions. I wanted her to suffer as her father had. To suffer for his sins. For hers. For the sins of the world. Wasn't that both what they really wanted?

"You thought Gracie was the one, didn't you?"

She turned finally, and noticing the gun in my hand, a gun aimed her way, smiled, ever so slightly. "We all make mistakes, Detective."

The bullet sliced into my leg before I could tell her that I had stopped making them. I fell forward to a kneeling position, my hands slapping against the concrete. My gun taking a slide. The pain not limited to my left thigh, but shooting off in every direction. Bouncing off my bones like sound off a tuning fork.

He stepped from the shadows, giant steps forward. Holding a .38 automatic in his right hand. He aimed it right at my face.

"Gabe," I said, my teeth clenched. "I've been meaning to tell you: I've accepted Jesus Christ as my Lord and Savior?"

"It's too late, Detective," he said, not so much as cracking a smile.

I saw trembling blue stars in the daylight. "I thought it was never too late."

"It is for you."

Gabe stood over me. Theresa now by his side. He looked to her, as if for permission. She nodded. He spoke. "My father had a plan," he said.

I glared up first at her and then at Gabe. And then it made sense. The resemblance was even there. And I realized I deserved to die for being so stupid. Margaret Deegan's words coming to me now. *She and her sister are eating breakfast with their cousin.* Their *cousin.* What she meant was: their *half brother.* Gabriel Travers. Leslie's youngest son. Who so adored his real father—Deegan, not *Uncle Kilgore.* Who was following in his father's footsteps—quite fucking literally.

"That plan included the murder of innocent girls," I muttered, trying not to retch. To just hold on. Leaning back up, pushing myself back from the concrete. Not wanting to look down. Not wanting to, but—If only I'd heeded his warning. If only I'd listened. If only I'd gone to Disney World instead.

"The plan was to rid the world of promiscuity," he corrected, lifting me to a standing position, the pain exploding now. He half dragged me to the edge where Theresa had been standing. The Francesconi Building at four alarm. There was nothing to do but stand back and watch while it burned.

"Heather," I said, forcing out the word. Anything to kill time, anything—

He laughed. But then a look from Theresa cut that short.

"You hire her for a couple of hours," I said. "So, there's plenty of time. Get her comfortable. Get her drunk. Maybe even fuck her."

"I never fucked her," Gabe said. "This has nothing to do with fucking."

"When she's showering, or in the bathroom, you drop O'Toole's badge and Sorrentino's room number into her purse," I said, ignoring him, thinking how wrong he was. How this had everything to do with fucking. "After she's gone, you tip the Feds. Serial killer found. Case closed."

I caught a glimpse of him out of the corner of my eye. The bastard was smiling finally.

But it was Theresa who spoke, her voice tinged with sarcasm. "You do catch on quick," she said.

H e raised the gun to my face and took a step back.

"Tell us where she is, Detective," Theresa said.

I laughed that they had such faith, in me of all people. "You've got to be kidding me," I said.

Gabe lowered his aim and then pulled the trigger again.

Same leg. I swore, the same spot. Falling forward again. No chance this time of standing. Would I ever stand again?

"She looks so much like *her*," I screamed, pressing at the wound, trying to stop the blood, trying to feel my leg.

But that got Gabe's attention. "What are you talking about?" he said.

"The girl who killed your father," I said. "Looks just like *Mary*. You wouldn't believe the resemblance."

"Who's Mary?" Theresa asked.

I ignored the question. "Your father was *so* obsessed with her."

I could see the red flushing Gabe's tree-trunk neck. "He couldn't have cared less about that little—"

"Four hundred seventy-nine videos over three years," I said, amazed that I could remember the numbers, amazed that I hadn't yet died from the pain. I did a quick calculation. "One and a half million dollars spent on those tapes alone, and I'm being conservative." Yeah, Mr. Conservative. "There were over six hundred pictures of her on his laptop. I mean, c'mon—if that isn't obsession."

Theresa looked back and forth between us, repeating her question. Demanding an answer. "Answer my question. Who is Mary?"

"You know nothing about my father," Gabe said, shooting her a nervous look. "*Our* father."

I played back the card he dealt me. If this had nothing to do with—"He fucked her," I said, "Then—"

"He didn't fuck her," Gabe said, his voice agitated. He turned, looked around.

"You didn't know?" I said, staring up at the back of his head, ignoring Theresa. "He was fucking her as he tried to bash her head in with a rock." I forced up a laugh. "Your father didn't give a shit about this religious crap. He just wanted to get laid."

"Gabe," Theresa said, her voice shaking ever so slightly, "kill him and get it over with."

"We need him to find the girl," Gabe muttered.

"We'll find her ourselves," she said. "Do it."

Gabe obeyed. He nodded once and then turned back. He took a step toward me—then another. He aimed the gun at my head, arm straight out. Then he began to pray. "This is the gate of the Lord through which the righteous may enter—"

"Look," I said. "You don't want to do this."

He wasn't listening.

"I will praise You," he said. "For You have answered me, And have become my salvation."

"Do you understand any of this?" I asked, trying to remember how long this particular psalm ran. Trying to calculate how much time I had left.

"The stone which the builders rejected has become the chief cornerstone."

"I'd especially like for someone to explain to me that 'Abba, Father' line," I said, wondering if I'd be better off jumping and making a run for it, with my shattered leg.

"This was the Lord's doing; It is marvelous in our eyes. This is the day which the Lord has made; We will rejoice and be glad—"

A single gunshot silenced him. I watched as Gabe dropped to his side, gasping as he hit concrete, a hand pressed to the side of his neck. Theresa screamed and lunged for his gun, but a shot to the shoulder knocked her backwards away from the gun. I scrambled for it, ignoring the pain. Reaching it taking longer than forever.

Turning, expecting Brown or Mazz or—instead I saw Albert Larsen walking toward me. My gun held out in both hands. He was rigid. Shaking. Crying. Mumbling. He dropped to his knees beside Gabe and made a sign of the cross.

"Join me," Larsen said.

I looked at him for a moment, wondering if he were serious, then moving slowly, excruciatingly, lifting myself into a kneeling position, or something at least resembling one, I pressed the palms of my hands together around the butt of Gabe's gun. And I spoke to God for what was probably the first time in my adult life.

"May these sons of bitches die—and then burn in hell," I said. "Amen."

SATURDAY

Discharged. Limping down the hallways of Yale New Haven Hospital on a crutch. She was in room 3617. The door was mostly open. She was propped up in bed. The TV on. CNN, not very loud. She looked pale and tired and as if she'd been through a long wash cycle. But she smiled when she saw me. It was the most beautiful smile I'd ever seen.

"Will," O'Toole said, her voice soft and hoarse. "You got shot."

Walking to the side of her bed. Moving the tray table out of the way. Holding onto the railings. "Just a flesh wound," I said, lying. The bullet had nicked the bone. "What about you?"

"Me?" She tried to laugh. "I've learned that it's best to call first."

"No, Gracie it wasn't like that. I'd been drinking all night. So pissed about them taking my badge. I wanted to show them up. I wanted to find the girl who'd killed Deegan. I was calling these online escort services I'd found on his laptop. Daphne answers, she was the girl on my couch. She sounds like maybe she's the one. But she shows up and she's got an alibi. But she starts drinking with me anyway. We're talking about the case, talking about what she does for a living, and the next thing I know, you're—"

Gracie reached out and squeezed my hand. "Reader's Digest, Will," she said. "Reader's Digest."

Dreamt is the only English word that ends in *mt*." Mazz and Brown were bringing her flowers. They smiled when they saw me. They shook my hand.

"I hear the Sons of God changed their mind about moving to the Elm City," Mazz said.

"No kidding," I said. "That's too bad. Now who's going to save the Ninth Square?"

"Didn't think you cared," Mazz said.

"I don't," I said. "Fuck the Ninth Square. They should just level it and be done with it."

"Nice to know some things never change," Brown said.

On the way out Mazz was talking about taking some time off. "Just a break," he said. "Me and the wife. Just to get away, y'know. Away from all this." A shrug. "Gracie's gonna be fine."

"Where you going, Mazz?" I asked.

"Aruba," he said. "I hear it's nice and quiet."

"It's beautiful," I said.

EIGHTY-EIGHT

The station house was empty. Sixty thousand plus at the Yale Bowl could drain manpower. They were needed there. The crime would be there. All those pockets to pick. All those tourists to scam.

I entered Klavan's office, sitting in chair opposite his desk. Staring at the framed pictures of Klavan's wife and their eight kids. I wondered if she held secrets from her husband. Or if she knew about his indiscretions? Had I known all along about Charlene's? There had to have been signs. Did we all know and either understand and forgive? As we wished to be understood and forgiven?

Klavan shook my hand. He congratulated me on a job well done. Then standing, he opened one of his file drawers and removed a few items. He returned, handing them to me. Pressing my gun and my badge into my hands. He leaned back then against the front edge of his desk. Folding his arms across his chest, casually.

I ran my fingers over the face of my badge. I never thought I'd miss it so much. I never thought it would be taken away. Staring at the shield number. Remembering what it meant.

But then forcing myself out of the chair, so that we could be eye to eye, I handed my badge and my gun back.

"Why don't you hold on to these for me for a while," I said.

EIGHTY-NINE

Time to go home.

I arrived at the front door carrying Gloria, wearing just the clothes on my back. Both my mom and dad gave me tremendous hugs. "Stay as long as you like," they said.

The official count: 64,220 people. Or at least that's how many pushed their way through the turnstiles on this blessed spring day. Mid-eighties. Not a cloud. Perhaps someone upstairs wanted to hear what these sons of bitches had to say after all.

Watching it on TV. Listening to the speeches bounce off the concrete-on-concrete Roman Coliseum design. They were all so well behaved. All so respectful. Polite. Committed, as they were supposed to be. Praying in unison. Cheering when James Crawford took the stage. And in hushed respect, bowing their heads and listening.

"I'm sorry," Crawford began.

Between the *Register*, the *Times*, and the six o'clock news, they pretty much got it right. Both papers printed excerpts from Richard Deegan's intended speech. They theorized that Deegan believed the murders would canonize the Sons of God in our eyes. And that we'd welcome them to our town as saviors. Gabriel Travers was paralyzed from the neck down from his gunshot wound. Theresa Deegan, who had always been a little unstable according to friends, fell off the deep end when her father died and had yet to utter a word since her arrest in that Ninth Square parking garage. Both were named as codefendants, responsible for the five murders, for the two fires. They cleared Louise Heather Karg.

No one mentioned Barbara Boyle's ties to the city. Or Questral's ties to the Sons of God. Perhaps it wasn't important.

No one mentioned Midori.

NINETY

My dad bought the white clam and garlic pizza. I paid for the beer. We got caught up. I told them parts of what had happened during the past few days. They told me how they planned on spending the rest of their lives. They were going to re-open the bakery in a big shopping plaza on Washington Avenue. They'd been wanting to move. The fire was a godsend. I told them I didn't think God had anything to do with the fire at all.

Calling it an early night. Sitting on the edge of my old bed, in my old room. Stuffed. Relieved. Confused. In pain. A little buzzed. The beer was my painkiller tonight. It had cooled off just right. A light wind was blowing. I had the windows opened. The world smelled fresh.

My old phone, shaped like a Gibson Les Paul—no matter how far and wide she searched, Mom could never find a Telecaster phone—rested on one of the pillows beside me. Daphne's phone number on that slip of paper alongside it. Gloria's case lay now on the floor in the middle of the room. Looking back and forth between the plastic Les Paul phone and the real Telecaster. Shaking my head. Ready for another beer. Ready for—

I leaned forward, kneeling slowing, painfully, and flipped two of the latches. Then taking a deep breath, the other two. I lifted the lid.

"Hey, baby," I said. Reaching for Gloria's neck.

And maybe it was the beer, but I could swear I heard her say something back.

"About time," I thought she said.

It took me a good ten minutes to get her in tune. My old tuner's nine-volt battery was missing. I needed to borrow one from my dad. The strings were a lot dead, mostly from age. But they'd do for now. Putting on a fresh set wasn't something I was up to. Just yet.

I held her in my lap for a beat. The old black leather strap still in place. So soft, from all the years. I'd bought it new with the guitar. Never took it off. Never changed it. I held a once-bright yellow extra-thin pick between the thumb and index finger of my right hand. At first just tuning her was enough.

Then reaching over, I picked up Daphne's phone number. Tuesday night seemed like such a long time ago. A lifetime ago. Staring at the Les Paul phone. Who did I want? What did I need? Maybe she'd want to get a drink sometime. Make like none of this ever happened. We could start with a drink. Somewhere quiet, just to talk. Or coffee. Or a movie. Anything, really. Sure there were complications. There were always complications. O'Toole was a complication. But still. But still.

"But still," I said out loud.

I placed the slip of paper back down near the phone; then I barred the index finger of my left hand over the third fret. Placed the tip of my middle finger down, third string, fourth fret. My ring finger and pinky down, fifth and fourth strings respectively, fifth fret. It felt like cut glass against my skin. But I strummed nevertheless. Again. And again. I banged on that G chord. Moved the whole thing up to the eighth fret, and strummed that C chord even harder. Something simple at first. Something easy. A progression to half the rock songs ever written. I'd play for a while. Staring at the phone. Or scrutinizing my stiff attempts on Gloria's neck. I'd play until my fingertips couldn't take it anymore. And then I'd call. Then I'd know. I'd tell Daphne I took Gloria out to play. And that the dreams weren't completely dead. They were still there. And there were new dreams along with them. Hiding under the pickguard, with the faded piece of masking tape marked: GLORIA 9/15/53.